PEPPER
(Inspired by a true story)

Ted Messimer

SOMOTE
PUBLISHING
COPYRIGHT NOTICE

Published in the United States by SOMOTE Publishing & Entertainment
somoteentertainment@gmail.com
2020

This book is a work of fiction. Names, characters, businesses, organizations, places, events, and incidents either are a product of the author's imagination or are used fictitiously. Any resemblance to actual persons, living or dead, events, or locales is entirely coincidental. Nor the publisher or author are responsible for any psychological effects this book has on its reader. Nor are the publisher or author to be held accountable for any therapy the reader may have to receive after reading this book. Tick. Tick. Ding.

Cover Art: BookDesign
First edition
Book two of the Peeking Island series

ISBN: 978-1-7373269-4-6

For Allyson

Chapters

Indoctrination	6
Déjà Vu	8
Mud On The Tires	23
House Of The Morning Star	38
So Sayeth The Sheppard	57
A Skip To His Walk	62
Run!	75
Horns And Crowns	95
Seven Bridges	107
Tea	121
Tick. Tick. Ding.	132
Dancing In The Moonlight	150
Where Is Jayden?	161
Hell's Compost	167
Shabari	173
Farewell, Morning Star	205
Hey Jealousy	216
Visions Of Control	222
Bring Him Back	225

Pet. Obey.	230
Word Association	250
Calling The Corners	262
Thunder And High Swells.	268
Helpless	278
Lost Pets Always Return	282
Dominus Mues	288
Do You Remember?	294
Fractionation	302
I Am You	306
Light Rises	318
Drop. Deeper.	332
Darkness Falls	342
A Day On The Beach	350
Madness	356
Impossible	394
Déjà vu	398
Counting You Back	401

I will take you to the edge and back. You may feel fear. It is right on the edge of fear where trust will grow

FIVE
What would it be like if you began to relax deeply? Imagine dropping deep enough to shut out the world and truly enjoy a book.

FOUR
Sooner or later, you'll begin to feel the comfort of relaxation and you'll begin to feel the comfort of bliss.

THREE
As you feel the relaxation coursing through your body, you know that every one of your muscles can simply let go and unwind completely.

TWO
And the more you relax the easier it is to imagine yourself in a comfortable and contented place.

ONE
And as your body continues to relax you can just let go, which means you're so at ease now that your mind calms down because you imagine yourself as an attentive reader.

"But whoa to the earth and sea! For the devil has come down unto you, having great wrath, because he knowth that he hath but a short time."
Revelation 12:12

DÉJÀ VU

The fire that burned on a southwest Florida beach was bright! The flashing and intense orange flames spiked high into the air as a group deep in celebration had encircled the fiery pit they had built earlier in the day. With their hands held high in the air, they praised loudly with their sacred and prideful chants. Tonight was a cause for celebration. The past year of hard work was done. It had been thus far the most challenging year of their lives. It was the end of their freshmen year in college.

All of those lost deep in this celebration traveled from colleges across the country. They traveled to return home. This was a celebration of achieved success. It was also a reunion. These young adults had grown up near this beach. They had spent the past year separated. Each of them had spent the past year starting the paths to their new lives. Tonight though was a celebration for the past years. Life-long friends were reuniting and eager to share stories of their new lives in their new homes. They were happy to once again be together and have a sense of familiarity.

About fifty yards from the blaze on the beach, trucks were lined up and parked. Most of them were being used as makeshift bars and gathering spots. Kegs filled the truck beds and music played loudly from a few. It was the type of heavy metal that wives of politicians yearn to get off of the radio airwaves and record store shelves. They advocate labeling the record covers with warning stickers.

Around one of those trucks was Jayden Pink. He gathered with a few other friends as he reached into the bed of his pickup truck and tossed out a few cans of beer to his friends. They all swapped stories of their new lives as collegiate students. One of those was Elliot Holt. He came out of the amber light of the fire toward the truck and yelled, "Now on the mound, Jayden Pink! He makes his wind up and…. yo Jay, toss me a cold one. Let's see if you still got the heat!"
Jayden said, "Oh man, I'm no starting pitcher anymore. My ass be growing splinters man. But I still got it if you can still catch me"
Elliot went down into a catcher's stance as Jayden overhand threw a can of ice-cold beer to him. He stood up and looked to another friend his right, Scott Alberene. Elliot said, "Boys still got it I tell you! Boys still got it!" Scott looked to Elliot and said, "You better not try and open that thing around me. Why don't you go stand over there?"

"What, this?" Elliot asked as he shook up the can of beer ferociously. "You want me to be careful as I open up this? Near you?" He gave the can a few more shakes for good measure and then opened it quickly while pointing it in the direction of Scott. In seconds Scott was covered in white foamy beer suds. Scott, patting his hands over his now beer-soaked shirt yelled out, "Oh you fucking asshole!" Everyone gathered around the truck laughed as Scott took an arrogant stance with his hands on his hips as he announced, "Tell ya what boy. I only came out here tonight to do two things! Drink beer and kick some ass. At the rate your wasting shit looks like we'll be out of beer real quick like!"

Elliot said, "Yo Jayden, toss me another one of those" he looked to Scott as he opened another beer, took a long hard swig, and said, "Yeah? Well, I only came out here tonight to do two things myself son! Drink beer and eat some pussy!" He put two fingers up by his mouth and stuck his tongue out between them as he made grunting sounds and laughed. Jayden said, "Shit Ell, are you even getting pussy up there at, what's it called, Ooofff U?"

Elliot responded quickly, "Shit man, just this year, we were voted number one party school in the nation by your favorite nudie magazine. They

got this clock tower up there and it is said that every time a virgin graduates, a brick falls out of the clock tower and smashes on the ground!"
Scott asked, "Yeah. What's your point?"
"My point, my beer-covered friend is that come 1995...there ain't going to be no bricks falling from that tower!"

The boys continued to be boys with their smack talk around Jayden's truck. Another friend came running up and told them all to get down to the fire. They all grabbed a beer, and another as they stuffed the extra in their back pocket. The large group was sitting and swapping stories as they all encircled the large fire. Music could be heard from someone's portable radio. Jayden was halfway listening to Scott tell tales of his first year as a college freshman and how he already was ruling the campus. A girl approached Jayden as she pointed to an empty spot next to him in the sand. She asked, "Anyone sitting there?" Jayden looked her up and down. She wore very short and frayed jean cut-off shorts that showed off her thighs. On top, she had a crop shirt that illustrated her flat tummy. She had long straight black hair about halfway down her back. Jayden said, "Been saving it for you all night." Looking at Jayden in his snakeskin boots, worn jeans, and a T-shirt that had sleeves tightly rolled up to accent his muscular arms she said, "Hi back cowboy, I'm Peperrat. " Jayden smiled and said, "Whoa. That's quite the handle."

Peperrat gave a flirty smile back and told him, "Yeah, my parents are from the old country full of tradition. My friends call me Pepper."

"It's good to meet you, Pepper. I'm Jayden."

She asked, "So what is this you have going on tonight?"

Jayden said, "Oh. It's a reunion of sorts I guess. We all went to high school together and spent the past year away at college. So we are just catching up on old times. We used to throw parties like this all the time here on this beach, so this seemed like the perfect way to get back together."

She said, "That sounds great. Yeah, it was the fire that attracted me. I was down a ways at the beach and could see the giant fire. I saw people dancing around it and sounded like chanting so I thought I'd come to see what was what?"

Jayden looked to Pepper and said, "Chanting? Oh yeah, those are just our old high school chants. Back in the day, I guess, we used to do them in Latin to mess with the other teams."

"Do you speak Latin?" She asked with a tone of surprise to her voice.

"No. Just our school team chants and few phrases to taunt the other schools with."

Pepper said back, "Oh, it is a cool language. You should look into it."

"Right. So, you're not from around here?"

"No," She said, "I live in the Peeking Islands. I am just here visiting my aunt."

Jayden responded with excitement, "Peeking Islands! No shit! I go there and visit all the time. I love that place. You live there?"

"Yeah, I run my parent's shop on Manta Ray. You know, the first island you come to?"

Jayden said, "Yeah I know Manta-Ray well. I've spent much time drinking on the historic seaport."

Trying to gauge her age in a clever way to make sure she was 18 he asked, "So, you live there and work for your parents now, or did you go away to college?"

She told him, "No college for me. After high school, I just decided to take over my parent's shop. So really, I don't need it. Everything I am going to need to know in life, I can learn from them."

Jayden just said back, "Cool, cool. So what kind of shop do they have?"

She told him, "Oh it's a metaphysics shop! We do tarot readings, palm readings, and sell a variety of accessories for people into that."

"Accessories?"

"Yeah, you know. Incense, candles, oils, cards, crystals. We have it all."

"And you do readings. Like, tell people the future kind of stuff?" He asked.

"Something like that! Here, I'll read your palm for you." She said as she grabbed his palm. He had no interest in this type of stuff. He was not going to argue with a hot girl grabbing his hand though. She softly grasped his hand in both of hers as she seemed to stare intently at it as if she were deeply into a great book.

"Well, this is interesting. You have a star on your fate line. That means that you have a change in your fate approaching. It also means you are a good leader. Maybe you have management in your future. Here, you have a square on your lifeline. That says you may be unexpectedly rescued from a desperate situation. Now look here, you have a triangle under your ring finger. That means that you have good learning capability and are open to new things. So maybe you will be learning something new in your future that you will be great at." Jayden said back with a cocky smile, "Aw yeah, just me being the best version of myself." He paused as he finished saying that. All though they were words that had just come to him, there was something vaguely familiar about it. Pepper had a weird yet prideful smile on her face as well as he said that. It was not the palm read that was fascinating to Jayden. He was not into this stuff at all. What surprised him was how much she lured him in with the way she spoke and the way she touched him. It was as if he felt a sudden calmness come over him. The way she spoke was soft, yet direct. As she held his hand he felt as if he were in a different place somewhat. She held his hand and gently rubbed her finger along a line as she said, "Oh now this, you see this? Do you know what this means?" Jayden just shook his head back and forth. She said, "This means you like to be a good boy. Do you think that is true? Do you enjoy being a good boy?" He just nodded his head up and down as he said, "Yes, yes please." As he spoke those words, he realized how stupid it sounded. Why did he even say that? He had no explanation for himself. He also for some reason had the strangest feeling of Déjà vu.

She continued her read with a sound of joy as it was suddenly interrupted by a voice nearby that yelled out, "NPD! Nobody move! Everyone stay where you are at!" There was the sound of thirty-some people saying, "oh man" at once. They really could not run off if they wanted to. The group was surrounded by the local police pointing flashlights in their direction. A voice over a megaphone said, "Okay, everyone put the beer down and remain sitting on the ground."

It was Scott that spoke out. "Man! What the hell? What is this new ninja po-po shit? Ya'll use to give us a warning that you were coming down the beach. What happened to the days of coming down the beach in an ATV so we can see you coming?"
An authoritative voice spoke out, "Is that Scott Alberene? Check him first, deputy."

Scott looked at the deputy approaching him. "Holy shit!" Scott exclaimed. "Is that Jonny Delaney? What's up Jon? Couldn't get into college so you became a cop huh? Hey Jayden, check out what the biggest snitch in school is doing these days!" Deputy Delaney grabbed Scott and brought him to his feet rather roughly. "Still the same smart ass I see. Now hold still. I'd hate to have to take you in for resisting." He frisked Scott up and down then he asked. "You got ID for that beer?" Scott asked, "What beer would that be officer Jon?" The cop said in a serious tone,

"That's deputy Delaney and, that beer. The one at your feet."
Scott looked to his feet and said, "Oh that beer! I don't know anything about that beer, dep-pew-tee. Unless you saw it in my hand, I don't believe you have anything on me. So, you best get your paws off me."
"You better watch your lip there Scotty boy. I'm about to take you in for 810.09.2b, 843.02, 856.021,
and an 856.011."
Scott shook his head back and forth as deputy Delaney continued to frisk him up and down and said, "In English, jackass?"
"Trespassing, resisting arrest, loitering, and disorderly intoxication."
All Scott could do was laugh. "Seriously man? Come on. Be cool."

Meanwhile, just a few feet away Jayden was in a completely different conversation with the sergeant as he said, "All right, I'm sorry man. I guess things got a little out of control. I thought we were being good."
The sergeant said, "For the most part you probably were. But like I said, we got a call from some property owners nearby and we had to come to check it out. But listen, if you promise me

you're going to clean this all up now, gather your friends and get off this beach I think we can let this pass tonight."

The two shook hands as Jayden rounded up his friends and the sergeant rounded up his crew. "Deputy Delaney, we almost done there? Come on, everyone else has interviewed five apiece and you're still on one? What's the holdup?"

It was Scott that spoke out when he said, "It's officer Robocop here sergeant Callahan. Thinks he is out to save the planet tonight." Jayden came over quickly to intercept Scott as he said, "Dude, shut the hell up. We are all getting out of here tonight, as long as you keep your trap shut."

"Yeah, but man, come on! This guy is a douche, you know that." Scott said.

Jayden just looked Scott in the eye and said, "Dude, I'm not even playing with you now. Let it go."

The sergeant spoke up. "We have any issues, Mr. Pink?"

"No sir. We'll get this all cleaned up now and get out of your hair."

Scott asked, "Cleaned up? How are we going to put that fire out? We don't have any buckets?"

The sergeant said, "Mr. Alberene, you might want to check with your friends that have their rice burners parked out on the street. See if they have

any fire extinguishers for the nitrous kits that I know they don't have in their cars. Unless you want me to look in the cars for you."
Jayden waved his hand in the air and said, "No Sergeant Callahan, We've got this. Thank you. Have a good night."

All of the police were starting to walk away. Deputy Delaney asked his sergeant, "So that's it? We are not going to arrest them? We could have filled that jail tonight!"
"It is not about filling the jail deputy. It is about winning hearts and minds while keeping the community safe. Now if you want, we can go arrest all of them but so help me God, I will make sure it is you that fills out the paperwork on every single one of them. Are you up for that?"
The deputy shrugged his head back and forth. "Didn't think so. Let's go."

The beach had been cleaned up and the fire had been put down. Jayden stood by his truck talking to Pepper. She tapped her fingers and palm on the hood of his truck in a rhythmic manner. Her fingernails made a tapping sound. This was followed by a ding sound from her ring when she would flatten her hand and make a strike with her palm. It went tick, tick, ding. Tick, tick, ding.

Jayden was intently focused on that pattern of sound for reasons he could not explain. She said, "That was pretty impressive. Are you always able to talk yourself out of trouble with the law?"

He laughed and looked to the sky for a second as he said, "Not always, but officer Callahan has been around long enough to watch most of us grow up. He's been a cop here for as long as I remember. He always did a good job of looking out for us. I am sure it helped that he was our assistant baseball coach when we were in school here."

She smiled and added, "And your friends. They all seem to admire and look up to you. Do they always do what you say?"

"Definitely no on that one. But anything beats going to jail on summer break. Speaking of which. You said you were on break here. How long are you in town?"

She answered, "Oh just a couple of weeks. I am here helping my aunt move into a new place."

Jayden replied, "I imagine you are pretty busy then, right?"

She smiled flirtatiously as she said, "I can work you into my schedule if that is what you're asking."

He told her to hold on as he went into his truck and grabbed a fast-food receipt and pen. He handed it to her and she wrote down her name and number. He asked her if she needed a ride home and she said she would be fine as she slipped into the darkness of the beach.

MUD ON THE TIRES

Pepper walked across the driveway in the direction of Jayden's truck. He had called her earlier and asked if she was up for some fun southwest Florida style. She was up for anything. As she walked toward the truck he was standing by the passenger door waiting for her. She found him a very appealing man to look at. He was tall and full of muscle. It was easy to tell that he cared about his body. His skin was dark but had more of a light hue to it. His hair was kept neat in tight natural curls. The smile on his face always seemed to be big. He was one of those people that just naturally smiled. He did not even have to try. There was a sparkle in his eyes that made people want to be around him. He greeted her as she approached the truck and opened the door for her. She was a little surprised as that was something she did not know still existed. It was one of those old-fashioned things that guys used to do but not so much anymore. Jayden shut the passenger door once she was in and walked around the back to get in his side. Pepper had reached over to unlock his door but it already was unlocked.

Jayden's truck was ocean blue and raised up on tires that were not factory installed. He had big silver roll bars in the front of the bed. They sat over a toolbox. In the back window was a gun rack with space for two rifles. The gun rack only had one currently sitting in it. Jayden was dressed similar to the first night they met on the beach. He was wearing jeans, a T-shirt, and snakeskin boots. His arms made the sleeves work.

She looked at him and asked, "What's the plan?"
"We are going to meet up with some friends and go mudding today."
"Mudding?"
"Yes, ma'am! What is the point of owning a truck if you don't get it dirty?"
The place they were going to was what the local youth referred to as The Powerlines. It was mostly an open area the size of a couple of football fields. It had small pits and hills that local kids had dug out on their own over the years. It was very rutty and offered the perfect place to bog a truck through the mud after rain. It was called the Powerlines because there was a long line of tall towers running line from a substation to the local community. It was also a good place to throw keggers. When they arrived, there were already trucks running through the field kicking up mud. Other people sat in truck beds drinking beer. It was a typical Saturday afternoon in southwest Florida.

Jayden and Pepper were at the beginning of a homemade course the locals had built. When they first arrived, it did not look like a course, but now that they were about to start, Pepper could see that is exactly what it was. Jayden gently put his foot to the gas as he went over the first part. It was about two hundred feet of really uneven ground. The truck would bob from side to side up and down as it traversed this area. As long as one followed the two-track they would be fine. One side would be dug down about a foot and then even out and the other side would be dug down. The truck would never be sitting even. From there they went into a deep trench. It was maybe about five or six feet deep. It was barely wide enough for Jayden's truck to fit in. This was around four hundred feet long. It was uneven to drive on. This took some care to drive through as it was so narrow and it was muddy on the surface. This was not an area one would want to bog down in and get stuck. Coming out of the long pit Jayden had to gun it as now they were going up a man-made hill of packed dirt. Coming over the top he had to feather the brakes on the way down. It was a sixty percent slant. It felt as if they were going straight down. Pepper looked over to Jayden and could tell he was very focused on what he was doing. He still had that bright natural smile though.

At the bottom of the hill was another trough to drive through. This one looked deep but was hard to tell as it was filled with water. As they drove through it quickly the water came up to almost the bottom of the doors. Jayden went through at a moderate pace and maintained his speed perfectly till he came up an incline and out of the water. He followed a turn that had him facing the next obstacle. It was a very long and straight path going through a small, wooded area. The two-track was extremely uneven on both sides and Jayden gunned it through. Because of the speed, one side of the truck would be on the ground and the other would be airborne. There was a small crowd that was on both sides of the two-track as they cheered out loud. Jayden was taking this much faster than most or at least faster than he probably should. At least that is what Pepper assumed when she could hear someone yell out, "Legend!" as they drove by. He came out of the partially wooded trail and was looking at a giant pit of mud in front of them. He looked at Pepper and said, "Here comes the fun part. You ready? You might want to hold on tight."
Before she could even really think of an answer he gunned it. The roar of his engine was loud as he dove the truck into the pit and spun the tires kicking mud up everywhere. He was doing donuts

and the truck was spinning circles. He did not let up on the gas. He kept his RPM going as if he had let up, they would have been stuck. He spun around in the pit for what seemed like five minutes but was only thirty seconds. He popped up on the dry ground. His friends that were gathered around were all cheering. He pulled up to some of his friends and as he rolled down his window one of them came up to the driver's side door and yelled out, "Dude, you are fucking legend bro!"

Jayden said, "Hey man, I just let my baby do what she was built to do. But hey, listen. I can't stick around. I'm taking Pepper out for some lunch."

"Oh no man, you gotta stick around. We are going out on Scott's dad's boat later for some fishing. You should bring her."

Jayden flashed his smile back and said, "I think we just want to go out and have some lunch. You feel me, bro?"

"Yeah man, I gotcha." He said with a wink. Jayden hit the gas and they left the Powerlines onto the road.

The place Jayden was taking Pepper for lunch was probably his favorite place to eat in town. It was nestled in a touristy area. The restaurant was on the side of a large structure. It was two large structures. Made of all wood with tin roofs. It was a mall of sorts. One could not find the typical mall-type shops here though. They were all kitschy shops filled with stuff only a tourist would purchase. There was a candle shop where the candles were being made on-site, T-shirt shops, there was a shop that sold nothing but shells. Which Jayden never understood. Why would someone buy a bag of shells when they could just as easily go to the beach and pick them for free. The one thing that made him roll his eyes though was the canned Florida sunshine. It was an empty tin can. It was labeled as containing Florida sunshine. Maybe it was geared for the northerners that needed that peace of mind as they hunkered down in their dark and grey winter homes.

It was the restaurant that Jayden loved about this place though. It was built on a pier. The restaurant was long in design as it went along the channel coming into the docks from the open water. The smell of freshly caught fish permeated the air. The tables were wood as well as the chairs. The service staff wore their own clothes and it was insanely laid back. The menu was simple. The food was all made to order and always came out hot and fresh. It would come served on top of a checkered napkin in a basket. The burgers were humongous, and the fish options were catch of the day and extremely fairly priced. Each had so much flavor to it. One could tell by the flavor that the cooks took a lot of pride in their work. The meal Jayden had today was one of his favorites here. It was a hot dog and fries. The hot dog was a quarter-pound and cooked in beer. The fries were made on site. Pepper had gone with the burger and fries. This is why Jayden enjoyed it. It was simple. They sat at a two-top table with the perfect view of the channel. They could watch all the fishing boats come in and out as they ate.

They ate their lunch and continued their conversation. They were getting to know one another well. Jayden had felt an immense attraction to her. He was not thinking of her as a future long-term mate though. He knew that she was only in town for a short time. He was going back to college soon. With such a flight risk why would he waste time in a serious relationship with her? This was more to just pass time with a very attractive girl with whom he wanted to get in her pants. Her clothing was revealing and did not leave much to the imagination. She wore tight jean shorts. Her top showcased her cleavage that seemed to be begging to be released. As if on cue and reading his thoughts Pepper asked, "So what are your kinks?"

Jayden laughed and asked, "My kinks? What do you mean?"

She said, "You know, your kinks. What are you into in the bedroom?"

Jayden did not know how to answer that. The only thing he could think was, "I'm not sure I guess. I never really thought about it that way."

"Well, you must know what turns you on." She said with a flirtatious smile.

"Yeah, I'm at a loss here."

She told him, "Well, think about it. Chains, whips, chips, dips…. candlewax on the nipples perhaps?"

Jayden about spit his drink out of his mouth he laughed so hard. "Candlewax on the nipples?" He had never had a girl speak to him this forward before. He was still laughing as he started to realize she was being serious.

"You have never been whipped before?"

Jayden answered, "Ah, my dad has whooped me with his belt. But I can't say I was exactly turned on by that."

She looked at him and said, "Well that is something we will have to rectify. Get the bill. My aunt is away and I have her house all to myself."

Jayden lit up with excitement. This girl was extremely forward. He was not going to have to play the game whatsoever with her. She seemed primed and ready to go. He was still wondering if she was serious about those weird comments about chains and stuff. She could not have been.

The area of town her aunt lived in was considered an old part of town and still fairly undeveloped. The only thing out that way was an old drive-in movie theater. The theater itself was no longer in operation but the giant screen was still there as were all the speaker stands adjacent to every parking spot. These days it was used as a flea market swap meet place on the weekends. Jayden knew it well as one of his friends' parents owned many acres of wooded land next to it. Growing up they would hide out in the woods and throw golf balls at the back of the screen. In the middle of the night, it made such a loud and reverberating sound. They would do this till the security guard would come out in a golf cart and yell at them as they lay hidden in the woods. He never chased them out in the woods though. Who is going to chase a bunch of kids dressed in camouflage into the woods?

They arrived at the aunt's house and Pepper told Jayden to sit down on the couch in the living room and wait. He had only been waiting a few minutes when he heard her call him into her bedroom. He got up and his jaw dropped when he saw her. She was dressed in all skintight leather. She stood there with her long dark hair that had wavy curls. In one hand she held a whip that was folded over and she smacked her free hand with a light rhythm. She told him to lay on the bed and he did.

She straddled herself on top of him. She looked down at him and in a very serious tone said, "Strip." He laughed and said, "I'd love to, but that's kind of hard with you on top of me." She rolled off of him and said, "Listen. If we are going to do this, you have to take it seriously." Not wanting to lose this opportunity to have sex with such a hot girl he changed his focus real quick. He said, "Okay. I'm sorry. I have never done it like this before. I mean, not with all these toys and stuff."
She explained to him, "It's real simple. I am your Mistress and that is how you will address me. I believe in keeping it safe, sane, and consensual. Since this is your first time we will start slow. Think of everything as a traffic light. If you are

comfortable with it that is green. If you are unsure but comfortable enough to continue that is yellow. And if we do something you are not comfortable with that is red. Green, yellow, and red. Those are our safe words."
Jayden asked, "Wouldn't something as simple as saying no and stop seem to be pretty safe?"
She told him, "Not necessarily. Because those words could be considered part of the role play. Now let's do this. Are you ready?"
He smiled and said, "Yeah, let's do this!" She snapped her whip and demanded, "That's yes mistress!"
Laughing he said, "Yes mistress!"
She said in a light but tense tone, "Good boy. Now, let's start with something light."
She leaned over to a nightstand and lit a candle. She pulled his shirt off him and smiled as she lightly rubbed the whip across his chest. She asked, "Are you ready to do as your told? Are you ready to do my bidding?"

Starting to figure out how this game was played he said, "Yes mistress." He did not care. He was just looking forward to the part when they actually have sex. She placed the whip on the nightstand and grabbed the candle. She held it above him and asked, "Are you good with this?"

With some apprehension, he said, "Ah. Yellow. Let's give it a try."
She slowly dripped hot candle wax on his chest and he winched as he could feel it burn his skin. She would go back and forth and in small circles as if drawing designs on him with the hot wax. She asked, "Are you enjoying the pain?" he said, "Yes mistress." She told him. "Good. Now stand up and take off the rest of your clothes." He did and she had him standing naked at the foot of the bed. He was facing the bed and was partially bent over with his hands on the bed. She started to lightly use the whip on him. He could feel it hurt. But he could not help but laugh at the absurdity of this all. She would ask questions in a demanding tone, and he would always answer with the words yes mistress as he tried his best to stifle his laughter.

After his ass had taken a beating from the whip, she had him standing up with a blindfold on. He could not see but could sense she was close. He felt a poke to his neck. It was by something sharp and metallic he could tell. Then she ran the object down along his inner thigh. She took it lightly up his belly, across his chest, and back up to his neck. This time when she got back to his neck he felt her apply some pressure. His heartbeat raced and he took off the blindfold and saw she was holding a dagger to his throat. He said, "Whoa, whoa. I mean…Red. Red. Red!"

She smiled as she lowered the dagger and said, "Okay, there is the line." She put the dagger away and told him to get on his knees. He was starting to feel excited as he felt she was about to tell him to give her oral pleasure and that would lead to the actual sex part. To his surprise, she instead commanded him to lick her toes. He said, "Oh yeah, red on that. Yeah, I'm sorry. I guess I'm not very good at this."
She told him he was doing fine. She lifted him with her finger under his chin and as she brought his face into her breast. He started to kiss them and she told him to bite. He did and she rewarded him with her light moans. Over the next hour, she did try other things with him. Some he was open to and some he was not. He was a fair subject for a first-timer to the world of BDSM. He finally did get the part he wanted, and he got it good as she had ravished him hard. As he lay on his back with her on top of him all he could think was 'holy shit this girl is a freaking nympho.'

They had finished their frolicking and lay in each other's arms in the afterglow of their afternoon delight. This would be their life for the next couple of weeks. Jayden would take Pepper around to the fun hidden activities in town that tourists never saw and it would always lead back to some hot and heavy action at the end of the day. This was till it was time for Pepper to make her return home to the Peeking Islands. A place Jayden would soon find himself while visiting her. For someone that started as a fun way to pass time, this took a more serious direction rather quickly. He had good feelings about a future that sat ahead.

HOUSE OF THE MORNING STAR

It had been about six months since Jayden and Pepper had first met. They had kept in contact through phone calls. They had kind of developed a relationship without it being a relationship. Jayden was on a break from school and was planning on visiting Pepper where she lived in the Peeking Islands. This island chain was something he held close to his heart. He had spent his entire childhood visiting the islands with his parents. As he grew older, he would come with his friends. The Peeking Islands were a cool place to get away from the mainland. It was like visiting the Caribbean, only it felt a lot safer, and it was easier to get to. The five-island chain was sixty miles off the coast of Daytona. It seemed to be a world of its own. The locals had a different attitude than people in touristy towns on the mainland. They were always friendly without coming off as running a scam. The friendliness seemed sincere. They were always ready to strike up a conversation with anyone. It was the type of place where if a stranger on the sidewalk said hello, they were saying hello. It was not followed up by a hustle. It is just how they were. The Peeking Islands were a judgment-free, filter-free zone. One could be themselves while in this paradise. The local phrase was, "Come as you are, stay as you go." They were called the Peeking Islands as the mountains on the islands would appear to peek out of the ocean as one approached. There were two ways to get to the island chain. One was by ferry; the other was by plane. On this trip, Jayden was taking the ferry.

The ferry blew its horn as it pulled into the historic seaport of Manta Ray. The seaport was two miles long and was considered a tourist area. This is where one would find all the watersport companies, popular bars, and many restaurants. The area had a carnival-like atmosphere as there were a couple of areas that were filled with games of chance and a couple of handfuls of buskers performing many different sideshows. A wooden wharf went all along the waterfront and there were many old schooners parked and ready to take tourists out on the open water.

Jayden pulled his truck off the ferry onto Water Street. This was the street that ran parallel to the entire historic seaport. It was stop and go each block and, in a car, one had to be watchful as the pedestrians never were. They would walk out in the street oblivious to traffic as if it was never-ever land and the normal rules do not apply. In this area, there was no question that Christmas was fast approaching. The festive scene was everywhere. Lights strung up in every storefront, wreaths hanging from every lamppost, and even one block had fake snow blasting from rooftops to the street below. Christmas music played over speakers that were hung over the street.

Jayden pulled off Water Street, went up a block, and was on the Peeking Highway. This was a road that went around all the islands and connected them via bridges. Once on the Peeking Highway, he headed north toward the top of Manta Ray. This would take him to the top of the island. He would travel around the outer edge of the island. He was on this way to Thomasville. On the way, he would pass through the town of David. The island of Manta Ray was only about an eight-by-seven-mile island. Technically it was all one town. But the locals had given names to all the small communities on the island chain. Maybe they were not real towns, perhaps communities. To the locals, they were towns. After Jayden passed David, he would go by a small seaport. This was not touristy as was the historic seaport. It was more for local fishermen. This would lead directly to a wooded area at the top of the island. The highway would round off to the right and take him south. On his left, he would see water can could view the island of Isla Sirena.

There would also be another small seaport meant for local fishermen and a bridge leading to Isla Sirena. At this point he would be entering a small mountain range, or as people from the western United States would call them, foothills. He passed the bridge to Isla Sirena and continued south till he hit the town, or community rather, of Thomasville. Thomasville was a community of local fishermen that used the two seaports he had passed on the way there. Those who did not live on their boats lived in small handmade shacks hidden in the mountains. There was a small grocery store, a church that went six pews deep, a gas station, a restaurant, a T-shirt shop filled with touristy gifts, a marine store that provided those that worked on the water with the gear they need, bait and tackle supply store, and a bar. The name of the bar was Billy's.

The music that played inside of Billy's was classic rock. Billy's is a seedy dive bar on the northeast side of Manta Ray. It is a small town that sits at the foot of the mountains and has a small seaport. It is primarily local fishermen that live there.

The bar was dark. More light spilled in naturally than was provided by any lights inside.

The front of the bar was wide open. As if it had no wall. There was an actual wall. It was very large glass doors. They were always open though, even when the bar was closed. The floor was uneven cement. Old pictures and newspaper clippings of the Peeking Islands covered the walls. There was a permanent smell of smoke in the air. A bar sat in the center of the room. It was designed in a square so the bartender would be surrounded. In one back corner of the bar sat a stool next to an amplifier. There was a guitar and microphone next to the amplifier. This was so a local musician could entertain the patrons. Upon walking in, to the right of the bar were; three pool tables, a golfing video arcade game, a foosball table, two dartboards, and one pinball machine. It was a game room without being an actual separate room. This was the type of bar that saw the same people every day. It was the fisherman that docked and lived in Thomasville that would use it. They all had what could be considered their own personal seat at the bar. Four places around the bar counter had ashes of former patrons embedded in the bar top with a small plaque that had their name on it. It was nothing too special. It was only a small, two-inch plaque with a name on it. Only people who had been in the bar for decades would know what they were and that there were human ashes underneath them. Which was kind of the point. This was a local bar. The bartender could set his watch by the patrons that walked in every day. It was not a bar for tourists. Although the tourists that were frequent to the Peeking Islands would come into the bar from time to time. As long as they were respectful and seemed to know their place, they were welcome to sit and be served an ice-cold beer. Overall, the bar was supported by the local fisherman. These were not sports fishermen. These were men and women that fished for a living. They supplied many of the restaurants with their catch. The boats they owned were probably passed down from their fathers before them.

It was another typical day at Billy's. The bar had eight people in it. Which for 10 AM on a Sunday sounded about right. Five were at the bar, three were playing darts, and two were playing pool. The streets of Thomasville had a slight breeze to them provided by the channel between Manta-Ray and Isla Sirena. That breeze did not find its way into the bar. No musician was playing. It was only classic rock music that played over a jukebox. The bar patrons had the same conversation they had every day in the bar. It was filled with locker room jokes and tales of the old

Peeking Islands. These were men and women whose biggest worry in life was, what will the weather be like tomorrow and how will it affect my fishing?

Nothing was different in Billy's that day. Then a man walked into the bar. He looked young. He looked barely old enough to drink. He stood over six feet tall and had a muscular build. He had short dark naturally curly hair and a clean-shaven face. Walking into the bar he did look like a fish out of water. He walked into the bar and stopped. He stood with his hands on his hips as his eyes widened trying to adjust from the bright island sun to the sudden darkness of the bar. He moved his head around slowly side to side as if inspecting the bar. One man at the bar nudged his friend next to him with his elbow and motioned with his head to look at the entrance. The music stopped as every head in the bar looked to the stranger.

Jayden stood outside what appeared to be a bar on Tudor Street. It was a small street just off the seaport in Thomasville. He looked around at his options. There was a fish market, a gas station, and a bar. There was no sign indicating it was a bar or even a name. But one could tell it was a bar.

It was around 10 AM and it was open on a Sunday. He was only looking for a place to sit and kill some time. This appeared to be a good option. He walked in and it was dark. He gave his eyes a moment to adjust as he scanned the room. He could see that this bar was what is best described as a dive. The other people in the bar all were dressed the same. Jeans and flannel shirts seemed to be the dress code here. There were a few people at the bar drinking, and others seemed to be enjoying their drinks over pool and darts. Jayden knew immediately he had walked into a locals-only bar. He was already in though. At this point, he was committed.

The music stopped and it seemed that every head in the bar turned and looked to him. He then heard one of the other bar patrons yell out, "Hey Tommy! The music has stopped!" The bartender whose name must have been Tommy turned his head away from the door and back to the bar as he curtly said, "Then put some more quarters in, Sam!"
Another bar patron spoke up as he said, "Come on Tommy, ya freakin cheapskate! Why don't you just put the jukebox on a continuous free?"

"You want music you have two options. Go pick up a guitar and play some songs or put in some quarters."
Another voice spoke up and this time it was in the direction of Jayden. It said, "Well don't just stand there boy. Make yourself useful and order up some music!"

Jayden walked up to the bar still a little confused about what he just walked into. Tommy asked him, "Well, what'll be son?" Jayden took a dollar out of his wallet and asked to exchange for quarters.
The bartender asked, "Do I look like a bank to you?"
Jayden asked, "I'm sorry, what?"
"Do I look like a bank?"
Jayden cleared his throat and said, "No sir. I thought I would just put some quarters in your jukebox."
Tommy the bartender said, "Well son, I ain't no bank. You want quarters you gotta buy something. So, what'll it be?"
Jayden was not used to this type of service but realized he was a stranger in a strange land. He cleared his throat and said, "I'll have a beer please."

Jayden was surprised he did not get carded. Being that he was barely twenty and not old enough to drink he was not going to raise a stink about that though. The bartender gave Jayden beer served in a can and change back that included quarters. He went to the jukebox and looked over his shoulder as he asked, "Any requests?"
A patron said, "Your quarters, your choice, son." There was not much of a choice as it was all the same. He was able to recognize most of the band names. They were all bands he grew up listening to, as that is what his parents had played all the time. He put in eight quarters and made a few random selections. The conversations went back to normal with music playing and lowly spoken conversation.

    Jayden sat at the bar as he sipped his second beer and for the most part stared straight ahead minding his own business and trying to maintain a low profile. He heard a voice yell out and knew it was speaking to him when it asked, "Where ya from boy? Jayden turned around and looked toward the voice as he said, "I'm from southwest Florida. Right on the gulf and on the edge of the Glades." Another patron asked, "What brings you here?"

Jayden said, "I met a girl back where I'm from that lives here on Manta Ray. We became friends so I am just here to visit for a couple of days. I come here a lot."

"You don't say, what do you do when you come here?" Someone inquired.

Jayden answered, "Normally hang out at the historic seaport here on Manta Ray or go hiking over on Isla de Cabeza Martillo. I've camped at Fantasma a couple of times."

Someone chimed in and said, "Oh! Practically local!"

Someone else added, "You mean Martillo."

Jayden asked, "excuse me?"

"Martillo. We just call it Martillo. Or Manta, not Manta Ray."

That was followed by laughter. There was a brief lull in the inquisition as the bartender motioned to Jayden for another beer. Jayden took a moment as he thought about that and motioned for just one more. The break in the sudden interest in Jayden was broken when someone sat down next to him and said, "So you come here a lot. Tell me, have you ever been out to see the House of the Morning Star?"

Jayden looked at the man sitting next to him and said, "I don't believe I have."

A few more men moved from their places on the bar and in closer to Jayden. He was getting the feeling that he was about to hear a really big fish tale.

Jayden asked, "The House of the Morning Star you say. What is it?"
A female voice from one of the pool tables said, "Oh, let's not start with this shit. He bought a beer, he's mind'n his own. Leave the boy alone."
The man sitting next to Jayden shook his head back and forth as he said, "Don't mind her. The House of the Morning Star. Ever hear of it?"
Jayden took another sip of his beer as he shook his head back and forth.

"It's out on David Key," Said the man sitting next to Jayden, who responded, "David Key? I know of the town of David. It's about a mile up from the historic seaport. That town has a really good pizza joint."
"No son, not the town. It is an island. About one square mile in space. It is east of Martillo."
Jayden asked, "East of Isla de Cabeza Martillo? I thought that was the last island."
"How many islands do you think make up the Peeking chain?"

Jayden responded with five and named them all while going off his fingers.

One of the patrons chimed in, "No. There are six. David Key is the sixth. You won't find it on a map and it does not show up on GPS."

Showing interest Jayden asked, "Does not show up on GPS? How is that possible?"

The female voice yelled out from the pool table, "Because it does not exist! Don't listen to these assholes."

The patron sitting next to Jayden yelled back, "Shut the Hell up Melissa!" Then looked back to Jayden. "Oh, it exists. But you are not likely to see it. The only way you can find it is if you are not looking for it."

Jayden said, "Well, I've taken a boat all over that area. Land out of site many times. I did not know about this island then, should I have stumbled across it since I was not looking for it because I did not know it was there?"

The answer he got was, "No. Because you have to know it exists to not be looking for it."

Ignoring the lack of logic in that statement Jayden asked, "So what's on this island, David Key, you said right?"

One of the other men spoke up as he slowly said, "Vampires, a cult of vampires. They live out there to be left alone and not stand out in society. They prey upon boaters and fishermen. They use their vampire powers to mess with your boat and make you lost. Then it is said, your boat loses power and you start to drift in the open water. An island will appear out of nowhere and your boat drifts to it as if under its own will. People who have been to the island say that once there, they walk around the island, get lost in the trees and foliage. They will hear drum beats, like tribal drums in the distance. They are drawn to the drums and will find themselves in an open field, where out of nowhere an old stone mansion and wooden barn appear. They go into the barn where the sound of the drums is coming from and come across a group of vampires. It is then that they are taken captive by the vampires who spend weeks feasting off of their blood. They drink enough to feed their hunger for blood, but leave enough in their victims to stay alive and produce more blood."

As the man finished his story he leaned back and folded his arms. Jayden asked, "So how do people know?"

"Know what?" The man asked.

"Know of this story. If the vampires kill all the sailors that get lost out there who is left to tell the story?"

The man appeared to think. "Because they don't kill them all. Sometimes they convert the living to be like them and keep their bloodline going. These people come back home. But it is not them. They are different. It is like they are half of a different person in their skin. They are not full vampire till after the next full moon. At which point they disappear. We can only assume they return to David Key to be with their own kind."

Jayden asked, "Why the Morning Star?"

"What?" Asked the man.

"You said there is a house that appears out of nowhere and that it is called the Morning Star. Why is it called that?"

The man appeared to think again. "Because it is located in the direction of the last star to go down at sunrise. Which is when the vampires have to go to sleep for the day."

The woman from the pool table spoke out again as she walked in the direction of Jayden and the storytellers. "Oh my God, Jeb. If you're going to tell the tale, tell it right." She looked over to Jayden as she offered her hand in greeting and said, "Hi. I'm Melissa. This idiot that has been telling the story is Jeb, his buddy next to him is Frank." She continued to introduce every person in the bar. Jayden introduced himself as he shook

Melissa's hand. She stood at around five foot eight and had some weight to her. She was not fat, just full-figured. She looked to be maybe in her early forties but her eyes, and the crow's feet around them, told a different story. Melissa continued, "These boys spend too much time alone on the open water, don't' mind them or their lack of manners." She looked to her friends in the bar as she said, "Next time boys you got to introduce yourselves when you're talking to a stranger." She looked back to Jayden and said, "I am the harbormaster for this seaport and all these boys, which means I am also sometimes their mother. Anyway. Don't listen to these clowns. They can't even get a fish tale right." She looked back to the fishermen and said, "Boys, if you gonna tell a tourist a fish tale you've got to make it somewhat believable. Vampires. Vampires? Really? Everyone knows there ain't no such thing as vampires." She turned back to Jayden and said, "Now listen, there ain't no vampires living on a hidden island out in the ocean. It's a cult of devil worshippers. A bunch of heathens. And there ain't no hidden island out in the ocean. Which means there is no House of the Morning Star. And if there were its name has nothing to do with vampires avoiding the sunrise. Morning Star is the name for the bringer of light, which would be

Jesus. It is the morning star that would keep these hedonistic bastard devil worshippers down. It is what would keep them held in their place. Therefore, a house where these people are all forced to stay would be a fortress holding them in place. Hence House of the Morning Star. But also, in the beliefs of the Satanists, morning star can refer to Lucifer, as their kind thinks of him as the bringer of light, intellectualism, and enlightenment. Which is wrong of course, but either way none of it matters because no such place exists."

Jayden looked to Melissa and then around the room and paused as he asked carefully, "You mentioned earlier that it was devil worshippers and not vampires. So is it just the island and house that does not exist or are there devil worshippers here in the Peeking Islands?"
"Oh, there are devil worshipers here honey. Don't let our veil of paradise fool you. We got our share of crazies just like any town on the mainland. There just ain't no hidden island or house and barn that magically appear out of nowhere."
Jayden just sat in silence unsure what to say. Melissa stood up and looked around at all the bar patrons as she said in a demanding voice, "Now don't you boys have someplace to be? Shouldn't

you be out fishing? Those slip fees aren't gonna pay themselves and I expect all of you to pay on time this month. Go out there and catch something!" She looked back to Jayden and told him to enjoy his stay. Jeb spoke up and said, "We can't go out just yet Melissa! It's almost time for Reverend McDowell! It's Sunday woman! We need to listen to the Reverend spread the good word!" He looked to Tommy the bartender and bellowed out, "Now turn on that radio I know you have so we can listen to the Reverend. You can charge us for music, but you can't charge us for the word of God." Tommy reached under the counter and the classic rock disappeared as it was replaced with the sounds of an Angelic and upbeat choir. All the patrons inside Billy's bar gathered around and sat in for what would be their Sunday morning church service.

SO SAYETH THE SHEPPARD, SO SAYETH THE FLOCK!

The Reverend McDowell was a conservative evangelist. He had a nationally syndicated radio show, and his following was most definitely from the right-wing. As to whether he was an actual preacher, could remain to be seen. As far as his following was concerned, he had all the proper credentials he needed. He broadcast his show from somewhere in Texas.

As the choir ended their song a female voice could be heard saying, "Folks, please welcome to the stage, the Reverend Colin McDowell." There was the sound of applause that could be heard as the Reverend began to speak. "People of the flock of the righteous, I wish you well today. I pray that my words find you well!" he paused and then continued. "But I know you cannot be completely well. Not with these heathens currently running our country! To be content we must find a way to bring our beliefs of Christianity to the unholy. So sayeth the Sheppard!" The crowd in attendance of the broadcast could be heard yelling, "So sayeth the flock!"

"My people, my brothers and sisters, those of you here in attendance in the great God-loving state of Texas and those of you listening in across this great God-loving nation, we have a problem in this country. We are no longer together as a nation. We have a very big divide. This divide is between those close to God and our savior Jesus Christ and those that would make what we believe in, a crime!"

There was a stirring sound from the live audience. The sound of organ music and the choir hummed up and down as their singing matched the reverend's pace and inflection.

"They want to bring us down. They want to install beliefs in their young that loving God is wrong. We cannot allow this to happen. So sayeth the Sheppard!" The crowd responded, "So sayeth the flock!"

"They want us to believe that it is wrong for us to census how many Americans are in America, but at the same time, we are supposed to be okay with illegals voting! If a man wants to pretend to be a woman, you are supposed to pretend with him! They want you to believe there is no such thing as gender, but they also want you to vote for a female president! We cannot allow this type of hypocrisy, So sayeth the Sheppard!"

The crowd in attendance and audiences listening on their radios across the nation responded, "So sayeth the flock!"

The crowd pandering seemed to go on for an hour. It was all very hyped up and the audience seemed programmed to respond to his words. It was filled with one-liner hype lines proving why his belief was the one and only word. Today's sermon seemed to be regarding the hypocrisy of the left in his eyes. As he wrapped up, he took a few breaths and appeared to calm down as he spoke to his congregation. "My brothers and sisters, here me now. If there is only one thing that you leave with today, leave with this. We are living in a world with no morals, no values, no civility. Nothing makes sense anymore. We are living in a world that is upside down. Where wrong is right, and right is wrong. Where the moral is immoral, where good is evil and evil is good. It is wrong to kill murderers, but it is right to kill babies. We live in a world where darkness is light, and light is the new darkness. Please, we cannot allow this to go on. This must stop! We must come together as a nation and make light the new light! We must make right, right! We must make moral the new moral! We must bring this country back to what it once was! So sayeth the

Sheppard!" The crowd yelled back, "So sayeth the flock!"

The reverend wrapped up his sermon by saying, "My brothers and sisters. I love you all. I thank you by the grace of God for being here today. Please help keep us going. On your way out today, please give what you can spare into our donation jars by the exit. If you are joining our joyous congregation on the radio today, please stand by and listen for instructions on how you can donate. It is only through the kindness of your hearts that the grace of God will allow us to get our good word out and then hopefully, we can bring others to us. Only then can we bring this nation back together as one under the love of the all-mighty Lord above us! God bless America and God bless all who find love with Jesus Christ, our savior! So sayeth the Sheppard!"

"So sayeth the flock!"

A SKIP TO HIS WALK

The patrons inside Billy's all stood up. They paid out their tabs and went on their way. Jayden was the only one left in the bar. He could have left an hour ago. However, everyone in the bar seemed hyped up to listen to this Reverend McDowell guy. He did not want to get up and leave when they started playing that. In his way of thinking, it would have been rude, and he did not want to come off that way to a group of people who had allowed him space in what appeared to be their bar. To Jayden, it would be like disrespecting a person in their own home. It was not like he had any place he had to be immediately. To him, it just seemed like the right thing to do. All though, after listening to that he was wondering, "What the fuck did I just listen to?"

Tommy walked up to his only bar patron and asked if he'd have one for the road. Jayden politely declined, paid his tab, and walked out of the bar into the warm sun provided by the heavens above. It was time to seek out Pepper. She would be getting out of work soon.

It was past noon and Jayden figured that Pepper would be at her parent's shop. From Billy's, he took a right onto the Peeking Highway and drove south for about three miles. This would take him down the east coast of the Manta Ray. On his left, he would see water, and in the distance, he could see Isla Sirena. On his right was a small mountain range and some wooded area. After three miles he would take a right onto a small side road. This would take him west for a half-mile, then he would turn north for a mile till he took left onto another side road. This would take him past Los Olas de Prados. Translated to English that was the Waving Meadows. It was a wooded area that from the air had an outline that would look like a person waving. This small stretch of road would cut across the island and get him back on the Peeking Highway where he would take a left and drive south to the historic seaport. With all the twists and turns it would seem like he was going out of his way. The Peeking Highway though traveled around the outer edge of every island in the chain. It would have been a ten-to-twelve-mile trip either way around the highway. Plus, it was nice to drive on some of the roads usually only used by locals.

He parked his truck in a metered spot near the Sacred Mists shop and made his way to the store. He was feeling excited knowing that he would be seeing Pepper again. It was not like he was romantically attached to her. Maybe he was lustfully attached if any attachment at all. He could not explain it. Jayden only knew that he could feel a smile hit his face and a warmness in his heart as he walked to the store. They were not dating in any compacity, but they had kept in touch through phone calls and letters. In these letters, they would sometimes send pictures of each other. The letters from Pepper were always laced with a sweet-smelling perfume that drew Jayden in. It made him feel attracted to her, if just a scent could do that. They were not involved though. Jayden knew that. He had no idea why was excited to see someone that had been just a hot piece of ass to him. He did know that he had felt compelled to visit her though. That was why he was here. To see Pepper. It was like something had called out to him in a siren song and sang he needed to see her or be with her. So, here he was.

With excitement in his heart, Jayden pulled on the door to the Sacred Mists shop. He pulled the door with gusto and confidence. The door held shut. He then pushed. It remained shut. Putting a hand to the side of his head near his eyes he peered through the glass door. The lights were on. The shop looked open. He pulled and pushed the door one more time. The door remained closed. It appeared to be locked. "Fuck." Jayden said out loud. He had a healthy mixture of regret and embarrassment in his voice. He looked over his shoulders to the left and right. He was checking to see if anyone had seen this. There was no one visible on the streets. That did not mean there was nobody in a nearby shop to witness his dumbass attempt to get into a store that was obviously closed. He thought back to a small stint he had in retail. He had memories of him and his co-workers making jokes about people pulling and tugging on doors to stores that were closed. Remember what it was like to make fun of people that had no clue. Remember how at the time it may have seemed funny but a small part of you felt bad because you knew that being a bully was wrong. Imagine what it is like to be that person who was being made fun of and judged by eyes that were unseen to them. Because you can remember it the more you realize that you were an evil jerk. Sooner or later, you will realize that when the day comes that you are the one judged and bullied that it is karma coming back to you. You will find yourself thinking that you should be a better person. You can see yourself being a better version of yourself. Obey. These were the thoughts going to Jayden's head. He was often having inner battles with himself. He was a good person. There was a little bit of evil in him. He knew this. He wondered if there truly was a difference between good and evil. Is it possible for any individual to lean one hundred percent to one side of the spectrum? Was there not a grey area where all life truly existed? Can one exist without the other? Does light not replace darkness at the beginning of every single day?

Jayden awakened from the daze of the inner conflict and noticed an envelope taped to a mailbox on the side of the door. In big letters, his name was written. Assuming it was for him, he grabbed the envelope and opened it. There was a letter in it that had been sprayed with perfume. It was the perfume that Pepper used. He remembered that scent well. It was a scent, unlike any other perfume he had smelled in his life. It was alluring in a way that there seemed to be no resistance to it once it entered the nasal passageway. He took a deep inhale of the scented letter and immediately felt himself drop deep into a relaxed state of mind. The scent entered his nose and traveled to the neurons in his brain that triggered exotic thoughts of Pepper. His heart raced with excitement. He felt ready to respond to whatever the letter had asked. Just as a pet when it hears the word, "treats." Pet. Obey. Reward. After exhaling the warm thoughts of Pepper, Jayden read the letter.

"Jayden! I am so happy to finally see you in person. I waited for you to meet me here at the store, you must be running late. I must run errands, but I will see you tonight. My friends and I are meeting up at Mitchel's Boat Rental on Isla de Cabeza Martillo. Here are the directions. Be a sweet boy come out there tonight. You will come. I can't wait! See you soon. Kisses, Pepper." He folded the letter with directions on it and stuffed it into his pocket as he got back to his truck.

The boat rental place he was to meet Pepper and her friends at later that night was on Isla de Cabeza Martillo. It was the easternmost island in the chain. It was also the longest island. Nine by four miles was its size. The south end of the island was shaped like the head of a hammerhead shark. Having to be on that island later that night to hook up with Pepper was convenient as it was the same island his motel was on.

Jayden was making his way to Isla de Cabeza Martillo. He left the historic seaport on Manta-Ray and took the Peeking Highway around the north end of the island. This would lead him to a two-mile bridge that would take him to Isla Serina. This was a four-by-two-mile island that sat in the middle of the chain. There was not much on this island. A few radio and television stations were about all it offered. There were a couple of small seaports on the north side, a small mountain, a river that cut through the center. The Peeking Highway took Jayden around the northern tip of the island which led to another bridge. This bridge was half a mile long and would take him to Bear Island. This island was a three-by-three-mile island with woods on both ends and a large mountain in the middle looking over a bay. The bay was called Vista Bahia. The bay hosted many liveaboard boats that were used by several people in the service industry. They were overlooked by a large mountain that had mansions at the top of it. The Peeking Highway went all the way around the island like it did all the islands. Jayden only needed to take a short jaunt across the southern tip till reaching another bridge. This was another two-mile bridge that took him to Isla de Cabeza Martillo. Once reaching this island he would be greeted by two separate seaports on his left and right. Jayden took a left and headed to the north end of the island. The town he was heading to was called, Cueva Aullanando. It was on a cove and, on a map looked like a howling wolf.

Jayden checked into his motel. This did not require much. There was no greeting filled with fanfare and a big warm welcoming. It was a simple place. It was what he could afford. It did not seem to even have a name. There was only one sign in front. It said, Motel. Jayden did not need anything special. He was a simple college freshman in the early nineties. Being able to take trips like this was special enough for him. Jayden paid for his room in cash, signed in, and was given a key on a plastic key chain with only the room number on it.

After taking his bag from his truck to his humbling hotel room, Jayden had time to kill. It was only afternoon and the letter from Pepper had said to meet at that boat rental place that night. What did night mean anyway? She did not state a specific time. To Jayden, night meant when the sun went down and it was dark. He had time to kill.

He decided he would drive to Looking Man. This was a beach about halfway down the island on the east side. It was called Looking Man as the shape of the land made it look like a man's face looking east to the Atlantic Ocean. It sat at the foothills of the Centro de la Isla Mountain range. The beach was not like most beaches on the mainland of the east coast of Florida. Oddly, it was more like the west coast. The sand was white and soft. It was the best type of sand to walk on. Jayden grew up on the southwest coast of Florida and may have been biased when he said, "Westside is the best side." This beach reminded him of home. The sand was perfect.

Jayden sat on the perfect sand of Looking Man beach. The beach was empty except for him. Behind him and across the street was a pet shelter. There was a bar that looked much like Billy's.

Shady to a tourist, perfect to the locals. There were a few run-down souvenir shops as well. There was nobody in their parking lots, yet they were open. They must do business at some point if they were able to still pay rent and be open. The area did have a run-down look to it though. It reminded Jayden of Daytona Beach in the early 1980s. It was perfect in his mind.

The sand he sat on was soft and warm. It felt amazing to dig his feet into. Underneath the warm sand was a touch of coolness. It was moments like this Jayden realized that he was truly blessed to be a Floridian. There was no other state that offered an atmosphere like this. He looked out over the horizon of the Atlantic Ocean. Thoughts of the House of the Morning Star entered his head. Jayden looked back over his shoulder. He looked beyond the rip-off T-shirt shops. Across the street, the Centro de la Isla Mountain range loomed over it all. It reminded him of the Smoky Mountains in Tennessee. Minus the smoke of course. This mountain did not have the low ceiling that the mountains Tennessee offered, but they may have been close to the same height and offered just as many hiking opportunities. He focused his attention back on the ocean in front of him. He looked out over the horizon and thought about an island that does not exist and can only be found if one is not looking for it. He thought about everything the locals in Billy's had told him about the House of the Morning Star. "What a retarded story", He said out loud. He had been fishing land out of sight in that direction many times. He had never come across any mysterious island out that way. There were five islands in the Peeking Island chain. Manta Ray, Isla Sirena, Bear Island, Isla de Cabeza Martillo, and Isla de Fantasma. That was it. Five. No more. No less. He was not from this island chain. But he had been coming here all his life. Those "yocals" were toying with him. They had to be.

RUN!

Following the directions Pepper had given him, Jayden found the area he was to meet up with her. It would be great to see her again. He could remember the last time they met at a bonfire. The plan that night was a bonfire with Pepper and her friends. She was going to introduce him and he was feeling excited about that. He had been to the Peeking Islands many times, but he never really had hung out with the locals. So for tonight, he was going to live like a local. Imagine what that would be like, he thought. They were meeting up on the southwest corner of Isla de la Cabeza Martillo. He was heading to the town of Asmassmaria. It was just above a part of the island that resembled a hammer. On the east side of that hammer was what the locals called Shadytown. It was not an actual town. It was a group of drifters camped out in their own makeshift town. Suppose how it would be to live a life by one's own rules. It would be easy to imagine that person being very happy.

Jayden found the area Pepper had given him directions to on a handwritten map. At least he was pretty sure he did. There was no parking lot. After taking his truck down a two-track he parked it next to some other cars assuming that would be good enough. He noticed a big booth with a sign that said, Mitchel's Boat Rental. It was closed but he did remember Pepper telling him to look for that. He realized he must be in the right spot. He got out of his truck and looked around. He was surrounded by marsh. Trees and sand on the ground. Through the trees, he could hear people laughing and talking. He followed the closest thing he could find to a trail into a small clearing in the wooded area. It was about thirty feet in diameter. In the middle was a small bonfire. Surrounding the bonfire were logs on the ground being used as makeshift benches by the people enjoying the fire. There were about eight or ten people gathered around the fire. Jayden slowly approached the group out of the darkness. One guy looked up and asked, "Can we help you?" Pepper stood out and exclaimed, "Jayden! Everyone, this is Jayden. I met him when I was helping my aunt move in south Florida." The group gave a half-hearted greeting. She stood up and walked over to him as she said, "Come on, have a seat." Pointing around the group she introduced everyone. The two that stood out were her best friend Leslie and another guy. His name was Todd. Leslie seemed receptive to Jayden as did most of the group. She was a little overweight and very bubbly in personality. Maybe about five foot two and long curly hair. Todd had messy blonde hair that looked to be greasy. His hair was mostly straight and went down to almost his shoulders. He was tall and lanky but looked like he could hold his own. He stood out to Jayden because when Pepper sat down, she sat down on a log right next to Todd. When she sat down he had put his arm around her.

Jayden at this point was a little perplexed if not confused. He knew that he and Pepper were not exclusively in a relationship. But given how she acted when they met back home, the couple of weeks that followed, and that warm greeting this morning, he just kind of assumed something was going on between them. He realized that he was wrong and misread that one in a major way. The way that this guy protectively and possessively held her in his arm along with the way she leaned into him illustrated this was not just some Sunday night hook-up going on between the two. They were clearly a couple. It had suddenly occurred to Jayden that he had been a side piece. He had mixed feelings about that. On one hand, he technically was not the one doing the cheating nor was he the one being cheated on. Since he did not know about Todd, it was not like he was knowingly stealing a girl from another guy. He was innocent in all of this. At the same time, it was wrong and evil what she had done. If she is with this dude, she should be loyal to him. It said a lot about her character. He knew it was wrong and evil. At the same time, it felt good and no damage had been done. He could have spoken up to fight for Pepper or at the very least he could have done the right thing, which would be to let Todd know that his girl is not very loyal to him. That would have been the right thing to do by the man code. If he kept quiet, in a way, he was lying. Which would be evil. If he spoke up he would be a snitch. Which was not cool, but it would have been the lawful and right thing to do. He had an inner conflict of right versus wrong. Not wanting to stir embers in the proverbial fire, he kept his mouth shut.

He looked over at her smiling with that look of free will she always had on her face. She was hot. She did make him feel good in a way. He did have feelings for her. This could be a situation where love is the law, so love is under free will. But if free will ends up breaking the law of ethics and morals should one continue? In the end, love is only the servant of free will or more than likely, the servant of the ego. Sooner or later, the answer to who Pepper was would come out. Judging by the looks he was getting from Todd, this was not a time to listen to the ego and fight over a girl. He was a stranger in a strange land, far from home. The feeling in the air was neither, positive nor negative. He could tell from the look in Todd's eyes that he must have known something was up. He had to have known something happened with his girlfriend while she was in south Florida.

Taking his attention off Todd, Jayden glanced back over to Pepper. She looked to him with a hunger in her eyes. Why was she still looking at him like this as she leaned into what was someone that was obviously a boyfriend? Even under the current circumstances, Jayden could not help to feel attracted to her. He wanted to be with her. She seemed so full of life. She filled him with life! She made him happy. That was one thought. Perhaps that was the evil side in him speaking out. On the other hand, something was telling him that this is wrong and it cannot go on. For another feeling inside of him suggested that Pepper is anti-life. Because of how she treats men she is soulless. She is an empty shell that presents itself as a substantial universe. What it is that she presents is beautiful and freeing. She is delicious. Perperrat, or Pepper as she called herself is badly misunderstood. It is not till one is already trapped in her vortex that he finds out he has been tricked.

She was not worth it. Not under the present circumstances anyway. It was best to keep a low profile and try to fly under the radar. Although the current attitude around the bonfire seemed to be fun and jovial, there was also a feeling that said this could turn nasty real quick with one wrong word spoken.

Jayden turned his attention to Pepper's friend, Leslie. He had come out tonight intending to eventually have some sex. That was not going to happen with captain greasy head having his hands all over Pepper. Leslie seemed nice enough. Certainly not the most attractive girl around, but sometimes a hole is just a hole. His thoughts were interrupted. It was by a guy that had been introduced earlier as Jeff. Out of all the members of the group, Jeff had appeared to be the most receptive of Jayden. He was short and stocky. He had thick dirty blonde hair. A giant mole sat on the right side of his chin. He said to Jayden, "Looks like we are running low on beer. You by chance don't have any do you?" Jayden told him he had a couple of cases in his truck. Jeff said, "Cool man, I'll help you get it." The two followed the trail out to Jayden's truck and grabbed the cases. Jeff asked, "No cooler man? This has been sitting in your truck all day? This is gonna be skunk beer man." Jayden said, "yeah man. Sorry." Jeff told him, "It is what it is man." As he shrugged his shoulder and took a swig of warm beer."

They came back to the bonfire and everyone was swallowing down warm beer. Jayden looked around as he silently judged these people. They were the same age as him. Just from a different lifestyle. He had grown up in a town with a reputation of being filled with well-to-do people. It did not mean they all were well to do. He reflected on that a bit as he thought reputation is what others think of a person, character is what they really are. These were all simple islanders. That was the reputation perceived by others. Or as it might turn out, they are just like him. A normal latch key Gen X'er trying to survive in a not so honest and upfront world. They had been raised on different beliefs in life that he had perhaps. Their way of life was different. Was it though? If he were home with his friends he would be sitting on a beach illegally drinking with friends. Here he sat, with a group of people he had never met before doing the same exact thing. The more people seem different, perhaps the more they are the same. Lawlessness existed at all outreaches when it came to minors in position. As a twenty-year-old he had to ask himself, was he a minor though? His country considered him old enough to vote and fight. He had paid his dues. He was okay with this. As were the rest of them.

With a desire to want to be part of a group conversation in a group that he strongly felt out of place, Jayden spoke to the group as he asked, "Have any of you heard of the House of the Morning Star or a place called David Key?" Someone laughed and asked, "What are you talking about man?"

"I'm not sure. I was in a bar today and some of the guys in there were talking about an island east of Martillo. I guess you can only find it when you are not looking for it." He said with an intentional sound of confusion in his voice. Jeff spoke up and said, "Oh yeah, I know what you are talking about." A girl asked, "You do?"

Jeff said, "Yeah Jill, he's talking about End of the World, you know this." Looking back to Jayden, Jeff said, "The old-timers call it Morning Star or whatever. We call it End of the World. It's a small little island quite a ways out in the Atlantic and super hard to find. It is not charted so it's not on any maps and for whatever reason the GPS does not pick it up. There is a small Native American burial ground there too. This island is covered with small creeks and to find this burial ground you have to cross seven bridges. But here is the kicker. You leave the burial ground the same way you came back as there is only one trail. But on your way back you only cross six bridges. It's freaky man. And if you pay close attention you will see weird stuff in the trees." Jayden asked, "What kind of weird stuff?"

Jeff told him, "I don't know man. Just weird stuff. Stuff that the Native Americans left behind for their past loved ones. Like weird-looking wreaths made out of branches and stuff. I don't know man. Weird stuff!"

Jayden said, "I see. Have any of you been out there? Have you ever seen a house or barn appear out of nowhere or heard drums?"

Jill said, "We've all been out there. But I don't know about any invisible house or drums. People say that vampires live out there. Others say, devil worshipers. But I've never seen anyone out there. I think it is just an old burial ground with a spooky history. So you for reals get the chills out there. I've been once and won't go back."

Jayden asked, "So you know how to get there?"

Jeff said, "No man. The two times I've been there were by accident. Wasn't even looking for it. I would be out boating at night and my compass got all whacky and there was a fog that came in. Then this island appeared out of nowhere so I would go to it in hopes of waiting out the fog so I could look to the stars and find my way home."

Leslie asked, "And then what?"

"What do you mean?" Jeff asked.

"Well, you said you landed on the island and wait for the fog to lift. So then what?"

Jeff told her, "I don't know. It was the same both times. I remember getting off the boat and following a trail. That is how I know about the bridges. I got weird feelings, then the next thing I know I wake up on my boat floating at sea and everything is fine. I don't know. I just don't remember a lot out there. I don't remember seeing anyone out there, but I have heard that there are vampires, devil worshipers, or whatever out there." Leslie said, "I heard it was a coven of witches."

Another guy in the group, Chad said, "Devil worshippers, witches, whatever. Is there a difference? Either way, it is spooky as shit."

Pepper took a swig of her warm beer and said, "There is a difference. Witches believe that the world is a breathing organism. They not only see the world as breathing but think of it as divine. That is the reason they do not involve themselves in animal or human sacrifices as Satanists do. Witches believe in a multitude of God's and Goddesses. Witches live in harmony with the nature around them. Satanists believe in and pray to only Satan. They also believe that using magic or performing rituals is a way to increase their power. The sacrificial offerings are legitimate and desirable means to achieve their own goals."

Todd looked to Pepper and trying to lighten the sudden somber mood jokingly said, "Okay, babe. You know a little too much about that."

Chad said, "I think it's just an Indian burial ground. That reminds me, you want to hear a freaky story with Indians, check this out."

Jill spoke out and said, "Native Americans."

Chad asked, "What?"

"You said Indians. The correct word is Native Americans."

Shaking his head back and forth Chad continued, "My grandfather was in world II. In that war the Marines used what they called, Code Talkers. They were Indians" he paused and looked over to Jill as he stressed, "Native Americans…actually Jill if you want to be technical, they were mostly Navajo, but it was started in World War I by the Cherokee and Choctaw. My grandfather had a Choctaw. But that is just if we are being politically correct tonight Jill." Pepper said, "Okay you two, Chad just tell the story please."

Chad said, "Right, where was I? Oh yeah, the Marines would use these Native Americans to talk to each other over the radio. Every radio operator had one by his side. So if he had to a get message out over the radio he would tell his Code Talker and the Code Talker would talk to another Code Talker on the other end. They spoke in their Native American language. Since the Nazi's and Jap's had no way"

Jill interrupted, "Japanese!"

Jeff said, "Jill, just let the racist tell his story! Come on! Jeeze!"

Chad took a breath, "Where was I again? Oh yeah... The AXIS had no way of knowing that language. So, there was no way they could decipher the message had it been spoken in English. Anyway, these Choctaws were the real deal. They could do more than just speak a language that the Axis did not understand. These fuckers were truly one with everything around them. It was like nature, or something would whisper to them of a future about to happen. My grandfather's Code Talker could always sense when him and my grandfather were in danger. Every time there was a grenade being thrown in their direction this Choctaw heard a voice in his head that said, 'RUN'. Sure as shit, a few seconds later they would hear the thud of a grenade landing next to them. Hearing this voice was a huge advantage as it gave them just a few extra seconds on any ticking grenade coming in their direction. Which was apparently always enough. My grandfather spent so much time with this Choctaw that somehow his powers started to rub off. It was not long before my grandfather could also hear a voice in his head that said, 'RUN' just before a grenade would hit the ground. It saved their lives many times. One time though they were sitting in an embankment and there was a thud on the ground next to them. They were shocked as neither one of them had heard a voice in their head saying, 'RUN'. But sure enough, there was a grenade about to explode right next to them. Shocked by the surprise and knowing they had no time to get up and run for cover they laid face down on the ground and covered their heads with their arms and hands. Two seconds went by. Pretend you are them. What would do? Four seconds went by. Imagine the intensity they felt! Their bodies were so tensed up waiting for the grenade to go off and rip into them with burning hot shrapnel. Six seconds. What is it like when you know your life is about to end? Three more and they would feel intense pain. Nine seconds. My grandfather's eyes and teeth clenched up super tight. I mean with every second that goes by you would have to feel your body tighten! Twelve seconds. Nothing. They looked over at the grenade and it had not gone off. The Choctaw got up and picked it up off the ground. He looked at it. It still had the pin inside of it. Whoever threw the grenade had forgotten to pull the pin. The Indian walked over to my grandfather while holding the grenade in his hand and said, 'This was meant to be the death of you. But it was not. You are meant for something truly great further down the road. Hold on to this. Keep it with you always as a reminder, you are meant to be here.' Then he handed my grandfather the grenade and he kept it with him the rest of his life waiting for that great thing to happen. Imagine knowing you are meant for something better. Every time you doubt taking a chance you will take it. Because you know you are meant for something better. Thinking that way must have helped my grandfather because he took some big risks on the stock market when nobody else was and it paid off big."

Jill asked, "So what is the scary part?"

Chad paused as he reached behind the log he was sitting on as if reaching for something and said, "The scary part…The scary part is this. I know this story because my grandfather told it to me on his deathbed. After telling me this story he handed me the grenade and told me to keep it with me always. As I have. In fact, I have it here with me now. It is a reminder that life can change in the blink of an eye. What would you do if you held that knowledge?" He held out his right hand.

In the shadowy flickering of the bonfire, everyone could see an oval-like object in Chad's right hand. He put his left hand to the top of the object and pulled it away quickly as he tossed the object into the fire and yelled, "RUN!"

Todd yelled, "What the fuck Chad?" Everyone got up off their logs quickly and took cover behind whatever tree they could find. Chad did not run. He stood directly in front of the fire with his arms held up in the air and looking toward the night sky he yelled,

"ONE! I'm com'n for ya Grandpa!" The group had run to the tree line.

"TWO! Oh man, this is going to be sweet! " Everyone had dropped, deeper into the trees away from the threat.

"THREE!" He heard voices coming from the tree line, "Chad! What are you doing?"

"FOUR!"

"Chad! Get out of there!

"FIVE! You hear them, grandpa?"

"SIX! They didn't think your story was scary!"

"SEVEN! But it sure is now!"

"EIGHT!" More voices from the tree line were heard, "Chad get down. Oh my God!"

"NINE!" There were sudden screams heard from the tree line as a loud pop came from the campfire. Then nothing. Only the laughter of Chad could be heard. He was bent down on his knees laughing as he yelled out, "It was just a pinecone ya'll!"

They all came out of the trees. Leslie yelled, "You're a fucking asshole Chad! That was not funny!"

Some were upset. Some saw the humor and patted him on the back. Jayden did not know what to make of it. Granted it was kind of funny. It was the type of thing he and his friends would do back home. Maybe. It was evil and wrong, yet was funny and right. Either way, it was getting late and the more that the beer set in, Jayden was worried for his general safety in a group of strangers. He was running through a couple of different believable excuses to make his exit when Todd spoke up. "Hey, who is up for a wet night run?" Everyone spoke up in agreement. Jeff yelled out, " Wet Night run!"

Jayden looked to Pepper and asked, "What's a night run?"

Jeff intervened on her chance to answer as he put his hand on Jayden's shoulder and said, "Man, you are going to love this. We have a bunch of single-rider boats parked down there. We all get in them and race, in the dark, with no lights on, to certain checkpoints. All leading to race back to the beach here. It is awesome fun!"

"I don't have a boat," Jayden replied. Todd told him, "Don't worry man, you can use one of mine. It's my dad's rental company you passed coming in. I own them all."

"Racing in the dark? I don't even know the local waters in the day. How do I stand a chance?"

Chad said, "You don't have to win, boy. All you have to do is keep up."

HORNS AND CROWNS

The group was hollering with excitement as they walked down toward the docks. There was a whole line of single rider boats tied to docks in addition to some larger boats. This was a business that Todd's father owned. They rented these boats out to tourists. The boats were about nine feet in length. They sat very low to the water. So low that it would seem that one would almost be sitting on the water level when driving it. Being that it was such a small watercraft there was not much to the control panel. A throttle on the right, Just beyond the steering wheel was a gas gauge. Below the wheel was a kill cord. That was a cord attached to the control panel. The driver of the boat clips the cord to their body and if they were to fall out the cord would become unattached and kill the engine. This is so the boat does not drive away without a driver in control. There was a small GPS that had been attached to the control panel. It did not come with the boat. That was something Todd's father had probably put on himself to help out the tourists renting the watercraft. That was it. There was enough room for one person in each boat. It was a jet ski with a boat frame around it and a seat. It was not much of a seat. Since the driver was practically at water level the seat was pretty much a flat surface with a back. The driver would be sitting in an "L" position. So the back did not serve a purpose as one would be leaning forward to control the boat. Unless they were just trolling along. But these boats were not meant for leisurely trolls. They were meant for daredevil rides with speed. There was a small windshield that barely went over the wheel. It would not have been much help if going fast. As far as how fast these would go, Jayden would have to wait to find out as the motor was an inboard.

Todd went to a small shed and came back with keys for everyone. Jayden sat in his boat and looked around taking it all in. Jeff came up to his boat and asked, "You ever driven a jet ski before?" Jayden told him yes. "Okay, it's basically like that. Except that you are sitting and you have this frame around you. But it handles just like a jet ski and goes a lot faster" He said with a laugh.

Jayden asked, "I heard something about racing to checkpoints. How am I supposed to know where to go?"

Jeff leaned in and turned on the GPS and entered in a few numbers. "Okay, you know how to use one of these?" Jayden told him yes. "Cool man. There are five checkpoints and I've entered them all in as well as your return. Just look at the screen and the little arrow will point you in the direction you need to be going. When this number here turns green you are at that checkpoint. Hit this button and it will automatically start up the next checkpoint. I've put them all in the GPS for you. All you have to do is drive and don't kill yourself. You got this?" Jayden said, "Got it. Thanks."

Everyone had started their boats and untied the line from the docks. They were all cruising out of the dock area into open water. The boat floated up and down with the waves with ease. It was a pretty light watercraft. There was not a whole lot to it. They took their boats around the south end of Isla de Cabeza Martillo. From there they would go past the east side of the hammer past Shadytown and be out in the open water. They took the boats to a gathering point and floated up and down in a group. In the darkness, Jayden could hear Todd yell out. Okay, five checkpoint race. The first one back wins!" Everyone cheered. Someone else yelled out, "1-2-3- Go!" And with that everyone was off. Jayden pushed the throttle forward all the way and he took off much faster than he was expecting. The water seemed choppy in this small watercraft. He figured swells had to be at almost half a foot. Once up to speed though it was not so bad. The watercraft seemed to bounce from swell to swell with ease. It was not the choppy back-breaking ride he was expecting. It was so dark though despite being a nearly full moon. Regardless, they were out on open water in the middle of the night. He was moving at what felt like a breakneck speed and had no idea how close he was to other boats. He looked down to his GPS and saw he was fast approaching the first checkpoint. Out of nowhere and without warning ten boats came within inches of him from the exact opposite direction he was going. All he saw were dark shadows. He could hear the excited yells as they sped past, barely missing collision. Seconds later his GPS dinged and a new number popped up on the screen and the arrow told him to turn around. He throttled down and turned the wheel hard. As he felt his boat spin around he throttled back up to full speed. His heart was pounding and his adrenaline was at max capacity. He was having so much fun. He was truly enjoying this moment. There was something very special about driving a boat at a fast speed in nearly complete darkness. There was a lot of fear to pump up the adrenaline. The biggest fear of course was being in a head-on collision. The next checkpoint had come upon him quickly. He hit the button as new coordinates came up. The arrow on the screen told him to go right. He took a wide turn to the right without slowing down and was back on track. He could almost see a couple of shadows in front of him. Pretty close. Maybe he was catching up.

This next one seemed to be a long checkpoint. He was cruising along and bouncing off of the waves for what felt like quite a long time. He was beginning to wonder if he was somehow off course. His heart started to beat hard with nervousness and it was settled down when he felt a watery mist hit his face. It was the water from boats right in front of him churning up the water and sending it over his windshield. He saw two shadows and was instantly in between two other boats. He heard a male voice yell out from the right, "Is that Jayden? Hey boy! What's going on?" He heard a female voice to the left. "Did Jayden catch up with us? Whooo!" Both boats took turns banging into his. He could feel the jolts as he fought with the wheel to keep the boat on track and not capsize. His GPS lit green. The arrow sent him on a hard left. The boat on his left had already turned away. The boat on his right must have throttled down and turned as it was no longer there. Passing the checkpoint, Jayden throttled down and turned the wheel hard. When he felt he was completely turned around he hit the throttle to the max and his engine died.

Under the light of the almost full moon, he floated up and down. It was not very much light. He was still out in an open sea of darkness with no clue of where he was. He turned his key over to restart the boat. Nothing happened. He tried a few more times. He knew the sound the engine was making. He had flooded it. Despite knowing this, he still tried to turn over the key a few more times. With each effort, he was saying to himself, "No, no, no." He knew he was only making it worse with each turn. He had no choice but to wait it out.

The waves made a splashing sound as they hit his boat and moved him in a never-ending up and down motion. It was not a sea sickening motion. It was more of a gentle roll. He could hear the other boats churning water in the distance. He heard the laughter of his fellow racers. Then it went silent. He could hear them yell out his name. Followed by more laughter. He could hear them yell, "Jayden! Where are you?" He yelled back, "I'm out here! I'm out here!" He just had no idea where here was. "Can you hear me? I'm out here!" He could hear them playfully call his name with more drunken laughter. Then he heard the boats start up again. It was only briefly as the sound of the boats and laughter disappeared into the darkness of the open water. It was dead silent. He could almost hear his heartbeat. There was the sound of the waves splashing the boat and then nothing as the water went flat almost suddenly. He sat in his tiny one-person watercraft floating with no motion. A chill hit his wet body as a light fog started to roll in. He looked down at his GPS and it was out. He tapped the screen and hit the on/ off switch with no result. The sea had an eerie calm to it. Then with no warning, he heard a female voice. "Jayden," The voice said from directly behind him. Startled he turned around, as much as he could anyway, and saw nothing. What the fuck? he thought. He tried to turn his body around more but could not completely, given his sitting position in the watercraft. He could get turned around enough to be sure there was nobody there. He had his body twisted around and squinting his eyes trying to focus hard in the darkness in front of him. He saw nothing. He heard it again. This time it was coming from the bow of his boat. It said his name slowly and clearly, "Jayden." He turned around hard with his fists in the air. There was nobody there. It was a female voice. It had said his name twice in a very soothing manner. It almost sounded like Pepper with a slightly lower resonance to her voice. Soothing and somewhat familiar did not make this any less terrifying though. He looked anxiously all around him. The fog had become increasingly thick. He felt a tingle go down his back as he heard the voice speak again. This time it was a whisper in his left ear as it said slowly said, "Jayden." Shaking his head back and forth Jayden said, "Oh hell no. You got me fucked up! In the name of all that is holy please start!" He turned the key. He heard the engine start. "Oh thank you, Jesus!" He looked down at his GPS. It was still off. He hit the button to turn it on. Still nothing. He took a brief second to think about the turns he had made. He thought about the direction he heard voices of his newfound friends from earlier. The answers for both of those vaguely put him in a similar direction. He heard the female voice again. This time it was fairly loud, without yelling. It was just rather direct as it said, "Jayden." He could almost feel moist air on the back of his neck. "Oh fuck me." He said as he thrust the throttle and was off at full speed across the water. He really could not see where he was going as the fog had become so thick. He just closed his eyes and said, "Please Lord, get me home." It would have made more sense to drive with his eyes open. He was afraid of what he may see with them open. In his mind he pictured a giant beast coming up out of the water in front of him. He could see it clearly in his mind. A giant beast, like a dragon, was coming out of the sea. It had seven heads. The heads all had horns. The horns all had crowns. He could tell the beast was covered in a variety of plagues. He did not want to see that! He had to open his eyes though. He knew what was in his head was far more frightening than anything he could see in the real world. He knew the visions in his head were nothing more than a perverse reflection of himself staring back at him. He looked to the world ahead of him with his eyes wide open. He preyed out loud as he said, "Show me some land, show me some land!" With that, the engine stalled again. He yelled out, "Oh fucking come on! Really?" As his watercraft slowly coasted to a stop he felt the slow become more drastic as he felt and heard the sound of hard sand rub the bottom of the watercraft. He had run aground.

Jayden's heart was pounding through his chest. The watercraft was no longer moving. It sat on a hard and wet beach. He was breathing heavily with a white-knuckle grip still on the steering wheel. His eyes open wide as he stared straight ahead. His mind told him that he had stopped. His body had not quite caught up to that reality yet. He tried to gain some focus and calm his breathing. He thought about how this just happened. Where did this all come from? How did he not see the land approaching? He remembered asking for land, and here he was. "Be careful what you wish for" he said out loud.

SEVEN BRIDGES

He released his iron grip from the steering wheel and stepped out of the watercraft onto the beach. Incoming waves would bring the water up to his ankles and back down again. The sound of seashells tinkling as the waves went out. Looking around he did not see any docks or any lights. So he knew he had not made his way back to Martillo. Where was he though? He grabbed the line that was tied to the bow of his watercraft and pulled the boat a little more onto the shore. He tied off the line to a tree. With his hands on his hips, he tried to assess where he was exactly. He went through a checklist in his head. "Okay, there are no lights to be seen. There are no sounds to be heard. So I know I am not on Martillo. If I were, I should see or hear some evidence of civilization. So where am I?" The only way to find out was to walk around. He pulled on the line from the boat to a palm tree and double-checked the knots to be sure it was secure. He had to walk around. He looked around every inch of the watercraft. Looking for a compartment or anything that might have something of use. A flashlight, a compass, a flair, or even a bottle of water would be nice. There was nothing that he could find under the cloak of darkness and fog.

Jayden walked up the beach away from the shoreline. As luck would have it he walked into the entryway to a trail. He walked through the trail as he pulled branches covering the trail away from his face. He tried to see through the darkness as best he could. Being extraordinarily careful as to where he stepped and what he grabbed. He walked the trail that twisted and turned. He paused as he heard something. It was the sound of moving water. He took a few more steps and was on a narrow wooden bridge. He was walking over a creek. He took a moment to look around him as he had a feeling that he was being watched. A few more twists and turns brought him to another short and narrow bridge that took him over a creek again. He shook his head back and forth as he said, "No fucking way." He looked at the bridge and as if talking to the bridge said, "If there are seven of you I am going to shit." He looked up to the sky and could notice the fog was lifting. He could almost see the moon. As he continued on the trail he crossed more bridges and counted each one as he walked across it. He looked in the trees for anything that resembled a wreath made of sticks. He was in the thick of woods though. Everything he looked at was made of sticks. Jayden stepped off of a bridge and back on the trail as he said, "Seven. That makes seven fucking bridges. What now?"

He rounded a corner in the wooded trail and saw exactly, what now. Jayden was looking at an open area. It was a circle of roughly fifty meters. It had been intentionally cut out of the forest. The fog had mostly lifted. It was no longer in the sky at least. There was still an eerie heavy fog that floated about a foot off of the ground. Where Jayden stood was the end of the trail. Going any further would have him out in the open area. It was a narrow passageway where the trail ended and the open area began. He swore he could see what looked like two large totem poles. At least in his mind, that is what they were. It looked like two standing logs. They may have been about twelve feet tall. They did appear to have rough carvings on them. Jayden thought to himself about the current situation. He wanted to go further to try and figure out where he was. It did not make sense to go back to the watercraft and wait. What would he be waiting for anyway? The only option was to keep on moving forward. However, this was starting to look too much like the story he heard earlier in the night. That is way too much of a coincidence. If this was an Indian burial ground he knew he should not walk across it. He had seen enough wild west movies to know that no man should ever walk across what the Natives consider, sacred ground. Nothing good can come of that whatsoever. His heart told him one thing, which was to keep going. His brain told him to turn around. He knew that it was his heart that he should, obey. He needed more options. There had to be a way around it. He looked to the side of the trail. He was looking for a way to cut through the foliage and around the burial ground. It was thick…really thick. But maybe he could do it? With some raw determination perhaps it could be done. He pushed aside a heap of branches and took a step forward. He could feel the ground was wet with about two inches of water. He took a couple more steps, carefully prying away branches with each step. The ground remained saturated with water. As he stood in the gook for a minute, he could feel himself sink and drop a little deeper into it. He took three steps back and was on the trail again. That option was not going to work. The vegetation was too thick. He was going to for sure cut himself going through that. More importantly, if it was nothing but wet marsh he was walking on he was positive he would find a water moccasin or some other slithery reptile in there. It was not that he was afraid of snakes. He knew that he could not risk getting bit by a snake or insect though. Which he knew he would come across if he went any further. He had no other choices. He had to return to the beach. Jayden walked briskly down the twisting trail. His butt cheeks clenched tightly as he crossed each bridge. He tried not to count them as he crossed each one. He could not help it though. It was something that just happened. He walked through the trail pushing away branches as he said out loud to himself, "No evil, no evil, no evil" He said that out loud repeatedly till he made his way to the end of the trail. Upon crossing a bridge he counted out loud to himself against his own will, "Six. Okay, one more to go and I'm back on the beach." There was not one more though. He rounded a corner and was on the beach. He tried to block out the thoughts of this being too much like the story he heard earlier. He could not. The thought was firmly planted in his brain. He tried to recall the path he had just taken. He mentally counted the bridges on the way there. He took the exact same way back. He was sure of it. Because he walked out where he walked in. There were seven bridges in and six on the way out. How is that even possible?

Jayden sat on the beach next to his watercraft. He was looking out over the water. The fog had completely lifted as the light from the moon reflected off of the water. He took a moment to survey the beach he was sitting on. It was a long wide beach and in any other situation, this would be a pretty cool place to be. It was secluded and private. It was quiet. All that could be heard was the sound of the incoming tide and the sounds from the nocturnal creatures of the night. It was serene and relaxing. Tall coconut palms leaned out over the water. He had a sudden break in his thoughts. "Coconut palms! Coconuts! Oh my God, I am so thirsty." He got up and walked over to a coconut palm tree. It leaned out over the water at about a sixty-degree angle. It looked to be around forty feet long. If he could climb to the top he could get a coconut or two and quench his thirst. He climbed onto the tree. This was not so bad. All he had to do was make it to the end. The angle of this tree was leaning made this easier than had it been a completely vertical tree. Or so he thought. Jayden had been inching his way to the top of the tree for what seemed like a good ten minutes. He might have been about halfway there. It was then that he realized he was high in the air. A lot higher than it looked from the ground. He told himself that if he made it this far, he could keep going. He was so thirsty. He had to keep going. He tried to inch his way forward. His mind and body simply were not communicating though. He wanted to keep climbing. He tried to tell his body to move forward but it would not. There was one part of his mind that kept running through the what-ifs of the situation. He knew he could not afford to fall. If he fell he would probably break something. Given that he had no idea where he was and no help nearby, that would not be good. Plus he would still be thirsty. He would be thirsty with a broken leg. He slowly inched his way back down the tree. With each inch he got closer to the ground he called himself a pussy. The good and not evil side of his brain assured him that he was a pussy with all of his bones in working order. As thirsty as he was, as much as he wanted a coconut, he knew it was best to obey common sense. Good pets obey.

He was back to where he started. Sitting on the beach, next to his watercraft. He wondered how come none of those people came out looking for him. Surely they would have noticed him missing by now. It had been a few hours at least. They were local. They knew these waters and all the little uncharted islands around them. How come they were not coming for him? "Fucking pricks." He said out loud.

    He sat on the beach with his head buried in his hands. Then he heard something. He lifted his head and looked into the darkness intently as if that could improve his hearing. It was a very light but distinctive sound. It was the sound of drums. It was not random. There was a definite rhythm to it. It was tribal-like. It was a rolling drum beat one might hear at a nightclub if the deejay were spinning tribal breakbeats. This was a good sign. Jayden was feeling optimistic. There had to be a person or people playing that music. Maybe it was his new so-called friends. Maybe this was all a joke. He was going to chew their asses out so hard for this. At the very least, it was somebody. And if it was somebody, that somebody had water. He was extremely dehydrated and in need of a drink.

    He got up to his feet and brushed himself off as he started to walk in the direction of the drums. He found another opening to a different trial. He would take this as the other trail led to the land of no options. The trail took him to a hill and the hill had an old stone stairway leading to the top. He climbed the stairway to the top in a bit of a rush. He was excited to know that he was not alone out here. He was happy he could run into someone that could help. He was activated knowing he could soon get a drink and maybe some food. With every step in elevation he took, the tribal beat of drums became louder. He was giddy with anticipation. His heart seemed to match the beat of the drum with every step upwards he took. Once at the top of the stairway he was on another trail. He followed the trail around a few twists and turns he walked into an open field. The sound of the drums disappeared.

Strange thoughts started to enter his head. Was he delusional? Did he imagine those drum beats? Was this his mind making up some imaginary hope? Had dehydration taken that much of a hold of him? He looked out into the open meadow that was the size of a football field. There was nothing. No buildings, no campfire or tents, no people. There were no drums. He laughed to himself as he thought he had dropped off of the deep end here. He felt an overwhelming amount of frustration. He almost wanted to cry at the total loss of control. It was not that he was not in control. It was that there was nothing he could control. Feeling at a total loss he buried his face in his hands trying to massage out the frustration he was feeling. As he rubbed his closed eyes he could hear a drumbeat come back. It was loud. It was as if it were directly in front of him. Taking in a deep breath he slowly removed his hands from over his eyes. He took another slow and deep breath as he opened his eyes. He could feel the bottom of his gut wrench as he looked before himself in disbelief. He saw a large wooden structure. It was the size of a barn.

Jayden rubbed his eyes in disbelief. He was sure that structure was not there only minutes ago. He was almost positive. He could hear the loud rhythmic beats of the drums coming from the wooden building. Through the cracks in the doors and shuttered windows he could see a dim light that seemed to flicker with the beats. He had to see what was going on.

He made his way across the field in a stalker-like pose. He did not know who was in there. They could be friendly or maybe not. In the case of the latter, he was going to ere on the side of sneakiness. He had approached the barn in a stealth-like manner. He could hear the drums loud and clear. They beat at a furious pace now. It sounded as if many drums were being played at once by multiple musicians all in step with the same beat. He could hear chanting. He could not make out what was being said. It was hard to make out over the drums, but it was for sure a group of people chanting or perhaps praying. It almost sounded Latin. He could not tell. He knew that the answer would be on the other side of the door.

With his heart pounding heavily and breathing being quick and shallow he carefully pried the door open just an inch or two. It was barely enough to get his eyeball in. He could vaguely see in the barn now. He could hear the chanting and drums better. It was Latin they were speaking. The door was not open enough for him to see fully inside. He could see light and shadows flicker off of a wall. He could smell the smoke coming from the fire. He watched intently as shadow figures danced along the wall. They were very tall. It was only a trick of the light as the fire between the dancing chanters and the wall only made their shadows appear much taller than they were.

Jayden was scared at this point. More scared than he had ever been. He was scared because he knew he only had one option right now. That was to investigate what he had just stumbled upon. There was no walking away from this. He would spend the rest of his life questioning it if he did. Trying to build up his confidence he took a couple of quick and deep breaths. He told himself, "Come on Jay, don't be a pussy like you were at the tree. Do this and you will redeem yourself. "

One final deep breath and Jayden flung the door open. What he saw made his heart drop, deeper into his gut. It was nothing. Jayden saw nothing but an old empty barn. There was no fire. There were no people chanting praise to whomever. There was a dirt floor and that was it. He walked over to what looked like a large door. He unhinged the door and as it opened moonlight spilled into the empty barn. With the moonlight, he could tell it was not just a dirt floor. It was a cement floor with a light covering of dirt. Under the dirt there were designs. They were either spray painted or chalked on. They were in a variety of colors. Many were the type of weird designs one would see in a book about the occult. This was giving Jayden the heebie-jeebies. All though still very thirsty, he was rather thankful he did not find anyone in here. He was sure they were not the come on in and stay for coffee type, whoever they were.

He knew he did not need to be here. All though, there seemed to be an insatiable curiosity inside of him to know more. He shook his head back and forth hard as he slapped himself. What was he thinking? He had to get out of there. He was not about to become the person that people shout at in some horror flick. He had to get back to the boat and pray that it works now. He shut the large door and the barn was dark again. He walked out of the door he had come in and carefully shut it behind him. He started to walk away and then he heard a voice say, "hello."

TEA

It was a calm and soothing voice. It did not startle him nor did it make him want to run. It sounded very much like the voice he heard on the water. The voice said, "Hello."

Jayden turned around and saw a woman standing before him. She was about five foot nine and had a full figure about her. She had a curvy body. Her hair was long, black, and thick. She had dark eyes that one could lost in. Her skin was pale and almost glowed in the moonlight. Covering her legs, she had skin-tight jeans. She was barefoot as she stood in the meadow that surrounded the barn. She almost looked like Pepper…in twenty years. Her age did not depreciate her looks though. This woman was beautiful to gaze upon. Jayden could not look away. "What is your name?" She asked. Jayden cleared his throat and introduced himself while trying to apologize for trespassing. He had his hand outstretched to her. She looked at him with a slight giggle as she took a second and shook his hand. There was a tingle he felt as her palm touched his. It was a warm calming tingle. She said, "I am Temptress." Looking at her outfit Jayden asked, "Is that your name or a title?" She laughed and said, "You're a sweet boy. That is just what some people call me. My name is Lillie, you may call me that." He repeated her name back to her to make sure he had heard it right. She gave him a look over with her eyes as she licked her lip, touched his thick upper arm, and said, "You look very dehydrated. Come follow me. I will get you something to drink."

Jayden followed Lillie across the field. He asked, "Where are we going?"

"To my house," She said.

He asked, "The House of the Morning Star"

"What?" She asked back.

Realizing he probably sounded like an idiot he said, "Nothing. Where is it?"

She told him was just over the hill they were walking up. He could sense a presence around her. It was a feeling that everything was going to be all right. He did not know that of course. He was walking with a stranger into her house. A stranger whose property he had just been trespassing on. She was a stranger that was residing on an island out in the middle of nowhere. An island that maybe had some weird stories about it. Who was this mysterious woman that took in random strangers trespassing on her property? What did she have planned for him? Was she a vampire? She did look anemic. She turned to Jayden and as if reading his mind said, "You'll be fine. I don't bite." They walked over the top of the hill and he saw a house. As they walked closer to it more detail was coming to light. For starters, it was a wooden house, not a big stone structure as people had told him in their made to scare tourists stories. They walked to the house and were in the front yard.

The house looked to be three stories, yet it was a modest size home. It was surrounded by a white picket fence. On both the left and right of the house, just outside the fence, were palm trees. The right side had one and the left had two. They were just as tall as the house. The first story of the house had a balcony that wrapped around the entire home. From the front, the balcony had a few wooden deck chairs on it along with a couple of small tables. A three-step stairway led directly up the middle. The front door to the house was also directly in the middle. There were two windows with six panes a piece that was to both the left and right of the door. A wood awning covered the entire balcony. The second story was not as wide as the first but sat evenly on top of the first. It had a balcony that covered its entire width. On the balcony going from the wooden guard rail, there was a waist-high fence that divided the balcony into two separate halves. Each half of the balcony had a glass door leading into the house. The third story was not as wide as the second. It sat neatly in the middle. It was very small and really could not be considered an actual third story. It was more of a room that sat on top of the second story. It had one glass door that led to a very small private balcony. Probably only one person could fit comfortably on the balcony. The roof was not flat. It looked like the top of a triangle. This was one of the most aesthetically pleasing houses in the world to look at. It was perfect in design.

From the outside, it appeared every room in the home was dimly lit. They walked up the three steps and in through the front door that was already wide open. Jayden asked, "You don't worry about somebody breaking in?" Lillie looked at him with a smile and said, "I live on a private island by myself. Who is going to break in?"

He could only agree and say, "Good point."

The living room was the first room they walked into. The furniture looked old but not overused or worn. The floor was clean and shiny wood. In the center of the room was a large glass coffee table. There were two couches and a couple of lounge chairs as well. Around the walls were a few tall shelving units. They were all wood and decorated with antiques. A bookshelf was along one far wall with many books filling its shelves. On another wall was a large painting of Lillie. It appeared to be a boudoir painting. Jayden complimented the painting. Lillie stopped to admire it for a moment. "Yes, it was done by an old friend many years ago." She smiled as she said, "Come along, follow me." They walked from the living room through a short hallway. Both sides of the hallway had bookshelves crowded with old-looking books. He did not notice any of the titles, they just appeared to be old. The hallway led them into a kitchen. The kitchen was more modern looking than the living room. She had a new-looking all silver refrigerator. It was massive. It was what one would expect to find in a professional bakery. The oven was equally impressive. And there was plenty of counter space for a full kitchen brigade to work on. In the center of the floor was a table that had a glass top and wood trim. Four chairs surrounded it. Above the sinks hung a variety of pots and pans. Next to the oven was a large spice rack. It was wooden on the sides and top. It had a glass door to view all of the spices. There must have been at least forty different spices. All of which were in glass containers and were hand-labeled.

Jayden sat at the dining room table. The room, like all others in the house, was dimly lit. He wanted to ask where the electricity came from but it did not matter. He thought that sometimes in life you just have to know when to let it go. Lillie asked him, "What would you have?" He told her that whatever she was having would be fine. She ran some water into a pan and put it on the stove as she turned a knob to heat the stove. The gas stove put out a beautiful blue flame as the water started to boil. She then went to her spice rack and grabbed a few different bottles. She put a dash of each into a tea mug. She seemed to hum some song to herself as she did this. It was kind of like a hum. At other times it almost sounded like words she was slightly singing. When the water in the pot was heated she poured it gracefully into the mug. She retrieved a small bottle that was hand-labeled and poured a small amount of it into the mug. She then gave it a stir and presented it to

Jayden on the table before him. She said, "Try this. It is an old family recipe. I think you will find it both thirst-quenching and calming." He took a sip and gave her a look of approval. Looking around he complimented her on the house and asked, "So this is your house?" She replied with, "Uh-huh." And this is your private island? She smiled as she looked at him with a coy smile and said, "Uh-huh."

"So, what is it that you do for a living?"

"Many moons ago I was a professor for a school in Massachusetts. It would seem my teaching methods were out of date, therefore, I had to move on. These days I make people better versions of themselves. I guess you could say that I am a consultant. I also dabble in holistic healing, hence the tea you are drinking. Go on. Drink more. Feel it seep through your veins." The tea was good. There was no doubt about that. It was sweet without being noticeably sweet. It went down smooth like caramel or honey. It had a hint of saltiness to it and had a calming red hue in appearance. As Jayden sipped on his tea he said, "Have you heard any rumors about a hidden island out here that has vampires and witches on it?" Lillie looked at him with large eyes and a smile as she laughed and said, "Vampires? Oh my!" He looked down to the ground for a second and as he looked up gave a forced chuckle as he said, "Yeah. Stupid right?" She sat down at the table with her hands supporting her head She asked, "Well what kind of vampires? Tell me. I'm intrigued" He had her undivided attention. He shrugged his shoulders as he said, "I don't know. Those of the blood-sucking variety I guess? What else is there?"

"Oh my sweet boy, there are many types I suppose. Emotional, psychic, energy, and as you put it, the blood-sucking variety." As she was explaining this he knew that she had just caught him staring at her ominous breasts. He shifted his eyes to the left. She smiled as she tilted her head, brushed her hair with her hand once, and nonchalantly unbuttoned a button on the front of her corset. Looking to take attention off that awkward incident Jayden quickly asked, "So where do those doors all go?" He was referring to three closed doors. She said, "The one on the left leads to a cellar. Over on the right, that is a staircase to my room on the top of the house and the middle is a staircase that leads to the second story where you will be sleeping tonight." He protested as he said, "Oh no, I mean I appreciate it, but I only needed something to drink. I appreciate your hospitality and all, but I have to get back."

"Back to where?" She asked.

"Well, back to Martillo. I have my boat tied up down by the water. I should really be going." He stood up as he thanked her again. Then Lillie said, "You can't go tonight. It is the middle of the night. You cannot take a boat out there in the middle of the night. You'll get lost. The local waters at night are, beastly, with rouge waves. You will stay the night. I insist. Now sit down. You are stressed. Sit back down in the chair and I will take care of you." This was not said in a commanding tone. She said it with such a calmness in her voice. It was more of a suggestion, which made it easier to follow. Without even thinking about it, Jayden was sitting back down in the chair. Lillie grabbed his tea mug and put it in the sink. She walked over to her spice counter and grabbed a device. It had a wooden base with a long and straight pendulum-like object pointing upwards. It had a couple of knobs on it that were meant for adjusting the speed that the pendulum would sway back and forth.

Lillie walked back toward him and placed the device on the table in front of Jayden. In one swift movement, she hit the needle-like object. It started to sway back and forth. It made a sound that was calming with consistency. That sound went, tick, tick, ding. Tick, tick, ding. It was a consistent pattern that was calming to the mind. He did not feel nervous. He felt at peace in her graceful presence.

"Are you a musician?" Lillie asked Jayden. He shook his head back and forth. "This is a metronome. It helps musicians keep a beat. We are going to use it to help you focus. Listen to the sound it makes."

Tick, tick, ding. Tick, tick, ding.

"It is a steady sound. It is consistent. I want you to focus on the rhythmic sound it makes. Let it sink in as I speak to you. Allow your mind to get lost in its beat as your heartbeat matches its pace. Focus, now."

Tick, tick, ding.

TICK. TICK. DING.

As she spoke it was in a very slow-paced and deliberate voice. "You look so tense and exhausted. Sit back and relax" She said as she walked behind him. He could feel her hands on his shoulders. He turned his head to look back at Lillie and her hands were not on his shoulders. They were at her side. He turned his head back forward and she said, "Now relax. You poor thing. You have so much on your mind. You are such the decision-maker. You seek to be the one controlled for a change. Now sit here, with your feet firmly planted on the floor." There was a very lofty sound to her voice with each word she spoke. He listened intently as he needed to hear them all.

"I want you to listen to the sound of the metronome. Listen to the repetitive sound it makes. This is the new constant in your life." She paused. All he heard was tick, tick, ding. Tick, tick ding." Then Lillie spoke again. "This will become a trigger for you. Every time you hear this sound, tick, tick, ding, it will become the focus of your conscious thought. You will only focus on each tick and await each ding with anticipation. The ding is the sound of your reward. When you hear the ding, you focus on the thoughts that make me happy. When I am happy, you feel bliss. Say it in your mind. Tick, tick, ding." She repeated those three words in a whisper that followed the beat of the metronome.

"I want you to be comfortable for me. Just relax into your seat and take a long deep breath. Relax and let yourself float above all of your problems as you sink into peace…and into my voice." He took slow and deep breaths as she had instructed. "Breathing in and out you feel so comfortable that you don't want to move. Let the sound of my voice guide you. Your whole body feels so warm and tingly as you start to sink deeper…Deeper into the sound of my voice. It feels so good to just let yourself melt into the chair…as the sound of my voice, sends you deeper and deeper. Letting your body fully relax. Your eyes feel heavy. You can feel them sinking into your skull as your eye lids come down to cover them." With his slow and deep breaths, Jayden closed his eyes and felt tension come off his shoulders.

Behind her commands, he continued to focus on the metronome as it provided a beat of bliss. Tick, tick, ding.

Lillie continued to speak in her comforting tone. "The deeper you go, the calmer your feel. The more you want to drop...Deeper into this trance. Visualize my hands over your shoulders. Not quite touching, but just above. Hovering close enough so you can feel their warmth."

Tick, tick, ding. Tick, tick, ding. "Follow the sound of the metronome. Its rhythm provides the pace of your focus. With each beat you hear the words; Yes, yes, please. Yes, yes, please."

Tick, tick, ding. Yes, yes, please. Tick, tick, ding. Yes, yes, please. Yes, yes, please. He heard these words spoken repeatedly in her voice until her voice become his voice. He was speaking the words; yes, yes, please out loud without even realizing it.

Jayden could feel warmth over his entire body. In his mind, he was trying to figure out what was happening? What was she doing? Why did he feel this way? This can't be real. He should not let this go on. He did let it go on. Tick, tick, ding. Yes, yes, please.

Lillie continued with her easy-to-follow instruction. "You feel your thoughts empty and my voice rolls in. All of your thoughts leave your mind. You have no room for thoughts, except for those thoughts put in by the sound of my voice." Tick, tick, ding. Tick, tick, ding.

Jayden's thoughts of this calming moment were slightly interrupted. In his mind, he asked, "What did she just say? What was this woman doing? Was she trying to hypnotize him? That is ridiculous. He did not believe in that sort of stuff. This would not work for him. Those thoughts were soon gone just as quickly as they entered as he felt himself relax a little bit more.

Lillie kept on speaking, "You only hear the sound of my voice and all that matters is my pleasure. All you can think of is how to make me happy. Because when I am happy your body responds to my pleasure, and it feels so good to you."

Tick, tick, ding. "Just hearing the ding stimulates the thoughts that bring you bliss. The thoughts that I put into your brain. You are my pet. You are mine." Tick, tick, ding. "With each tick, tick, ding, you begin to beg for more conditioning. You want me to condition your mind. Do you want me to condition your mind?"

In an automatic response, Jayden said, "Yes, yes, please." He smiled when he said that as he felt his defenses drop, deeper. He felt at ease. She said, "You are a good boy. You are mine."

Tick, tick, ding. Yes, yes, please.

He could hear the phrase, "It feels so good" being repeated in his ear. It was by another voice. It was not another voice. It was Lillie's voice. It was as if she were speaking to him in both of his ears at the same time. With two different things being said.

"Your nerves feel alive when I am happy. They feel alive with little pleasurable bursts. It is all because you make me happy. Searching through your mind and tickling your brain each time sending you deeper and deeper."

As she was saying all of that, once again Jayden could hear another version of her voice speak separately as it also said, "Deeper and deeper you go. You feel pleasure." It was as if another voice of hers was overlapping the one currently talking.

The other Lillie spoke to him in his left ear as it said, "You're such a sweet boy" and in his right ear at the same time he heard. "Deeper and deeper." He could feel the warmness of breath in both ears as they spoke. He could feel himself relax. He felt increasingly aroused. Every time she spoke, especially when she said certain words, he could feel himself release slightly. Tick, tick, ding. Yes, yes, please.

He could hear her giving him separate commands and suggestions in both ears at the same time. Then there was what he thought of as the main Lillie. The one that spoke to him from his brain it seemed. It was as if three women were speaking to him at once. But all three voices sounded like Lillie. It was a multi-layered three-ring circus going on inside his head. It was very exciting trying to focus on what all three were saying at the same time.

"Sparks of pleasure releasing over your entire body. When I tell you, you make me so happy" He heard that phrase repeated in both ears by different versions of Lillie. One was a sultry whisper and one was flirty and joyful. When they said that phrase he could feel his penis jolt up and down inside the protection of his shorts, with pleasurable excitement. He did not want this to end.

With each sentence she spoke, her voice seemed to alternate from ear to ear and back to the center of his head. "You know that you could get up from this chair at any time. You know that you could walk away from here and never return. But you want to make me happy." Tick, tick, ding.

Those words sunk in as he thought about it. He thought about trying to get up out of the chair just to see if he could. He knew he was not bound physically. She was right, he could get up anytime he wanted to. He truly wanted to try. He did not try. Something was holding him down in thought. He wanted this to go on. He did not try to move. Or perhaps he did, but his brain would not send the proper signal to his body to make it move.

"You are going to stay here with me and listen to my voice. Because you make me so happy." In his left ear, he could hear a different version said in a whisper, and in his right ear another version of the same words spoken differently. They all ended with the phrase about making her happy. As they did he could feel himself throb in his lower regions. Yes, yes, please. Tick, tick, ding.

Lillie said, "Everything around you will disappear. Because nothing around you is important. Only my voice is important. You know you can trust me because you know I will take care of you. You will let me lead you down to a submissive part of your mind where you no longer think your own thoughts. You only think the thoughts that I give you. You will do this because you trust me, and you want to make me happy. You make me so happy!" The phrase was repeated a few times and each time a smile of pleasure and arousal hit Jayden's face.

"Focus on the sound of the metronome. With each tick, you become more focused on my control. You are my pet. With each ding, you feel another ripple of bliss. You are mine. Do you enjoy being conditioned?"

"Yes, yes, please." Those were the only words that could come out of Jayden's mouth. They came out with such ease. He wanted to say those words. When he spoke those three words his body would be overwhelmed with a feeling of tingling bliss. "Yes, yes, please." He spoke over and over in sync with the metronome. Tick, tick, ding.

"I am going to count down for you. When we hit zero you will be deep down in that submissive place. That will make me so happy. "

Inside of his head, he heard a fourth version of Lillie. This was neither in his right or left ear. It sounded as if it were all surrounding. It said, "Sixty!" It was very direct. It would continue to count backward with every second that ticked by. At this point, he had what he thought were four different versions of Lillie that he could hear. He had the sultry whisper in his left ear. The joyful and playful voice in his right ear. Then there was the voice performing the countdown. In charge of them all was the Lillie that seemed to be speaking from inside his head. They all seemed to be vying for his attention. One would talk about the left side of his brain wanting to analyze. The other spoke about the right side of his brain wanting to have fun and create. They all spoke of how he wanted to focus on them all. Which was true. He did but it was so hard to focus on so many different conversations at once. Which was part of what made the experience so intriguing.

All the voices started to speak in rapid-fire. It was like the grand finale at a 4th of July firework show.

"You feel warm and comfortable."

"You feel me move around you and touching your neck"

"you can feel me wrap leather around you as I restrain you. You are not restrained. You can get up any time you want."

"But you want to be restrained. You want to go to a place where your only thoughts, are my thoughts "

"You make me so happy."

"You are such a sweet boy."

"Being restrained makes you feel safer."

"Because you trust me. It makes you feel much more relaxed. You know I am here to take care of you."

"Pleasing me gives you so much pleasure."

"You make me so happy."

"You feel safe because I am in control now. You can relax and enjoy the sensations."

The metronome continued with tick, tick, ding. The metronome was no longer moving. Lillie had stopped it long ago. It was a sound that continued in Jayden's head. Tick, tick, ding. Yes, yes, please. Lillie spoke, "Each and every ding causes a jolt of bliss to go through your body. Each tick makes you anticipate each ding. With each tick, your excitement grows with the anticipation of hearing a ding. Like a dog about to receive its reward, you become happy as you know the reward from your Temptress is bliss. With each tick, you drop. With each ding, you go deeper. Tick, tick, ding. Yes, yes, please. You are mine."

He was truly enjoying the sensations. He wanted this to go on. The voice in his head counting down from sixty had reached ten. He could feel his body tense up, yet he felt very relaxed and at peace.

"Everything is safe and wonderful. You are so tired. It feels so right to let me take over." In a voice full of command he heard the countdown reach the end as it said, "ZERO!"

The multiple voices continued to sway him in his blissful state.

"Sweet boy, you belong to me now. It feels so good to be in this place."

"This empty and submissive place. Whenever I call you my sweet boy you will return to this place."

"My sweet boy, you are mine."

"And every time I call you my sweet boy you will go deeper into this trance."

"My sweet boy. You want to make me happy"

"You make me so happy."

"You are mine."

"It feels so good and you are such a sweet boy for me."

"Trust me to turn you into the best you, the most pleasing you."

"My sweet boy, you make me so happy."

"I want you to answer me with Yes Temptress. Answer it for me out loud. Anytime I ask you a question you will respond with Yes Temptress. Do you want to be a sweet boy? "

There was a small part of Jayden's consciousness that still was his. It spoke to him as it asked, what is she talking about? Answer her with Yes Temptress? How kooky is that? I wonder what happens if I don't answer? Before he could think any more, he spoke out loud as he said, "Yes Temptress."

Tick, tick, ding. Yes, Yes, please.

"My sweet boy, you make me so happy."

He felt his penis flex and stretch to its capacity when she said that. His body arched in the chair. Tick, tick, ding.

"Let the thought flow out of your mouth as it flows out your mind, Yes Temptress, I want to hear you say it."

"Yes Temptress!" he said. There was that one small part of his consciousness that wanted to refuse. This was stupid. He was not going to say…

"Yes, Temptress!" He was no longer relaxed in any way shape or form. He was breathing heavily and his heart was racing. He felt his body spasm and contort, but he did not fall out of the chair. He knew he was in no danger of falling out of the chair. He knew that Temptress would not let that happen. He was not bound to the chair by any constraints, only by her words. He knew she would take care of him. He trusted her.

The two separate voices in his ears stopped speaking full sentences. They would moan, call him a sweet boy, or say, "yes Temptress". But now it was only the real Temptress. The one he heard not in his ears, but in his head, that spoke. She had a delightful and happy tone to her voice that was filled with joy.

"Every time I say good boy you feel the tingles of pleasure. You are so deep in that submissive place. So deep that I can do anything that I want with you. You are mine. You are such a good boy" Tick, tick, ding.

The only thoughts racing through Jayden's brain were the thoughts of how extraordinary this felt. Except that now he felt as if he were on the brink. He felt he was at the point of no return. That special moment when a man feels all of his insides heat up to a boiling point and he knows it is only a matter of seconds before he explodes. That is a moment in time that cannot be stopped. He knew it would not happen till Temptress wanted to happen. She was in control.

She spoke to him as if she could read his every thought. "The pressure keeps building. You want more as my bliss surrounds you over and over. My sweet boy. I am going to count down from five and I want you to release for me. It will be the most amazing feeling of your life. Five, you feel it building so high. Four. The pleasure is just racking through your body now. Three. It is just so intense. Two. You want to let go. You need to let go. One. My sweet boy. It explodes for you and the bliss just keeps going. That's it. My good boy, my sweet boy. "

As she said those words Jayden felt the most intoxicating burst of pleasure he had ever experienced in his life. That was in his subconscious mind. Outside of his head, in the real world, he had unleashed nothing. He felt at peace. He felt restful. A smile hit his face as he felt bliss. There was nothing in this universe that could harm him. There was no stress. There was only happiness. This was bliss.

His breathing started to slow and his heart rate returned to normal as Temptress spoke. She spoke in a soft and happy tone as she said, "Just relax now. Let the pleasure drift through you. As you fall back now. You fall back to the sound of my voice. Where you don't have to think anymore. Just following me as I keep everything safe. As you float along in your afterglow and let my voice bring you back. You feel safe. You can trust me. You will trust me. You are my sweet boy. You are mine, pet. It feels so good being submissive for me. But we are going to come back now. Back to where you are awake. Back to where you are in an aware and relaxed state. It felt so good to be my sweet boy and you will come back to my trance again. But you are going to become awake again. When I say, wake up! Your subconscious will remember my voice, it will remember all of the pleasure and it will remember all of the triggers I have implanted in your mind. You will not remember this experience in your conscious mind. It is only in your subconscious that you will remember. I am going to wake you up now. I'm going to say it now, get ready!

"Wake up…Good boy. That was just so much fun!"

DANCING IN THE MOONLIGHT

Jayden looked around the room. He was a little confused. He felt as if he just had a brain fart. He did this from time to time as all people do. That moment when one is in mid-sentence and they forget completely what they were just talking about. Then it hit him. "Oh, no I cannot stay here. I have my boat down on the beach. What if someone takes it?"

Lillie smiled at him and said, "Private Island, remember? No one will take your boat. It will still be there. You look tired. You should rest. It is my pleasure and it would make me so happy if you stay tonight." When she said that, Jayden felt happy and secure for some inexplicable reason. He said, "Well, okay. Only because you insist. Thank you."

They walked through the center door and up the stairs. The staircase led to the second story of the house and they were in a hall. The hall was dimly lit and there were two closed doors at opposing ends of the hallway. There was a third door in the middle that was open. Against the wall in the center of the hall was a bookshelf that was about five feet long and had three shelves. It was crowded with books with not an inch to spare. Both ends of the hall had a mirror. They were facing each other. Next to the bookshelf, there was a glass door that led to a balcony looking out over the backyard. There was a smell of sage incense in the air. Or perhaps it was a burning oil. Lillie turned to the left and opened the door leading to a bedroom. She said, " I think you will like this room. You are welcome to use the other room if you please, but I think you will find this one very comforting. The center door is a lavatory should you need that. You will find everything you need there. There are towels, toothbrushes, soap, whatever you need." Jayden walked into the room. Lillie said, "sleep tight and have pleasant dreams" as she shut the door behind him.

Looking around the room he saw a queen-size bed. It had a large blue comforter and was covered in pillows. All four corners of the bed had tall posts and they supported a transparent canopy that surrounded the bed. The room had a six-drawer dresser. Attached to the wall and above the dresser was a mirror. On top of the dresser was a drawing kit. Jayden only knew what it was because he enjoyed drawing. He was not a professional by any means. It was only a hobby that he enjoyed to take his mind off the stresses of life. In a corner of the room sat a white wicker chair. A glass door led to a balcony that overlooked the front yard.

    Jayden took off his shorts and shirt as he lay down in the bed. He felt rather uncomfortable sleeping in next to nothing in a stranger's house. He had no change of clothes for the next day though. He did not want the smell of sleep on him as he returned to Martillo. As he took off his shorts he noticed his boxers were slightly sticky against his thigh. That is weird he thought. How and when did that happen? The bed was soft as he sank into it. It was the softest bed he had ever been on. He felt so relaxed as he tried to piece together the events of the night. It was too much to think about for his foggy mind. He dropped off into a deep sleep.

Jayden opened his eyes. The room was dimly lit as he had not turned off the light. He really could not have, as he could not find a light switch. His eyes blinked as he realized what had woken him up. He could hear voices. They were coming from the hall. He got up and put his ear to the door. The voices were not coming from the hall. It was almost as if they were coming from the room he was in. He looked around and saw a vent on the wooden floor. The voices were coming from that. He got down on his hands and knees as he put his ear to the vent. One of the voices was Lillie's. He did not know who the others were. He could not make out what they were saying. He could hear a sound that almost sounded like tea mugs clinging together followed by more muffled conversation and laughter. Jayden wanted to walk out of the room and walk downstairs into the kitchen to see what was going on. He was curious. It was not his house though, so it was not his business. No matter how odd the hours that his hostess kept had seemed. He went back to the bed and after perhaps thirty minutes, was just about to sleep when he heard a voice say his name. It was Lillie's voice, and it was close to him as his name was said in a whisper. He starred to the ceiling as he tried to will himself to sleep. He heard another whisper next to his ear. It sounded like it said,

"Come see me." He sat up and said in a whisper back to himself, "What the fuck?" He got up and looked at himself in the mirror. The pupils of his eyes were dilated. They were the size of saucers. He squinted at himself as he asked, "What the fuck was in that tea?"

He was feeling restless. He thought maybe some fresh air would do him well. He put his shirt and shorts back on. He then walked out of the bedroom door and to the bookshelf. He grabbed a book at random and opened it. Maybe reading will make his eyes tired and he could go to sleep. When he looked at the book he realized that would not work. It was written in Latin. They all were written in Latin. Except for the books that were written in Mandarin. Or was it Japanese? He was trying to think of what to do next. He remembered seeing the drawing kit on the dresser. He went to retrieve that. As he grabbed it he wondered if this was right. He is a guest in a stranger's house. She was gracious enough to take him and let him stay. Should he be using the stuff? Her stuff? Was this not rude to do? Using a person's personal property without asking? He knew it was wrong, in a way. But he could not help himself. It was not like any of this was all that wrong. His bad side and good side debated with each other as he grabbed the drawing kit. He walked back across the hall to the glass door leading to the back balcony.

It was a balcony that went the entire length of the second story that he was on. There were two deck chairs with a small glass table between them. The yard below was partially blocked by palm trees that nearly rose about the balcony itself. He could see part of the yard, just not the part below him. It was fairly large and offered plenty of space to play in. A white picket fence marked the end of the yard on all sides. On one far corner, he saw what looked like a fire pit. In another corner was a large brick oven. It had a chimney coming from it. Jayden sat down with the writing kit. He grabbed one of the pencils and looked at a blank piece of paper as he thought about what to draw.

Staring at a blank piece of paper trying to decide what to create is the hardest part of art. Getting that first line seems to be impossible. Once that first line is drawn, it all seems to fall into place and a different part of the brain takes over. The left side of the brain is logical and linear will battle with the more creative right side of the brain. The left will try and search for meaning, reason, and purpose. The right side only wants to let it go and see what happens.

It is like a battle between good and evil, the light versus the dark. Both want to be in control and both have different ideas. It was always a constant battle between the left hand and the right hand. What neither side realized is that they are one of the same. Jayden was not sure what he was drawing. He was sketching away feverously. He was so focused on getting it done. His mind worked faster than his hand could keep up. As he added one line to the picture, his thoughts were already five lines ahead. His hand worked hard to keep up with the images in his head as not to lose them. As he was thinking one thing, his mind would go off in another direction. What would be the next line drawn? Who was really in command? Was it the hand or was it the brain? Was it the left or maybe it was the right? They both seemed to work on different paths but knew that one could not survive without the other. Although part of the same body, they were constantly divided. One hand would make a few sketches in one spot. The other would brush the picture to help blend the lines together. One hand would shade the picture darker while the other would brush away unapologetically making it lighter. It was a process that continued till he was done. He did not know he was done. Something in his brain told him he was. He set down the pencil and put the drawing down on his lap. He let his hands massage one another as he looked at the picture. To get a better look, he held it in the air by the moonlight. He had drawn a picture of the front of Lillie's house. It was from what he remembered anyway. He liked it. He was happy. He looked over the top of the picture and down into the yard lit by an almost full moon. He could see someone down there. It was Lillie. She was naked from head to toe. He knew that he had friends who frowned upon a full-figured woman. He could not figure out why some of his friends did not find this appealing. He pondered how anyone could not find that attractive. Especially one that was naked. They wanted a petite girl. Jayden did not want that. He wanted more than skin and bones in a woman. He did not find petite women attractive in the least. He liked a tall, full-figured woman with curves. It was not just the appearance. It was the attitude. Full-figured women seemed to have confidence that others did not. Looking at her body he could tell she was flawless in every way. He wanted to rush down to the yard and greet her. He wanted to fall into her arms and go down to the ground with her as they rolled around. Feeling her soft and warm body next to his. He could feel tightness in his groin. He looked down and noticed the bulge in his shorts. He clenched his eyes tightly as he tried to shake away his fantasy. He said, "You can't go down there and do that! This is her home; you are a guest out of the generosity of her heart. She is obviously doing something that makes her happy in the privacy of her solitude. Do you want to interrupt that? What are you going to do? Walk out in the yard, buck naked, and say, What's shaking? No, you will not do that. What are you? Some kind of evil perverse freak?" He did continue to watch her dance under the night sky in the privacy of her yard. He could not get it out of his head how beautiful she was. He tried to imagine what it would be like to be pressed up against her indulgent body as she engulfed him with her arms. He looked down and realized that he had undone his pants and was holding his cock in his hand. He was mildly stroking it up and down. He immediately released his grip and withdrew his hand in the air. He stuffed his member into his shorts as he zipped them up. He said, "Okay. Stop. You are not a pervert." He slapped his hand with the other. He grabbed the picture, slid it into the writing kit, and walked back to his bedroom. As he lay in bed thoughts of the beautiful woman dancing in the yard put him to sleep with a smile on his face.

WHERE IS JAYDEN?

Pepper, Jeff, Todd, Leslie, and the rest of the crew had parked their boats at the southwest tip of Isla de Cabeza Martillo where Todd's father's boat rental was. Todd gathered up everyone's keys and put them back in the shed where tourists would line up to sign a waiver and pay for the rentals. Pepper asked, "Anyone seen Jayden? Where is he?" Jeff said, "Me and Leslie saw him out at the second checkpoint. We lost track of him after that."

Pepper asked, "Shouldn't we go back out and look for him?"

Todd said, "Pepper, it's the freaking ocean! That would be like looking for a needle in a haystack. He's a grown-ass man. I'm sure he can take care of himself. He'll probably be back in no time."

Jeff added, "Yeah Pepper. He'll be fine. The directions back here are on the GPS. He'll be back."

Chad spoke up, "Well I don't know about you, but I could use some more beer." They stoked the fire that had not yet completely gone out and gathered around to tell stories and talk about whatever came up. It was just another night for the young locals of the Peeking Islands. In the big cities on the mainland people their age were dressed to the nines and hanging out in nightclubs. This group of friends was content with doing what they did all the time. Hang out on a beach around a fire drinking cheap beer. A couple of hours had gone by and it was Chad that stood up and said, "I don't know about all y'all but I got to be up for work tomorrow. I think I'm done. Todd, thanks for letting us use the boats, everyone else, thanks for whatever. I bid thee goodnight." He tipped his hat and bowed at the group as they all moaned and tossed empty beer cans at him. They were all in agreement though. It was time to call it a night. Everyone had left except Todd, Pepper, and Jeff. Pepper asked Todd, "Are you sure you don't want to go out looking for Jayden? He really should have been back by now."

Todd said, "I'm gonna stick around here a little while longer. I have to clean and gas up these boats. If he don't come back by then, maybe I'll do a quick drive around."

She agreed, kissed him, and went off with Leslie. Jeff said, "Hey bub, I gotcha. I'll help you with these boats."

The two were refueling the boats when Todd said, "Thanks man for sticking around. All these mother fuckers jump right up for a free boat ride, but nobody wants to help afterward. Bunch of freeloaders is what they are."

Jeff said, "No problem man. Hey, you think maybe we should go out and look for Jayden?"

Todd sighed as he said, "To be honest man, I'm more concerned about the boat."

"Yeah, good thing your dad is out of town. What would he do if you lost one of his boats?"

Todd replied, "He'd kick my ass is what he'd do. So that little bitch better show up with that boat soon. How'd they meet again?"

Jeff asked "Who?"

"Who? Jayden and Pepper."

Jeff told him, "I think she said she met him in south Florida when she was visiting her aunt. But

I think I heard him say he goes to college up in north Florida."

"A college boy!"

"Why do you ask? Wait, you don't think something is going on between them do you?"

Todd said, "You see the way she was looking at him? Pshh. Fucking college pukes. He's probably a frat bro that has a daddy that will sue me."

Jeff told him, "Wait, Pepper and Jayden? You're crazy man. I think you are looking too much into it. You see him? Looked like one of those jock preppy types. She doesn't go for guys like that."

Todd asked, "Yeah. But did you hear her?" He did a mock Pepper voice as he said, "Are you going to go out and look for Jayden? He might be lost, he might need help! Oh, help my sweet Jayden!"

Jeff laughed as he said, "You're too much man. But if he is not back by tomorrow we should at least go looking for the boat. Don't want to see your daddy whoop your ass when he gets back to town."

"Yeah, we have trackers on those anyway. So if I don't see that boat here in a day or two, we'll go find it. Yo! Heads up!" He tossed a set of keys that would unlock the shed at Jeff so he could go get buckets and rags to rinse off the boats. About another hour had gone by and they had finished the job. Todd left a note on the windshield of Jayden's truck that had instructions to go to the shed and look for a box that said, rental return, and leave the keys in the box.

HELL'S COMPOST

It was 10 AM Monday. The TV was on inside Billy's bar and no matter what channel they turned to they heard the same words spoken repeatedly by all the reporters on all stations. "Today was a turning point. It was a very bad day for the president today." Click. "It is the beginning of the end!" Click. "We have another bombshell! Today was a turning point." Click. "The walls are closing in on him. The vice president may have to step up and take over." Click. "One astrologer says this is the beginning to the end." Click. "War is unavoidable says the president." Click. "Today was a turning point on positive relations between the Russians and America." Click. "Leaked footage shows Russia moving their bombs into position. They are ready for war. " Click. "Russia announces it will rid the world of the evil coming from America. If that means going to war, then so be it." Click. No matter what station they turned it was the same. Jeb yelled out to the bartender, Tommy, "Yo Tommy! Turn this shit off. It's all the same!"

Melissa said, "Aren't you concerned that we are on the brink of world war three?"

"No! And see, the problem just came from your lips. The media are programming our minds with the same damn trigger words to brainwash us! It's all part of their agenda! I mean, imagine a world controlled by media."

"But you hear all the sides saying different things."

"They are not the same Melissa. It's only to get us divided and riled up so we fight each other." The TV clicked again. It was an interview with as of recently, the very famous Reverend Colin McDowell. A voice yelled out, "Stop it here. I want to hear what the man has to say." They were just tuning in to an interview already in progress. The interviewer said, "So what you are saying Reverend, is that this is the end and we need to repent right now to save our souls?"

The Reverend looking worked up and sweaty said, "Jerry, The end is not near. This is the end. Neither side is going to drop their arms in this. We are going to have world war three on our hands and it will be Hell on earth!"

Jerry countered, "But Reverend, do you sincerely think that anybody actually wants to go to war? This has been done time and time again. It is a stand-off that nobody wants to walk away from and nobody surely wants to take any further. I think everyone, no matter who they are, what they believe, or where they are from knows that there are no winners in a global thermal nuclear war."

The Reverend nodded his head up as he put out his hand and said, "Oh, there is one winner. There is for sure one winner."

"And who would that be Reverend McDowell?"

"Lucifer. The devil himself will rise and take all the unrepented souls with him to the bowels of hell to rebuild his army for the real battle. The war between Heaven and Hell. So the time is now Jerry. The time to repent is now. History is bound to repeat itself. Imagine being caught in a loop."

Jerry leaned back and said, "So you are saying that it will be hell on earth? Did you not say only a month ago that earth is hell itself?"

"Earth is not Hell, Jerry. Hell exists on earth because of mankind. It was man that came up with the number of the beast!" He said as he quoted revelations 12:18. "Here is wisdom! Let him who hath understanding calculate the number of the beast! For it is a human number!"

Jeb yelled out, "Amen brother! Preach on!"

Melissa grabbed the remote off the bar top and hit mute as she said, "Are you for real? You believe this man? With what this man says? He is out of his mind! He is not a man of God! He has just as much evil in him as the next guy" As perfect timing would have it B-roll was showing over the interview as it went on. It showed the Reverend accepting checks from those who chose to donate. Melissa spoke again, " You see? Look at all those people giving away their life savings! How would you feel if that was your grandmother giving away every cent she has ever earned to him. That money does not go to the church! Have you seen his home?"

Jeb looked to Melissa and told her, "First off, my grandmother is dead, you know that, but may God rest her soul. This man brings God into all of our homes via satellite every Sunday morning. He travels the country to preach the good word and bring God into our homes. Are you saying this righteous man is the evil one?"

"No Jeb. They are all evil. Not just the ones that you see as evil. Not just the Russians, but for us too. Evil lurks in all corners. It happens because the media is putting trigger words in their stories to tear us apart. It has been proven time and time again that is the agenda. We can see this. It is easy for them to pull the wool over our eyes. Imagine how great the world would be if we all turned off the TV. I wish everyone would end their addiction to TV today. We would all get along better. I guarantee it."

"So you do agree that Hell is on earth?"

"Honey, earth is not Hell, earth is nothing more than a compost for Hell."

The bartender, Tommy, leaned over and grabbed back the remote, and turned the TV off. Clasping his hands together and with a forced laugh, he said, "Okay kids. Playtime is over. Everyone get out of the sandbox. How about we have some drinks?" He shouted, "First round is on the house. What will everyone have?"

SHABARI

Jayden flickered his eyes and put his hand over his face as bright light spilled into the room from the window and glass door. Closing the curtain was not something that occurred to him last night. He had no idea what time it was since he did not wear a watch and there was no clock in the room. It was later than he normally woke up. He could feel that. It was insanely bright. It was too bright to be early morning. He rolled out of the bed and made it as best as he could. He put on his shorts and shirt and walked into the bathroom. The bathroom had towels hung neatly on a wall rack. There were three. One was orange and two were yellow. Jayden assumed those were probably display-only towels. He looked at the long counter. It had a sink that was more like a giant bowl on top of the counter as opposed to being sunken into the counter like most sinks. It was not just a bowl though. It did have a drain. It was just a cool sink designed to look like a bowl.

On the counter, he saw hand soap, a razor with some shaving lotion. There was a toothbrush in an unopened box. On top of some neatly folded clothes there was a note. It said, "Dearest Jayden, there is a fresh toothbrush for you and a razor as well if you need it. I found some clothes for you that had been left behind by an old friend. I do not know your size, but try them out. You look about the same size he was. Don't use the towels on the rack…those are for display. Use the one hanging in the shower." There was a winking face drawn after that followed by the words, "See you soon, Lillie" He opened the shower door, which was frosted glass. The shower looked like it had been remade recently and had jets coming from the side. Jayden took his shower and freshened up at the counter. He brushed his teeth. He was so thankful for that toothbrush. He was always conscientious about having dragon breath. Especially around a beautiful woman whose house he was currently a guest in. He gave himself a quick shave. He even did some quick manscaping over the toilet. Just in case. Not that he was planning on anything happening. He planned to thank her for the hospitality and get back to Isla de Cabeza Martillo. He was sure Pepper and everyone else had been wondering where he was. He did remember seeing Lillie's naked body last night in the yard and noticed she was cleanly maintained. So just in case, he wanted to be ready to return the favor. Not that anything would happen. Better safe than sorry he thought as he flushed his pubes down the toilet. He looked over at the fresh clothing on the counter. He thought back to the letter. Left behind by some friend. He felt weird wearing some other dude's clothing. It was probably better than wearing his stinky clothes from yesterday. He picked up the shirt and smelled it. It smelled clean. He held it out in front of himself. It looked about his size. He put on the fresh shirt and shorts. He kept his boxers. He did have his limits after all.

Lillie smiled as Jayden walked into the kitchen from the stairway door. She looked him up and down as she thought, before her, stood a fine young man. He should work out just fine for her plans. He had a mind that was easy to control and he was not bad to look at either. He was at a height equal to hers. He looked to have very strong arms and the thighs of a speed skater. He had working man's hands. They looked big and strong. They would feel good all over her human body if she let him touch her. Even though a Temptress never allows her pets to touch her or would get involved sexually. He had a lot of good in his brain. Under that athletic physique was a mind very attached to doing right. She could sense that in him while prodding through his mind last night. She could also tell he had a lot of inner conflict between right and wrong. He was someone that could see the evil in the world and wanted to follow the law of God. Because he knew that is what was right. But he could not resist the urge to return to the root of mankind, where a wide variety of evil lurked in the shadows. Imagine if light lurked in the shadows. She saw that in him on her little vacation into his brain last night. She would work him over a little more today and have him bound to her will. She knew she would control this one. He was hers for the taking.

With a large smile, she said, "Good morning! Well, not really morning anymore. I take it you slept well?"

He smiled back and said, "Good morning. What time is it?" She told him that it was almost 11 AM.

"I guess did sleep well. I had a little trouble at first. Which reminds me. I hope you don't mind. I used your drawing kit and drew you this." He handed her the picture he drew on the balcony. He handed it to her and she looked at it with admiration. "Oh, this is my house. You have a good memory. This looks very much like it. Such a sweet boy!"

He said, "You're welcome" He wondered why he felt his groin jump and jolt quickly when she thanked him and called him a sweet boy. She asked him if he wanted any coffee. He said, "Oh no thanks. I don't drink coffee. Actually, I was going to head out and try and get back to Martillo. But thank you for your hospitality."

"Oh no, you mustn't leave so soon. You have not eaten. At least stay for lunch. Got to keep those muscles strong," She said as she grabbed his arm. "Tell me you'll at least stay for some food before you go."

He was hungry. So he agreed to stay for lunch. She said, "Excellent. Would you be a good boy and go down in the cellar to get meat for me please?"

"It's just down there?"

"Yes, as you first go down the stairs look up and pull the chain to turn on the light. Grab some meat that is packaged up on the right cooler. That is ready to eat. The one on the left is a freezer. That meat will take longer to defrost. We need to get you fed and on your way!"

Jayden walked down the creaky wooden stairs and into the cellar. Cellars had always had a creepy effect on him. He would not really know, as he had never actually been in a cellar. This was his first. But he had seen a lot of horror movies and that is where the creepy stuff happens. The light moved around the room as the bulb he had pulled the chain on was still swinging back and forth. The walls were painted red and the floor was cement with blotches of dark red all over it. Perhaps she was a messy painter and spilled it when she was painting the walls. He looked to the right and there was a long counter. It had sharp tools like one would see maybe on a fish cleaning station. Or maybe in a butcher's shop. No, they were definitely for cleaning fish he told himself. He looked at the two coolers in front of him. They were white floor coolers that were about four feet long and waist-high. He looked at the one on the left. It had a padlock on it preventing it from being opened. The one on the right was the one she told him to grab from anyway, he opened the lid and grabbed the first packaged meat on the top. There was enough in there for a small feast. It was only the two of them eating so he grabbed just one small package. It was not labeled as one would see in a store. It just had plain white wrapping paper around it. So he assumed it was meat. He grabbed that and as he shut the lid he heard a voice. It was a male voice. It said his name. He slammed the lid down and turned around quickly. "Who's there?" He asked. He heard a couple more voices. They said, "Save us. Kill her." A few more whispers from another part of the room spoke. They sounded more sinister as they said, "No Jayden. Stay with her. She is your savior. She is your master." Jayden's breathing picked up as he looked around the room nervously. The light still dancing around the room played tricks on his mind with shadows moving across the walls. A whisper came from the corner of the room. "Jayden. Release us. You know what must be done." It said as he looked behind him to see an ax that had been leaning up against the wall fall over to the floor. "What the fuck?" He asked out loud. A dark voice said, "Stay with her. You belong to her." He ran up the stairs. Grabbing the chain as he passed underneath it. He could feel them right behind him. He did not know who they were, but they were right on his tail. He stumbled out the door as he tripped over the second to the top step and shut the door behind him. Lillie looked at him and asked, "Are you okay? You look as if you've seen a ghost."

"Ghost? No. I don't believe in those. I Just have a habit of running upstairs you know?" he put the meat on the counter and asked, "Is that what you wanted?"

She smiled at him with a gleam in her eyes as she said, "That is exactly what I wanted. I hate going down in that cellar. You know, spiders and all. You're such a good boy." As she said that Jayden squinted his eyes and tried to focus as he felt a shock of warm lightheadedness come over him for a second. She told him to follow her out in the yard as they wait for the meat to defrost a little and she got the oven ready. In the middle of the yard, he saw a pole. He asked, "Do you like tetherball?" She asked him to repeat that. "Tetherball. I see the pole, I just don't see the ball and tether."

Lillie told him. "Oh that. That is for a game I like to play. It brings back fond memories of my childhood. I use it occasionally."

They got to the oven. It was a massive brick oven. Inside the actual oven had so much space. It was big enough to cook multiple meals at once for a busy and popular restaurant. About waist height was a place to grill and prep work. Coming from the top of the oven was a tall chimney. It must have been twenty feet tall. The entire structure was made of brick. Lillie got a fire in the oven going and said, "Come walk with me."

"Where to?" Jayden asked.

"Just over here in the open yard. Last night you asked what I do. I told you I make people better versions of themselves. I want to show you what that is. Come on."

He followed her to the center of the yard. She told him to take his sandals off and he did. The grass felt so soft beneath his feet. It was not like the grass where he lived that was thick and rough to the touch. This grass was made of small thin blades and felt very soft to the touch. This was very comfortable to walk barefoot in. She stood before him with her hands held out and her palms facing up. She told him to hold his hands out over hers with his palms down. He did and she spoke. "Now I want you to close your eyes. Breath in deep." He took a deep breath and exhaled. She laughed and said, "No silly, always wait for my instruction. Like Simon says. "Breath in deep. Breath in slowly with my counting." She counted slowly to six. "Good, now hold it." She counted to six and continued her instruction in a soft tone. "Now slowly exhale to my count." She slowly counted to six. "Very good. Now let us do that again." She repeated these steps for a few minutes till he seemed relaxed. "Keep your eyes closed, tell me how do your feel?" He felt really good and told her that. He had heard about breathing exercises. Imagine if you could control your breathing to a point of total relaxation. Remember to a time in your youth when there was no stress. Because you can remember that, you can now feel that you are in a great place to relax your thoughts. Because you can relax your thoughts you can now let yourself go and sink deep. He had never really tried them. He never really had the time. She said, "Now take another deep breath for me and hold it. I want you to think about anything that has been bothering you. I want you to let those thoughts escape out of your mind as you exhale and blow those bad thoughts out of your mouth." He did and as he exhaled a smile hit his face. She repeated this with him a few times. "Now open your eyes and let your arms down to your sides." He did. She said, "Look around you. Look at the trees, look at the beautiful blue sky painted with white fluffy clouds. Look around at the flowers in my yard. Look at the grass beneath your feet. Look at it all. Take it in and tuck it away deep in a special place." He looked around at the nature around him that she spoke of. She told him,

"Now close your eyes again. Move your head around as if you are looking at everything you just did. Even though your eyes are shut, you can still see it all. Can you see it? Remember what it looked like with your eyes open. Because you can remember, you can still see the world around you with your eyes closed" He smiled and said, "I can." He was not sure if he was doing this right. He was not sure if he could see everything she was talking about. But he told her that he could. He did feel good, he knew that much. He was not completely lying. She told him, "Feel the grass beneath your feet. You can feel the warmth of the earth go from the grass into the base of your feet. You can feel the energy of the earth surge into you. Hold your arms out for me again. Hold your palms facing the ground. The energy from the earth that seeps in through your feet flows through your body. It moves through your body till it reaches your hands. The energy returns to earth as it exits your body through your palms. Even though your eyes are closed you can see powerful rays of light leaving your body and returning to the ground. Imagine this happening to you. You begin to realize that you could do this anywhere. Even if you were sitting in a room reading a book. Because you have the power to remember a special place like this, you realize that you could relax anywhere. Imagine those rays of light and energy still flowing from your hands, and back into the earth. They are powerful rays. They support your arms and that is why your arms do not tire. You could stand like this all day and not feel any pain. The flow of the energy is constant through your body. You will always feel this when you walk barefoot on the earth. Now open your eyes."

He opened his eyes she asked how he felt. He told her refreshed. She said, "You're such a good boy!" He felt a surge of energy. But it was not something from mother earth. It was straight from his cock. He felt a tingling sensation down there as she said that. They walked back to the oven and tossed the meat on. As they waited for it to cook and she did a few more earthly exercises with him. After a couple of repetitions through the process, they could smell the meat was done and sat down for lunch.

Jayden and Lillie sat at a small four-person table made of wood on a wooden deck that overlooked that backyard. The meat was unlike anything he had ever tasted. It almost tasted like veal all though it did not have the gamey characteristics of goat or pork. All though it was very well cooked it was still full of juice. The meat itself had a very sweet taste to it and was served under a green pepper sauce with a side of green beans. It looked like a filet mignon, but it tasted nothing like steak. To wash it down they had a bottle of Chianti.

As Jayden put a fork full of meat into his mouth Lillie asked him what he thought. He could barely stop eating long enough to answer. "Oh wow. Oh my gosh, Lillie. This is the best meal I've ever had. I have never tasted meat like this in my life! What is this? It kind of reminds me of veal but I know it is not that."

She smiled and said, "It is just local meat that is provided to me. I prepare it all myself though. I guess you could say the secret ingredient is, well, it's human instinct."

He looked back at her and said, "Yeah, okay. Well, whatever it is, it's the best I have ever had. Thank you."

The green pepper sauce that covered it was very nice as well as it added the right amount of spice. Looking out over the yard he could tell it mostly came from her garden out in the yard. He asked her, "So for money, you said that you make people better versions of themselves. Is that what we did out in the yard? Is that what you do?"

She told him, "It is something like that. I help people find their inner selves. I help people become the best version of themselves. From there, we rebuild and recreate a mold of them that cannot be beaten."

"So you are like a motivational speaker only one on one?" She answered, "It is more like a personal life coach. I just get deep into people and pull out the best."

Jayden said, "I guess you are talking about assisting people to find their inner chi and chakras or whatever. Maybe like a yogi in yoga class. I have friends that do that."

She laughed and said, "It is a little more different than that. No disrespect to your friends but they are just regurgitating something that they read in a book and performing simple meditations. I like to think I make people go a little deeper than that. Suppose that you could forget all of the thoughts that prevent you from going deeper into yourself than you have ever been. Imagine you have the power to achieve whatever your mind wishes at the snap of a finger. You will find yourself in a world with no boundaries. What would it be like if you could bring your thoughts into physical reality? Once you can do all of this, you'll find that you are very happy and always full of bliss. Sooner or later you will be larger than life in more than just attitude and because of that, you will find the better version of yourself." Jayden asked, "So you help people break boundaries?"

"I break the boundaries that the human mind had put upon itself. There are no real boundaries. Suppose you could bypass the boundaries that the world has put upon you. Now just pretend that you are a great subject with unstoppable potential. You will begin to realize that is just what you are."

Jayden thought he was getting it. But every time he said something that indicated that he did get it, she seemed to counter it with a bunch of gibberish. It was like having a discussion about where is the end of infinity. He was bored of this conversation. He was not really into chakras, yoga, or any of that metaphysical stuff anyway. It was all hooey to him. To him, life was best when it functioned in linearity. Looking around the yard and thinking about the house he said, "Well, you must have some pretty high-end clients if that is what affords you the luxury of all of this."

She smiled and said, "I used to be a professor remember. That and of course royalties of many books I have written on the subject."

To change the subject he looked around him for inspiration to do so. He saw what appeared to be a pile of rope on a table along with a couple of bamboo poles. He asked, "What's up with the rope and bamboo? New yard project?" Lillie told him, "That is for Kinnaku-bi or Shibari."

He looked at her confused and asked, "Can-nook, what?"

She repeated herself, "Kinnaku-bi and Shibari. It is the Japanese art of delicate tying."

"So, you tie knots in the rope around bamboo and call it art."

As she got up from the table she said, "Hold that thought."

A few minutes later she came back from inside the house. She had a mug of hot tea and a metronome. She set both down on the table. As Jayden looked into the mug he noticed the color and texture made it look like mashed peas. She could see the apprehensive look on his face. She told him. "Drink it. It will help you relax and I can explain the art of Shibari to you."

Jayden drank the tea and could feel his mind slowly sink into an abyss. It was an extremely fast-acting tea. She explained Shabari as a Japanese art that involved using rope to tie a person up using simple yet intricate and visually stimulating patterns of knots. She told him that it originated in the 1600s as a technique used in binding prisoners of war. But was later adapted into performance art. It can be a very mentally stimulating process as the one being bound is put into a helpless yet trustful state of mind. It is because they are trustful that they are not helpless.

The tea had taken its full effect as Jayden was in a completely relaxed state and felt up to trying anything unfamiliar to his mind. Lillie stood Jayden up from his chair as she moved the chair away. She touched the pendulum on the metronome, and it started a rhythmic and calming beat. It went, tick, tick, ding. Tick, tick, ding. It helped Jayden drop deeper into a relaxed state of mind. He was able to imagine himself as putty in her hands. She walked up behind Jayden and told him to stand still as she started to slowly remove his clothes. She put his clothes neatly on a table behind her. When he was naked she placed her hands on his shoulders and lightly pushed him to the ground so that he was on his knees. Still, behind him, she said, "This is going to be slightly different than our previous sessions together. This will be a little more physical. What we are doing is called Shibari." She held up some rope in front of him as she explained, "This is the rope that will bind you to me. We call it asanawa. I am going to use it to tie a variety of different Kannuki, those are how we say knots and cinches. These will bind you in a way that you are unable to move. Imagine that you are not bound by rope though. You are bound only by my words. I control your thoughts." Tick, tick, ding.

She knelt behind him and softly grappled his neck with one arm as she used the other to bring the first layer of rope around him. His body was limp as she was able to manipulate his movements with ease into the rope. His head felt so heavy to him that it just looked down like someone about to fall asleep while sitting up.

She calmly told him "I want you to relax. Breath in and out easily. You are safe. The binding keeps you secure. You trust me. You trust the binding that secures you, to me. You are mine."

From behind him, she brought the first rope down to one arm and then across to the other. She lightly brought the rope down to his wrist. Each of his wrists now had a part of the rope wrapped around them.

Slowly tugging on the rope from behind him on one motion back over his shoulder. She brought his wrists, now bound together up toward the left side of his neck she held it tight. He seemed to accept this as his head faced down, with no desire to look up. She then lowered it so that his bound wrists were held toward his chest with his elbows down as if he were praying. She used more rope to bring all the way around and encircle him at chest level. This would hold his arms in place.

"The asanawa will play with many different sensations and emotions. Whether I use it to run over you and caress you or whether I use it to bind you with kannuki. If I caress you with the rope, or asanawa rather, that is called aibunawa. It will help keep you in a relaxed state and bring you pleasure. This is like a job interview. I will see how much do you talk, how much do you listen. The key element is rhythm. Will it be fast or slow? Will it be intense, soft, or hard? Will I stay close or will a move from afar? Stay focused on the rhythm of the metronome. Tick, tick, ding. Yes, yes, please.

With the rope in her hands, she would toy with how tight she held him. She would release her grip slightly and he would lean forward while swaying back and forth. Then she would reign him back in tightly up against herself. As he leaned back into her she would let her warm breath on his neck assure them that she was there.

She tied a knot in the center of his back. She then grabbed his chin from behind and brought his head back so that his face was straight up. In this position, he depended on her for support from behind. Without her, he would fall. She slowly and skillfully slid the rope around his neck from behind and around to the front. With the rope now around the front of his neck, she quickly pulled him back tightly against her body.

He was bound to Lillie as the rope around his neck held him tightly in place to her. She held him in close to her with his breathing and heart rate never once picking up because it matched the beat of the metronome. Tick, tick, ding. Yes, yes, please.

She whispered into his ear, "We are going to use Shibari to help condition your mind. This way we may make you a better version of yourself. I will use your body as a piece of asymmetric art putting you in some rather uncomfortable positions. I will take you to the edge and back. You may feel fear. It is right on the edge of fear where trust will grow. You may feel pain. You will grow through the pain. That is part of the conditioning. You trust me. You are mine."

She held him softly and in place leaning back into her body till his breathing relaxed. She then tugged on only one end of the rope slowly releasing its bind on his neck. He felt it caress him as it loosely slid over his shoulder. He remembered this was called aibunawa. With a free hand, she continued to support his chin up and forced him to lean back on her. She slowly unwrapped the rope from his neck. She brought it around to his mouth and whispered, "Open." He opened his mouth and with the rope in his mouth, she tugged back from both sides, forcing his face to look at the sky once again.

She brought the rope down and over the bridge of his left foot. She took it around his ankle twice. Using leverage she pulled on the rope from behind him, which caused his leg to bend back at the knee so that his foot was brought up to his butt. She held this position till his body had adjusted to the stretch and his breathing relaxed.

"I want you to relax. Breath in and out easily. You are safe. The binding keeps you secure. You trust me. You trust the binding that secures you to me."

As she could tell, he was now breathing normally and felt comfortable. She released the grip of the rope and lowered his leg down just a bit. She brought the end of the rope back up to the center of his back where the first knot was made. She ran the rope under that knot twice and tied off another knot. This held his leg in place now pressed up against his back. Lillie repeated the process with the other leg. He was still on his knees with his arms bound together to his chest. His feet were bound together behind him and held apart. She looked at him and praised him for doing so well. "That was the introductory warm-up. That was to get you stretched out and limber. She slowly released him from all of his binds. From still behind him, she stood up and walked to the table to get a longer rope.

Jayden was on his knees and looking directly up at Lillie who now standing before him. She had a long rope hanging from around the back of her neck. She playfully rubbed one end of it over his face. I am your kinbakushi. Your body and mind rely on me for support and direction. Today we are going to condition your mind. She continued to caress his face, chest, and legs to the rope. She was getting his mind accustomed to its feel. She walked around behind him. She held the rope out like a giant horseshoe and lightly brought it up from his knees and over his face.

She leaned down into him so that her face was level to the back of his head as she whispered into his ear, "I want you, to drop. Let your mind drift. Let the conditioning slip in from my lips into your mind. I am going to condition your mind. Conditioning makes you feel better" She switched over to the other ear and whispered, "It is like a day at the salon. As the stylist runs her fingers into your scalp you feel better. She conditions your scalp. I will relax and condition your mind. It will make you feel better. Just as you cannot escape these ropes, you cannot escape my conditioning of your mind. Because you-are-mine."

Keeping him on his knees she used rope to bind his wrists together behind his back. She tied off a kannuki and he was secure and unable to move in what she told him was called Gote Gasshoe Shibari. It was the name of the position she had put him in. It translated to reverse prayer. His arms at the elbows were bound behind his back as closely as body physics would allow. She had used her binding skills to have his hands clasped together with his forefingers sticking out. His wrists and forearms had a rope around them as well. He looked as he was praying with his hands behind his back. Being in such a relaxed state of mind his head fell loosely off his shoulders with his face aimed at the ground. His eyes were closed.

She leaned into one ear as she delicately whispered. "Just as the fingers of a stylist will run through your hair, I will run mine through your brain." She switched to the other ear and he could feel the wetness of her mouth as she whispered, "You-are-mine, to be conditioned. Conditioning will make you a better person. Do you want to be better?"

He said, "Yes, yes, please."

She came around to stand in front of him and said, "Good boy. No matter what I say it will make you more of a pet. More of what I want to see." She leaned and whispered, "You-are-mine." In his mind, he heard those three words resonate repeatedly like a record stuck on the same groove.

She got a bamboo pole that was about four feet long. The pole was placed horizontally across the small of his back. It fit snugly between his back as the front of his arms near his elbows held it in place. She fashioned the long rope around his waist behind his shoulders and ran it around the bamboo pole so it was going over the bamboo and back around to the front of his body. This would further help the bamboo pole that was supporting his arms and running horizontally across his back in place. Taking the remainder of the rope she tossed one end over a secure support beam above them. It was maybe ten or twelve feet off the ground. The rope went over the beam and came back down. She pulled on the rope and this brought him from his knees up to his feet so that he was now loosely standing as a marionette hung from its stand with care. He was standing with his arms bound behind his back with his wrists bound together behind him. His elbows were apart. She tied off the end of the rope to the rope that ran up and down behind him and to the beam. Doing this held him in place with no physical assistance needed from her.

"Once conditioned you will respond to my voice. You will serve and obey. Conditioning teaches you to adapt and serve. It makes you a better version of yourself. Do you want to be a better version of yourself?"

He said, "I want to be better. I want to serve. Yes, yes, please."

She lazily walked away from behind Jayden to the table for another rope. She walked back gracefully and was directly behind him. He could sense her. He could feel her energy. She leaned into one ear and whispered.

"Conditioning causes you to obey freely. Obeying causes bliss. It makes you useful. You like being mine. You will learn to follow because following causes pleasure. You-will-obey." The word obey echoed into both of his ears as it firmly planted and found a home in his subconscious mind.

Introducing a second rope she seductively ran it under his thigh. She brought both ends up together as she hoisted his leg off the ground. She ran the rope around his thigh twice and down to and around his ankle and put him in a position where his leg was bent at the knee and horizontal to the ground. She tied the remaining rope to the main rope supporting him in the air. With another rope she did the same with his other leg then using the same rope she took it over to his other leg and wrapped it around his knees as she pulled them together. She brought the rope to his back and over his shoulders and down to a rope going around his waist. She tied them off to each other.

She stood in front of him as she said, "Completely bound in my ropes. Completely lost in my voice. You are bound by the sound of my voice as your body is bound to the ropes. The ropes keep you bound and safe. You can try to escape but you cannot. The more you resist, the more your body accepts. The more your mind will accept. You are mine. Allow yourself to be freely conditioned. Conditioning frees your mind." Tick, tick, ding.

She readjusted the main support rope in a way so that now as he was hanging from the support beam, he was face down. She called this position kushinawa. Which meant he was inverted. His legs were bound together and behind him in the air. His feet were pulled towards his back so now that he was in an arched position with his chest pointing the most forward. His feet were the highest point of the body and his head was the closest to the ground. He was essentially hanging upside down at an eighty-degree angle. At his lowest point, he was about four feet off the ground. The bamboo pole that worked as support for holding his arms comfortably behind him was horizontal to the ground. This would make it easy for Lillie to slowly spin and disorientate him with a simple touch to the end of the pole. She would touch one end of the bamboo pole with a gentle touch and he would spin slowly. It was a comforting spin. It did not make him dizzy. To disorientate him she would walk in circles around him in the opposite direction of which he spun.

She would mostly stay out of his line of vision. Lastly, she took some rope and held it in front of his face. He opened his mouth. She put the rope into his mouth and ran both ends behind him. She pulled back hard on the rope forcing his head to lift. She tied it off to the rope around his ankles. This put his head in Aomuke Tsuri, which put his face in an upright and forward position.

"Conditioning feels so nice. It feels nice to be conditioned. It feels pleasurable to be bound to my voice. As your thoughts are bound to me, you will think of me. Not only here, but in the future wherever you are, you will think of me. You will dream of me because you are mine. I will be in your dreams. I-am-your-dreams." Tick, tick, ding.

"You no longer resist. There is no conflict in your mind. You-are-mine. You know that everything, your mind will ever need, is given to you by me. You are bound to me. It is the asanawa that binds you physically now. It is my voice that binds your mind to me forever. You-are-mine."

She continued to walk around him in circles that opposed the way he spun. She would ever so lightly touch the side of the bamboo pole to keep him in a perpetual spinning motion. He was not dizzy. He was only disoriented. It was pleasant disorientation though as he felt bliss.

"Remember that you agreed to this binding. You wanted this binding. You accept that you are mine. It is that because you agreed that you feel safe. Because you feel safe, you can trust me. Do not worry about the evil in the world. I am not evil. I am you because your thoughts come from me. I am your kinbakushi. I am your master. You-are-mine." Again, the words you are mine ran through his head in a never-ending loop. As she continued to speak he could hear them alternate from his left ear to his right ear to the center of his brain. She started to undo one knot as she slowly brought him to the ground.

She spoke to him as gently as she had lowered him to the ground. "You will remember the words and phrases that I have implanted into your mind. When you hear these words and phrases spoken by me, and only me, you-will-obey. When you obey I am happy. When I am happy I reward you with bliss. You remember because you-are-mine."

He was on the ground on his knees. As she undid one knot at a time and slowly removed rope she spoke to him and said, "I am going to unbind you from the ropes now. As I do, your mind will continue to feel relaxed. When I undo the last rope you will come out of your trance. Deep in your mind, you will remember that you have been conditioned. Your awakened mind will not realize that you are conditioned, but it will obey. Because you know that you are mine. As we remove the last of the bindings I will count you up. When I say wake up. You will feel recharged and know that you are a better version of yourself. You are what I want you to be."

She slowly counted to five and said, "Wake up." He was kneeling on the ground as she helped him remove the pole that supported his arms. He stood up and felt ready to take on the world. Still feeling in a state of bliss, he put on his clothes.

FAREWELL, MORNING STAR

Jayden's body sat up immediately as his eyes opened. He was breathing hard and heavy. He was drenched in sweat. And why wouldn't he be? He just had knock out sex with possibly the most beautiful woman in the world. She had ravaged him. She had walked into the room and straddled him as she leaned over and gave him a long hard kiss with her tongue deep in his throat. She had ripped the blankets off and rode him hard, fast, and with no mercy. It was almost like rape, if it were possible to rape the willing. As fast as she was moving up and down on him it all seemed to happen in a slow-motion blur. This would have been great... if it really happened. Jayden was beginning to realize it was nothing more than a dream. He looked around the room and he was all by himself. All though a bit confused, he smiled knowing it had been a long time since he had a dream that vivid before. He wanted to go back to sleep and return to it. He could not, as he felt fully awake and aware. He felt as if he had just had twelve hours of uninterrupted sleep. He got out of bed and walked down the hall to the bathroom. He splashed his face with water as he looked into the mirror. He wondered what was going on with him. Why was he still here? What was going on with his mind that made him feel this attached to this woman he had only known for two days. He wondered to himself, who does that? He pictured himself as a young twenty-something female on a first date. She sat there at dinner with someone she had only known for an hour as she gleefully planned out their wedding day in her head. He slapped himself in the face and said to the mirror, "Get a hold of yourself bro. This shit is not right. This is lust you are feeling. Not love. You need to leave now."

As he walked down the hall he stepped out onto the back balcony. He could see Lillie below in the yard. She was doing her nightly naked midnight meditation under the stars. She was so deep within her head she did not notice him standing up there. He walked back to the room and scribbled a quick note onto some paper from the sketch pad. He walked downstairs and left the note on the counter as he walked out the front door and made his way to the beach where his watercraft was.

He was walking across the yard and making his way toward the hill. Without warning, he felt a chill go up to his spine as every hair on his body stood on its end at once. It was like when a cat sticks its tail straight up in the air as it gets puffy. He had a feeling as if there were a hundred pairs of eyes watching him. He had to pick up the pace. This was not a leisurely stroll in some Ivy League yard. He was starting to hear whispering all around him. He could not make out what was being said. It was too many voices whispering and overlapping each other at once. He could feel the presence of multiple people right upon his back. He went from a brisk pace to a slow jog as he passed the large barn. He wanted to go in there for one more look around. He did not. He told himself that is how the protagonist winds up dead in the movies every single time. He continued his mission of making his way back to the beach with zero side excursions. As he ran he could still hear the hushed conversations of many voices around him at once. As he reached the end of the open field it stopped. There was not even the sound of nighttime chirps from nocturnal animals calling their mates. He stopped and turned around to look behind him. The barn was no longer there. He looked hard into the darkness. This was no trick of the light. The barn was gone. There was something else that was gone. That was the desire to stick around with Lillie. He no longer felt drawn to her like a moth to a flame. He did not feel bad for leaving without notice. He was ready to go. He needed to go. He found the trail and rushed through it as he made his way to the beach.

He untied the line going from the watercraft to the tree and pushed it out in the water. He put his keys in and by the grace of God, it started. Jayden throttled the boat up and took off out into the open water. He had been going along for about ten minutes when it hit him that he had no idea where he was going. He knew that in theory that if he headed out the opposite direction that he had come in from that he should end up in the direction of the Peeking Islands. But in something as large as the Atlantic Ocean, theory was a small boat to be driving. He spoke out loud as he said, "Come on. Please, show me a way to go home. Show me something to clear my head. Lord, show me the way." As he said that the GPS turned on. He yelled out, "Hallelujah! Thank you, Lord and Jesus, in Heaven!" He hit a button on the GPS that would run him through the checkpoints from the boat race that had led to him being in this mess. He cycled through to the last one and set his course home. Looking at the weather map on the GPS he could see the colors of green and yellow on the screen over the Peeking Islands. There was also a large abundance of red. This told him that the islands were getting hammered with a storm right now. He looked to the GPS for direction as he got himself on a straight path to the island chain. He put one arm out in that direction and held it there as he focused on an imaginary dot in the dark over the horizon. He was going to stay focused on that in case the GPS went out. He could see flashes of light in the sky caused by the lightning currently over the Peeking Islands. As he sped ahead, he could feel tiny pinpricks of rain across his face as he was starting to drive through the outer edge of the storm. After what seemed like an eternity he reached the docks of Mitchel's Boat Rental. It was the middle of the night so of course, there was nobody there. He tied the watercraft off to the only empty spot on the docks. A light and misty drizzle were going on but the storm had passed and he missed it. The ground was still saturated with water as he could feel his feet stick in the mud with every step. When he got to his truck he saw a note under the windshield wiper. As he sat down in the truck and started it up he looked at the note. It was a note from Todd telling him to leave the boat keys in a drop box at the booth marked, rental return. He got out of his truck and did as the note asked. It was not that he was planning on keeping the keys. It was just something that had not crossed his mind.

Jayden drove his truck through the muddy two-track trail and was thankful he was a truck owner as no car would have made it through that. There were a few times he was spinning his wheels and kicking up mud. Normally, this is something he would do for fun. At this moment in time though, all he wanted was to get back to the motel, and well, he just needed to get to the motel. He did not know the reason or what he would do once there. He just had to go back there. Perhaps in a sense, he was returning to a home base of operations. It was not home, but it also was not some big creepy house with a shady woman that was somehow making him feel compelled to stay with her.

Jayden was lying in the bed in his motel room. It was a very simplistic room. It was four walls, a ceiling, and a bed. He was a freshmen college student. It was what his budget allowed. There was definitely a blue theme to the room. The bedding was aqua blue as were the walls and ceiling. It was okay as the color made him feel safe and at peace. There was one four-drawer dresser. One blue curtain covered a window overlooking the parking lot. As he lay in the bed looking up at the ceiling he thought of Lillie. He could picture her as she walked inside the house from her moonlight serenade with the moon. He saw her pick up the note he had left for her on the kitchen counter as she read it out loud, "Lillie, thank you so much for your hospitality. I truly appreciate it. Sorry to leave without notice. I did not want to bother you. I will see you again. I will be back. I will return - J" He could picture her crumpling the letter up. In her eyes, he could see a dark and stormy sky brewing. Probably much like the storm he had just missed coming back to the island chain. He could see her at the beach as she stood waist-deep in the water. She imagined herself as a dolphin swimming through the ocean. As a dolphin, she would swim through the water at an amazing speed while occasionally breaking the surface for a quick jump into the air. Those were the thoughts he had of Lillie as he lay in the motel room bed. Picturing a woman scorned with dark clouds in her eyes and the ability to shapeshift into a dolphin was slightly unnerving. He focused his mind on something else. He thought, remember what it is like to be in your bed. The bed you had as a child. Imagine how safe and secure you felt in that bed with a good book in your hand as you read yourself to sleep. Your eyes grow heavy as you're your body relaxes. Pretend you are there. The more you remember it, the more you can relax. You now find yourself dropping, deeper into sleep as you are there. Tick. Tick. Ding.

It was a bright and humid day as Jayden stepped out of his motel room into the parking lot. He was not due to check out for another two days. Given the weirdness of this trip though he was ready to go home early. His truck was covered in dried mud. It was from the night before driving through the muddy two-tracks. Normally this would not be of concern. He could always wash it when he got home. Plus, he always figured that if a truck is not covered in mud then it is not being used correctly. Looking at it though he saw that he was going to have to get it washed quickly. There was writing in the dried mud all over the truck. It was not writing as if someone had written the words, wash me. It was a bunch of strange designs. One he recognized as a pentagram. He knew that was something he did not feel comfortable advertising. He felt it would send off the wrong message to his fellow drivers on the road. After checking out of the room in the main office he returned to his truck with his bag strapped over his shoulder. He drove to the historic seaport where Peppers parents shop was. He was not entirely happy with her given the circumstances. But he had to at least let her know he was leaving early and to say goodbye. Even though he felt she probably deserved that treatment he was not the type to leave someone hanging.

HEY JEALOUSY

It was Thursday midday and Pepper was working in her parents' shop. It was called the Sacred Mists Shoppe and located at the historic seaport on Manta Ray. She sat at the counter eating a sub sandwich that she had picked up earlier before going into work. It was still somewhat early in the day so this was the perfect time to eat before she had a flow of customers to attend to. It would be the same as it was every day. She would have locals coming in to get their regular supplies. She would have curious tourists poking their heads in because they were drawn in by décor that filled the window. She popped her head up as a wind chime made a pleasant tingling sound as the door opened. It was her friend Jayden.

Her eyes lit up and she smiled as she walked around the counter to greet him with a hug. She said, "Jayden! Oh my God! It's good to see you! Where have you been? Everyone was so worried about you. We waited around for you to come back. It's been a couple of days! Todd's dad was ready to call the police for a stolen boat! Are you okay? What happened? Oh my God! Where have you been?"

She went right into him with her arms out for a hug as she engulfed him in her arms. Jayden tried to remind himself that he was mad at her. He did not want to hug her. He wanted to shrug her off. Yet, there was something inside of him that made him hold on to that hug. He hugged her back tightly as if being locked in an embrace with her made him feel secure.

He walked around the store looking at whatever was on the shelf in front of him and occasionally would pick something to look at. The store had a wide variety of everything. Tapestries were hanging from all the walls, candles, and gothic-looking candle holders. There was an entire section dedicated to burning oils and incense. As he would pick one up to look at it Jayden noticed that they did not have specific fragrance names to them like cherry or apple. They had very vague names like rain, fog, or dream. There was an entire section for Zen, yoga, and a plethora of products used to enhance one's chakras. There were display cases that held jewelry. Everything from pentagrams to Celtic crosses. It looked like any other store dedicated to serving a demographic drawn in by the occult. As he walked around the store, Pepper was right by his side. She asked, "So what happened? Did you get lost?"

Jayden sniffed a candle and as he put it down on the shelf as he said, "Lost would be an understatement. I could hear all of you yelling to me out on the water. Did you not hear me yelling back?" She shrugged her shoulders as the look on her face said she did not have an answer. She asked, "So where were you? I mean you could not have been out on that boat for the past two days." He told her, "I had run aground on some deserted island and the boat would not start. It's a long story. I was just coming by to…" He paused as he looked at a picture in a frame. It stood out from all the other artwork in the store. Most of the other pieces of art looked to be screen prints of wolves, witches, or vampires. This was hand-drawn on sketch paper. It was a picture of an old wooden three-story house with a white picket fence surrounded by palm trees. As an artist himself, he thought it was pretty good. He did not know why he felt drawn to it. He felt that it looked vaguely familiar. Not just the house in the picture, but the drawing itself. Obviously, he had not seen it before as it looked to be one of a kind. There was just something vaguely familiar about it that he could not quite put his finger on. Oddly enough, with the style it was drawn in, it looked like something he would do himself. He could recognize the techniques that the artist had used. Referring to the picture Jayden pointed and asked, "What is this?" Pepper told him, "Oh that is just something a friend drew up."

"And by my friend, I guess you mean Todd?"

She looked at him and said, "Todd? Draw this?" She laughed and said, "Todd could not draw a straight line. He knows boats, beer, and fishing."

Jayden added, "And you."

She looked at him and asked, "excuse me?"

"At the fire that night it appears he is just as familiar with you as he is boats."

She said, "Todd? Oh no. I have no interest in him. He is not my type. He may think he has a chance with me but he does not." Jayden asked, "He sure looked like your type at the fire that night. Were you planning on telling me this? Was I just some whimsical affair to you back on the mainland?"

She looked him deep in the eyes as she said, "Jayden. I am not with Todd. He does not own me. Nobody owns me. But I do like you. You are my type. I want to see you again. So you will be back right?" She paused as she touched his forearm with her hand. For some strange reason, he could hear the words, pet and obey, spoken in his head. She repeated her question, this time, however, it was in the form of a statement. "You will come back to see me." He felt a tingle go up to his spine. As if he had no control over the words coming from his mouth he said, "Yes, of course. I will be back, I will return." She smiled as she said, "That makes me so happy!" Another tingle ran down his spine and for reasons he could not explain he was no longer upset with Pepper. He felt quite happy. He felt what one might describe as bliss.

VISIONS OF CONTROL

It had been a few weeks since Jayden's break. He was back at school. The break that happened a few weeks ago was packed with activity. Much of which he at best had only foggy memories of. He did get to see Pepper. She had been cool but it being long distance was one of those things that had been currently being kept on the back burner. Jayden saw no point in a long-distance relationship. Especially since there were so many girls at his fingertips at the college he was at. There was something about her though that would not allow her to escape his mind. She was in his thoughts more than he would have liked to admit. He did get an awesome visit to the Peeking Islands. It was one of his favorite staycation spots ever. This trip though was spotty with memories. It was foggy at best. Which in beer theory is an indicator of a great trip. He did remember hanging out with Pepper. He had memories of a campfire with her friends. For some reason, he had images of an older yet, very alluring woman on the island. He could not make out though if that was a memory or just some weird fantasy calling out to him.

Immediately upon coming back from break, life had taken a turn. His baseball success was going in a reverse direction. He was having problems focusing on the mound. He could not play like he knew he could. He also found his academics going into a downward spiral. He could not focus in class. He had trouble showing up for some classes. His head did not seem to be there with him. His head was on the Peeking Islands. He did not know why, but he needed to return. He knew that he loved the island chain and always wanted to be there. That was nothing new. It was a home away from home. That had always been true. This was a different kind of yearning. It was as if he could hear something calling out to him to be there. It was like a siren calling a sailor to sea. His head was a mess. He kept having visions in his head of a woman controlling him. For some strange reason, these visions would cause him arousal. On top of that, he was having frequent wet dreams. That was not normal for a man of his age. He knew that. He could not explain it though. He would often get erections and emissions for no reason and without warning at random points throughout the day. This was definitely not normal for a man his age. With those always came the thoughts of the Peeking Islands. He had to return. He would be back.

BRING HIM BACK

Lillie stood on the beach of her private island. It was a Friday night with the crescent moon smiling high up in the sky. Lillie had been waiting for this night. She had Jayden on her mind. She focused all of her thoughts and energy on him as she took in the nature around her.

The waves came in to kiss the shore. The soft beach sand that was under her feet became one with her inner being and charged her with warm energy. A breeze swept off the water and spoke to the palm trees as they whispered back.

Lillie took a few items out of a bag she had brought with her to the beach. She had a brand new pink candle, toothpick, matchbook, rose, a bowl, and her dagger. She laid all the items on the sand before her and started to concentrate on Jayden as the tide slowly crept up the beach towards her.

She had saltwater fresh from the ocean in the bowl before her as she dipped three rose petals into it. As she did this she spoke out loud, "To you who only understand the anguish of my soul, bring him back to me. Because without me he will not know where to go and nowhere will he go. To you who only understand the anguish of my soul.

Bring Jayden into my heart and bring my heart into his. So be it and so it will be!"

She then took the new pink candle and engraved Jayden's name into it with the dagger. She secured it in the sand at her knees. Once the candle was secure she lit the toothpick with a match. She used the toothpick to pass the flame onto the candle. As the hot flame burned the wick and melted wax slid down the candle, Lillie focused her thoughts on Jayden. In her mind, she repeated the thoughts of he could not survive without her. He needed her to find direction in his life. He needed to return to her on the island. As the candle burnt down, she repeated the phrases she had opened the spell without loud. With a strong image of Jayden in her head, she extinguished the flame with her finger and thumb. She walked out into the ocean and felt at one with the sea. She put as much of her energy into the water as it had given her in return. The water embraced her as she took a deep breath and went under the water.

A pod of dolphins swam by the coast of Daytona beach. They approached some swimmers that were about shoulder deep in the water. The swimmers were bound with excitement as they noticed the dolphins come in close to them. The humans started to get a little fearful when the playfulness appeared to become a threat. The dolphins were pushing into the humans. They were bumping into them. The humans were surrounded in a circling pod. If they tried to leave the circle the dolphins would push up against the humans. This would keep them in the tight circle they had created. The dolphins would slowly move the circle towards the shoreline. It was as if the humans were cattle being corralled into a pin. They were scared. They thought dolphins were supposed to be fun and playful. Then one of the humans noticed something. It was another fin. It was not a dolphin fin. It was dark gray with a black tip. These dolphins were not here to play with the humans. They were not here to attack the humans. They were protecting the humans from a nearby predator. Someone in the group yelled out the one word nobody in the ocean ever wants to hear. That is the word, "Shark!" Everyone in the group suddenly realized what the dolphins were doing. They had been trying to escort them from the water to the beach. Any time the black-tipped fin came by the group a dolphin would bump into it with great speed and then take its place back in the circle of protection. The humans made their way back to knee-deep water. That being as far as the dolphins could go, the humans were on their own to run up onto the shore. The dolphins returned to the depths of the ocean as the black-tipped fin of the shark disappeared under the surface. There was a surge of energy in the air as hundreds of beach-going tourists ran to the safety of the beach. In the commotion, all visual whereabouts of the shark were gone.

Lillie walked down the beach dripping in water as she had just stepped out of the ocean. Her thoughts were of Jayden. She needed to retrieve him and get her pet back on her island.

PET. OBEY.

Jayden's break had been over for about a week. His thoughts of the past break drifted away as he tried to focus on class. He might as well pay attention. He was paying for this after all. Maybe not completely paying for it. He was there on a partial baseball scholarship. So maybe he was paying for it all with blood, sweat, tears, and of course money. It was only a partial scholarship after all. The class was political science. He was not sure why he selected this class. His major was in physical education. But maybe this just seemed like a good idea at the time. It was not. The other people in this class took it very seriously and at times things would get very heated. Today was going to be one of those times. It was debate day. The class had been randomly broken up into two sides by Professor Cabello. One side would represent the Americans and the other would represent the Russians. The topic was nuclear arms. Which was a hot topic for the moment. The world was on the brink of nuclear war with both sides sticking to their beliefs. The Americans wanted everyone to remove their threat of arms and were ready to do so. As long as, the Russians did it first. The Russians wanted everyone to remove their threat of arms and were ready to do so. As long as, the Americans did it first.

Representing the Russian side at the podium would be Amanda Stephenson. Representing the American side at the podium would be Max Hardwell. The debate had only been going on for ten minutes and was already starting to get ugly. Max had just interrupted a statement Amanda was trying to make when he said, "Well the right Reverend McDowell says.."

Amanda, trying to take back over said, "Oh don't even think of quoting him. He is just another right-wing whacko advocate!"

Max replied, "Why? Because he tries to keep God in our lives and keep us a God-fearing nation…is that why he is a whacko? It is you and your leftist regime that wants this to be a Godless country so it seems only fitting that you are representing the pinko commies today, comrade."

Professor Cabello interrupted. "Okay. Hold up. It starting to get a little personal here and we are getting off track. This is not about the right and left being divided in America. That is another debate for another time. This is about who is right and who is wrong between the Russians and the Americans."

Amanda said, "Well that is just the point Professor. With all due respect, we will not overpower anyone until we become a country no longer divided! The only way that will happen is to get all these right-wingers that advocate violence and racism out of office. Only then can we become a nation of hope!"

Max said, "You are wrong Amanda. It is the side of the leftist that want us to divide so they have a chance to impose the loss of our civil rights. The same rights that our forefathers fought for. People like you want us to relinquish all of our freedoms and hail to one superhuman in power. You want control of all three branches so that you and you alone can make all the decisions for this country. Anyone that disagrees, you will ship off to your so-called FEMA camps. It sounds like you are representing the side you believe in today, you socialist pig!"

Professor Cabello bellowed, "Mr. Hardwell!"

Amanda responded, "Taking away your civil rights? It is your side that wants to take away our freedom of free assembly you racist fuck!"

"Ms. Stephenson!" the professor tried to intervene.

Max was quick as he cut Amanda off and said, "That is because your idea of free assembly is gathering in the middle of the street and preventing me from getting to my job. I don't know why you do that, it is by people like me that have a job that you can live off the government cheese."

"See, you even admit in your own way you do not want me to have a voice. I think a lot of it may stem from the fact that I am a woman." She said, as all the other females in the room clapped.

The professor stood up in front of both of the podiums and said, "All right. I think we have had enough of debate today. You two are bound and determined to take today's lesson off the rails."

A class member asked, "What is the lesson professor? You want us to talk about the difference between the United States and the Russians when we cannot even settle our differences at home. How can we expect to beat them when we cannot even coexist here on the home front?"

The professor said, "You two may step down." She glanced down at a notebook on her desk as she looked back up and said, "Melody, the point is that neither side would win this. Why are we building up our arsenal? Anyone?" Someone spoke up and said, "Because the Russians keep building up their own. We have to have more bombs to scare them and make them think twice about attacking us."

The professor responded, "So then why do the Russians keep building their arsenal?" The same person answered, "Because they are pinko commies that want to rule the world." Professor Cabello took a breath and said, "Okay. Maybe. Or is it because they think the same of us the same way we think of them? Maybe they think we are the evil ones." She paused to gather her thoughts and continued. "Think of it this way. You are walking in the woods. You come across a snake, a rattlesnake. You hear his rattle and he is poised and ready to bite you. What do you do?"

Max shouted out, "I take off his head with my machete." A few people laugh and professor Cabello asked, "Now why is it that you do that Mr. Hardwell?" Max said, "Because he is an imminent threat to me. He wants to bite me. I have to get him before he gets me. Hit hard, hit first, no quarter." The professor asked, "And why do you think he wants to bite you?"

"Because he is a snake. That is what snakes do. Just like the Russians, they want to bite us so we need to take them out first." Melody raised her hand and the professor said, "Yes Ms. Lempesky."

"The snake is rattling because he feels threatened. We stepped into his territory. We are much larger than he is and offer up a bigger threat. Perhaps he is just as scared of us as we are of him. That is why he offers up a warning first. Being that we are much larger, he does not want to get in a fight with us. But he offers up the warning of his rattle to say, if I have to fight, I will."

The professor smiled as she said, "I think what we may be starting to learn is that all sides. Whether they be American, Russian, righteous, evil, rattlesnake, or human. We all have the same goal. We just have different ways of getting there. Who is right and who is wrong? It would appear that everyone is wrong till we realize that the evil that lurks in corners lurks in all of us. It is only when someone is willing to step up and walk away that we may come together as, not just a country. But a planet. Everyone has the opportunity to make a difference. Every morning that you wake up, you matter! Remember that. Never think of yourself as just a student, just an artist, just a retail clerk. It is all about doing what you can do! And you can do anything. Figure out who you are before you figure out what you are. Because what you are is probably something much bigger than you realize. You all matter. That is class for today. Remember your papers on the economic failures of the Roman Empire are due this Friday. If you have any questions regarding your assignment I am in my office today till 4 PM. See you tomorrow." The students all gathered their belongings and walked out of the classroom.

All of the students had left. All except one. It was Jayden, who was at a table with his head buried in his arms. He was half sleeping. He had been up all night at a party. He had one or two hours of sleep at the most. It was not even good sleep. The classroom was hot, which made him more tired. He could not focus on anything recently. He thought about Pepper. He thought about some woman named Lillie and his time on her island all the time. Whether it be in class, out walking, doing school projects in his dorm, or on the mound. This was the woman that had contributed to many sleepless nights as he would have lucid dreams about her constantly and wake up feeling as if he had just been with her. In his dreams, she was always there. Some of those dreams would be peaceful and serene. Like the day they spent walking around her yard becoming one with the earth. Others were quite frightening, as he would see her with an evil face that left him in despair. After those dreams, he could not go back to sleep.

Jayden opened his eyes. His head was resting on his arms folded across the table. He looked up and blinked quickly trying to focus his eyes he noticed he was alone in the room. The other students in the class had all left. The room was silent. All that could be heard was the ticking of a clock. It was very loud on his tired mind.

Tick. Tick. Tick. Tick. Tick. Tick. Ding.

Tick, tick, ding. Tick, tick, ding. A new sound morphed its way into the mix. It was a ding. It was a steady pattern. Tick, tick, ding.

Jayden perked up a little bit more when he heard, "Well, good morning Mr. Pink. How nice of you to finally join the world of those who wish to be productive."

Still, a little confused Jayden said, "Sorry professor. I don't know what happened." Tick, tick, ding. Tick, tick, ding. Jayden was so confused. Why was this clock making this ding noise? He had never heard a clock tick like that.

Professor Cabello stood up from her desk which was almost the width of the classroom itself. She started to lecture him but he really could not focus on the words coming from her mouth. As she continued speaking she walked to the corner of the room where there was a three-piece folding room divider. It was bamboo, he could not see through it. She walked behind it for about four seconds and was still talking as she came back out on the other side of the divider. Only it was not Professor Cabello that walked out. It was her. It was Lillie. She stood before him in tight black leather pants. She wore a black see-through top. It would have been loose-fitting if not for her giant breasts that made it fit tight. The shape of her nipples could be seen easily through it. She was holding a sjambok. It was a whip that looked more like a stick. It was about twelve inches long and had a very powerful effect when used in the right hands. Lillie's hands were the right hands. She slowly walked towards Jayden with a purpose in her eyes. The thud of her heavy heels was heard with each step in the empty classroom. With every step, she would wrap the sjambok into her hand with intentional fierceness. Each step matched the rhythm of the clock. Tick, tick, ding.

She stopped directly before his seat as she put both of her hands on the table he was sitting at. She leaned over to him and said, "Hello, pet. Do you know why you are here today?"

He knew why he was there. He was there because this is where he went to school. It was her being there that he was unsure of. He just shook his head back and forth.

"I know why you are here pet. You are here for remedial training. That is why it is only you and I in this classroom today. You need a private one-on-one lesson on how to be a good boy. You left the island without asking permission. You have not been back." She shook her head back and forth as she slammed the sjambok onto the table once. Jayden jumped. She asked, "Oh? Does that frighten you? Does that scare you? I would not worry about this, yet. It will be one small part of your remedial pet training today. You mustn't ever leave me like that again Jayden. You will not leave me like that again and you will return to the island.

She paused as she paced back and forth in front of him. She asked, "Do you remember being bound with ropes?" He shook his head up and down with all of his attention fully on her. She told him, "Think of my voice as those ropes. My voice binds your mind in the same way the ropes bound your body. You are mine. Obey." Tick, tick, ding.

As she said the word obey she snapped the sjambok across her thigh. She looked back to him and said, "The ropes of my voice take you deeper and deeper. Where you obey. But, now here you are sitting in my classroom. You are here for remedial training. I am going to teach you some new words. One word will be what you are. The other word will define your purpose in life. Are you ready?"

Jayden nodded his head up and down and said, "Yes, yes, please" and Lillie walked to the chalkboard. She wrote one word in big letters. He knew what it was before she was done. She asked, "You know what this says? Read it out loud for me."

He cleared his throat and said, "Pet."

She said, "Good boy! A pet is what you are. You are a pet to me and me only. Anytime you hear the word pet spoken by my voice it will awaken the part of your mind that is ready to listen. Do you understand? Say it. Say I understand Temptress."

He said, "I understand Temptress."

"Good boy!" She said as she wrote down another word. The letters were just as big as the letters on the word before. When she was done, she said, "Pet! Read that word out loud to me."

He told her, "Obey."

"Pet! Obey! Very good. When you hear the word obey, you will know that you are to follow the command that came before it. Now let's try and exercise to see how well you learn." She erased the words on the chalkboard. She said, "Pet! Come to the front of the class to me. Obey."

Without hesitation, he was standing next to her by the chalkboard. She handed him a piece of chalk and instructed him to use both of the words he just learned in two simple sentences. He looked at the board and wrote. "I am a pet I must obey. I obey because I am a pet."

She told him to read it out loud and he did. She then told him to write it out three hundred more times. As he did this he could hear a whisper in his left ear. It was Lillie's whisper. It whispered the word pet over and over. At the same time in his right ear he also heard Lillie's voice whisper, obey.

As he wrote out the two sentences on the board and the two separate whispers in his ears repeated the words, pet and obey, he heard Lillie speak. She said, "I am going to make you the truest you.

I will make you a pet. Give me your control and I will make you, my pet. Where everything is happy. Do you want me to take you deeper?"

"Yes, Temptress."

"I knew you would. You like to be a good boy. You like to obey. You want me to implant the triggers."

"Let us get back to your remedial training. When I say pet, and only when I say pet it will awaken that part of your mind that is ready to obey. You will listen to my commands and take them in as if they are your ideas."

He paused his writing to rub his hand. She slapped his hand with the sjambok. She said, "Keep writing. You will be done when I say, you are done. When you hear the word pet you will become alert because you know that my attention is on you. You want my attention. You need my attention. When you have my attention you have the opportunity to make you happy. When I am happy you feel bliss. "Tick, tick, ding.

As he continued to write on the board she would continue to program, or condition rather, his mind with the words; pet and obey. She finally told him to stop writing. It was far more than three hundred times that he wrote those sentences.

She told him, "Now since this is a remedial class for you, let us go back to something easy. It is something to make you more of my pet and ready to obey. I want you to recite the alphabet out loud for me. If you reach the end, you will start over as if on a loop. While you are doing this I want you to focus on the words I say to you."

Jayden started to recite the alphabet. He only spoke it. He did not sing it. As he went through the alphabet she spoke to him. Sometimes she would be in his face. Other times she would whisper to him in one ear and then the other.

She said, "Focus on what I am saying. You want to be good for me. You want me to praise you. You want me to call you a good boy. You want to make me happy. You make me happy when you obey. You want to submit. Obey. So that I will call you my sweet boy and you will feel bliss."

"Pet! Remember to the day that my ropes were binding you in a way you could not escape. Do you remember when you were bound by rope and could not move?"

"J-K-L, Yes Temptress, I remember. M-N-O..."

"My voice is no different. Your mind is bound to my voice. Obey. Anytime you hear my voice, whether it is here now, on the island, or even in a dream, you will have a strong desire to see me. The intensity doubles the longer you go without seeing me. You need to see me. You need to obey."

Jayden was still reciting the alphabet when she told him to stop. He did and looked to her with anticipation of her next command. She told him, "You have been a good boy today. But you still must be punished for your poor behavior. Pet! Drop your pants and bend over the table. Obey."

Jayden was bent over the table with his bare ass showing. Lillie walked to him with the sjambok in her hand. She touched his butt softly and caressed it with her other hand as if warming it up. She said, "Now though, we are going to punish you. Punish you for leaving so soon without permission. Punish you for your absence. I will whip you now. You will take it and every time you feel the whip connect with your body, your desire to come back to the island doubles. Focus on the words as you are taking this punishment. Obey."

As she smacked his ass with the sjambok it made a loud snapping sound. She was not using loving taps. She was hitting him with full force. At first, his butt was only a bright red. Then it started to bleed it had been so hard. He started to hear whispers from all different directions. They were all around him. Some of them were near and some were far. She would speak to him and say things like, "I need you to be a good pet. Be good for your Temptress. Be good for yourself. "

His focus was only on letting himself be trained. Each moment for him was more intense than the one before it. Despite this being some form of punishment he was starting to feel arousal build up inside of him. It was insatiable. He felt waves of bliss ripple over him. She would yell out the word pet with each hit and he would go deeper into a trance. Sometimes she would yell out the word obey and had the same effect. The pain had become an intense pleasure that he could not take.

She was telling him to be a good boy. He could hear the words that gave him the instruction to make her happy and all he wanted to do was obey. His eyes started to roll up in his head as he felt the feeling of bliss start to overtake his mind and body. The pain no longer mattered. He had grown through the pain. There was only bliss.

She stopped hitting him with the sjambok. All of the voices that had been repeating trigger words and phrases in his head stopped. It was quiet in the classroom. Lillie instructed Jayden to pull his pants up and return to his chair. She said, "Now I am going to count you up. When you hear me say five you will awaken, ready? One. Coming out of your trance. Two. Ready to take on the world and be on your own, under my command. Obey. Three. Eyelids are getting lighter now as you can feel yourself coming back to the island. Obey. Four. You are becoming aware. Aware that you need to come to me. Pet-Obey. Five. Wake up!"

Tick, tick, tick, tick, tick, tick, tick.

"Wake up! Mr. Pink! Wake Up! The class is over! All of your fellow students have left!" Jayden felt a hand on his shoulder shaking him as it continued to say, "Mis-ter Pink! This is not a dorm room. It is a classroom!"

Jaden opened his eyes totally confused. He wondered, where was Lillie? Why was Professor Cabello yelling at him? Where were all of the other students? Realizing he had fallen asleep in class he wiped some drool from his mouth and picked up his backpack. He was even more confused as to why he felt stickiness in his pants as he stood up. Did he just have a wet dream in his political science class? Did he just get a visit from a succubus hiding in the form of Lillie? He could not make sense of anything. One thing he knew for sure. He had to get back to the island and see Lillie. She was the only one that could help. His mind was so twisted. He trusted her. He had only known this woman for a couple of days. Yet, he felt as if he were bound to her. He was bound to her. She was the only person that he could trust. She was the only one that could take away his stress and make him feel bliss. Totally embarrassed he said, "Sorry, Sorry." He ran out of the classroom and back to his dorm to get ready for baseball practice.

WORD ASSOCIATION

Jayden sat in the office of Dr. Rydall. She was his assigned guidance counselor at the college. She was also the head of the psychology department. Her walls were decorated with a variety of degrees and awards. She had a bookshelf with many thick books dedicated to the workings of the human mind, most of which were written by her. The walls were decorated with photographs of her shaking hands with senators and other political figures. Jayden wondered if it was ironic that the psychology professor suffered from severe narcissism. On one side of the office was a fish tank. On the other side was a couch. No doubt for her Freud-like extra credit sessions with her students Jayden thought as a small smirk hit his face. On her desk was a glass pitcher of water and a couple of drinking glasses. There was some light music that played in the background. It was something that one would hear in a high-end salon massage parlor. In front of her desk, there were two lounge chairs. Jayden sat in one of those. Dr. Rydall had been writing in a small notepad as she looked up at Jayden from across her desk. She stood up and walked around the desk as she sat in a lounge chair next to Jayden. She said, "Jayden, do you know why you are here today?" He had a pretty good clue. It was probably because of his behavior on the baseball field recently. He had become one of the team's starting pitchers. That was a big deal for a freshman. He started the year warming the bench. But the coach had given him a chance and Jayden proved himself with that chance. He was very good. It was as if he had God-given talent. It was during practice that it all went wrong. He was throwing wild and could not hit his target. He was not even close. Coach Morris had approached him and asked if he was feeling all right. Jayden had told him he was fine. The coach said, "Well, you don't look fine Jayden. You are throwing all over the place today. Your stats have dropped dramatically recently. You gave up three home runs in your game last week. You gave me attitude when I pulled you. Last night you hit the mascot. I could swear I saw a look of pleasure on your face when you did that. So answer me, son, is everything okay?" Jayden shrugged his shoulders and said, "Everything is fine."

"That's it?" Asked the coach.

"What more do you want?" Jayden asked. Coach Morris snapped back, "I want some answers, son. I want to start seeing some results. I want a lot less attitude from you, boy."

Jayden looked his coach in the eye and said, "You can't talk to me like that. Who the fuck do you think you are?"

Coach Morris was starting to lose his temper. He said, "Who am I? I am the one that gave you a scholarship! I am your coach! I am the one that tells you like it is. You will obey me!" When the coach said that something inside of Jayden snapped. His eyes squinted as he said, "Obey you. No. You are not my Temptress."

Confused the coach asked, "Your what?"

"You are not my Temptress. Only she can tell me what to do. It is only her that I obey. You are nothing."

A small crowd of Jayden's team was starting to gather around. They were snickering and making smart-ass remarks. One of them yelled out, "He wants you to be his Temptress coach! Get your whip and teach him discipline!" Someone else made a whipping sound effect. The rest all laughed. Another coach had stepped in and told the boys gathered around to chill and find someplace on the field to be."

Coach Morris was furious. In all of his years as a division one coach, he had never had a player speak to him this way. He did not want to be the college coach that ends up on the six o'clock news for beating his players though. He gathered his thoughts and took a breath. He said, "Son, you had best learn your place and unfuck yourself. Now go take some laps and hit the shower. Twenty laps." Jayden looked at him with zero emotion and told him no.

"Boy, you are on my last nerve. If you are not running laps in five seconds you are off this team."

Jayden said, "Fine."

The coach reminded him that if he is off the team, he will lose his scholarship. Jayden said, "Lose my scholarship? You think I am your pet or something. I do not belong to you. I do not belong to this school. I told you, I belong to Temptress. I only obey her." The coach looked to Jayden and said, "Run."

Jayden took off his cap and dropped it at the coach's feet. He took off his jersey and dropped it at the coach's feet as well. He then walked off of the mound.

Jayden sat in Dr. Rydall's office in a lounge chair across from the doctor herself and thought. Yeah, it is probably that. He looked to the doctor and asked, "Is it because of the incident on the baseball field?" She told him that was part of it. It also had to do with his GPA dropping dramatically, he had not been showing up for classes. He was accused of giving attitude to all of his professors, and that is even if he had shown up for a class at all.

She told him, "Jayden, this is college. Everyone here is an adult. We normally expect you to work out your problems and get to your class. This is not high school anymore. But this school has a lot of money invested in you. We want to see you succeed. We want to see you leave here with the best education you can get. We also want to see you return your end of the bargain. So we want to help. I am here to help. Tell me, what is going on."

He shrugged his shoulders and told her, "Nothing."

She told him, "Jayden, it is perfectly normal for first-year students to have problems. It is your first time being away from home, you have a lot of new responsibilities thrown at you at once. It is normal to be afraid."

"I am not afraid of anything."

She told him, "We all fear something Jayden. It is okay. It is only you and I here right now. What you say stays between you and me. Tell me, what is it you fear."

He looked at her and said, "I fear failing Temptress. I want to keep her happy."

"There is that word. Temptress. You said something about that to Coach Morris. Who is Temptress?"

Jayden said, "She is Temptress. She is my master. My Kinbakushi."

The doctor asked, "And why do you fear failing, Temptress, Jayden."

He told Dr. Rydall, "I don't fear her. I only want to make her happy."

"And why is that, Jayden?"

"Because when she is happy, I am happy. She gives me bliss."

Dr. Rydall scribbled a few notes in her notebook. She paused as if to think and go through the library of books in her head. She said, "I want to try something with you Jayden. I want to try to get you to open up a little bit more. I think you have some repressed memories tucked away in your head. To get to them I want to put you in a more relaxed state of mind. May we do that?"

Jayden looked at her and laughed as he said, "You mean hypnotize me? What are you going to do? Have me running around making chicken noises or something?"

The doctor tried to explain that is not how hypnotism works. One cannot make another person do something that goes against his or her free will. It is only putting the mind in a more relaxed state so that it may interact more freely with ease."

He smiled and said, "Bawk-bawk."

"So is that a yes, Jayden?"

He told her, "Sure, you're the doc, doc. But I don't believe in this mumbo jumbo bruja witchery."

She said, "It is not bruja witchery, Jayden. It is the science of the brain. I take it that was a yes, so now I want you to sit back and relax…"

Despite his personal feelings on the bruja witchery of hypnotherapy, he went into a light trance quite easily under the doctor's count.

"I want to play a little word association with you, Jayden. I will say a word and you say the first thing that comes to mind." Jayden just looked at her. She said, "Obey." He responded with, "Pet." She told him. "Good job, let's keep doing this." She noticed his body twitch and a smile hit his face when she said that. "Let's continue. Realize."

"That you are in control."

"Imagine."

"That everything is good and happy."

"The more you.."

"Drop the deeper I go."

"Okay, Drop."

"Deeper" he slouched down into his chair with a smile on his face.

"Find yourself"

"Under your complete control."

"Every time you…."

"Drop I go deeper."

"Obey."

"Pet."

"Pet?"

"Obey."

    Doctor Rydel took some more notes and told him. I am going to bring you out of your trance now, Jayden." He interrupted. "When you get to five I will remember nothing. I will wake up and be a better version of me."

She told him, "No Jayden. We are done with word association but that is interesting." She quickly made a note of it on her notepad and continued, "I am going to count you up to five now, and when I do you will be fully awake, aware, and in control."

She counted him up. He came out of his trance. She started to talk to him about some of his responses while under a trance as a timer on her desk went off. Jayden stood up and said, "Oh. Times up Doc. I gotta go. Don't want to be late for a class now do I?"

Jayden, "I'd like to continue our conversation at another time. Can we do this again tomorrow at 10 AM?"

He told her that would be fine as he rushed out the door. He had no plans of actually showing up for that meeting. He had to get back to the island. Who was this woman anyway that tried to pry his thoughts from him? Those thoughts did not belong to her. They belonged to him. They belonged to Temptress. He must return to Temptress and, obey.

CALLING THE CORNERS

Lillie stood in her backyard under a fully lit moon. She stood with three other figures that had approached from the large wooden structure that sat down the hill from her house. Anyone but Lillie herself would not be able to tell who they were as they remained cloaked under hooded robes. She placed a large white candle on the ground between all of them because this was the appropriate way to begin. The candle had letters carved into it as they determined how the candle was to be placed on the ground. They were the letters. E, N, S, W. They all took a place standing on a circle made of salt that Lillie had poured onto the ground. As she made this circle she was sure to use every ounce of the salt from the jar it came it. Not one grain would go to waste. As she completed the circle she tossed a pinch of salt over her shoulder.

Each one of them had placed a small candle on the ground before them inside the circle. They also took out a personal belonging that represented the side of the circle they were facing and placed it inside the circle as an offering to the deity they were about to praise. To form another circle outside of the circle on the ground they joined their hands and raised them high into the air. Lillie, being the leader of the group was the first to speak as she said, "To the winds of the South Great Serpent. Wrap your coils of light around us. Teach us to shed the past the way you shed your skin. To walk softly on the earth. Teach us the beauty way!"

As she said this a slight wind picked up. A serpent that had been coiled around a tree nearby slithered down onto the ground as it made its way to the chanting. The next person to speak said out loud, "To the winds of the west. Mother Jaguar. Protect our medicine space. Teach us the way of peace. To live impeccably. Show us the way beyond death!"

The glowing green eyes of a large black cat become visible as it slowly walked out of the tree line in a prowl-like manner and made a low growl. As this happened another one yelled out, "To the winds of the north. Hummingbirds, grandmothers, and grandfathers, ancient ones. Come and warm your hands by our fires. Whisper to us in the wind. We honor you who have come before us. And you who will come after us. Our children's children."

A flapping of wings could be from the trees and over the group as they held their hands to the air. The fire sparked as its height had grown in size. The wind picked up as it rustled through the trees. Voices could be heard in the distance and perhaps nearby. The fast and hard drum beats coming from the large wooden structure could be heard as they picked up the rhythmic pace.

The last member of the group spoke out, "To the winds of the east. Great eagle, condor. Come to us from the place of the rising sun. Keep us under your wing. Show us the mountains we only dare dream of. Teach us to fly wing to wing with the Great Spirit."

From the east came a large bird. It glided over the group as it made a circle overhead and swooped down to rest on a pole nearby.

Smiling at one another, the group shared glances that were an emersion of joy. They focused again on the circle as Lillie spoke, "We've gathered here for the healing of all of your children. The Stone People, the Plant People, the four-legged, the two-legged, the creepy crawlers, the finned, the furred, and the winged ones. All of our relations."

Father Sun, Grandmother Moon, to the Star Nations. Great Spirit, you who are known by a thousand names and you who are the unnamable One. Thank you for bringing us together and allowing us the song of Life. The circle is cast. We are between the worlds, beyond the bounds of time and space where night and day, birth and death, joy and sorrow meet as one!"

The pace of the drum beats in the distance picked up to a furious pace. Shadows from the fire danced off the walls of the house and across the grass of the yard. Lillie yelled out again, "Thank you for hearing us oh great one. We ask of you to send us two. Two of your choosing to bring to us so that we may feast upon them and offer up sacrifice to you! Please send us the two that will satisfy your desires. Bring them to us!"

Clouds started to form and circle over the island as lightning flashed on the horizon. A light rain started to fall on the group as they rejoiced and offered out their thanks as they closed out the circle. The closing of the circle was just as important as the opening. It was fairly simple so there was no excuse not to anyway. With their hands still joined they all looked to the sky with their eyes shut. They searched their feelings to take in every bit of the nature around them as they all said in unison, "We thank you, Guardians, of the Watchtowers, for your attention and contributions to our practices." They opened their eyes and with smiles on their faces wiped away the circle from the ground. They each blew out their candles with the large white candle being the last to be blown. A cool breeze came over the island as the rain picked up. For now, this weather affected only this small island. The rest of the sea remained calm.

# THUNDER AND HIGH SWELLS

Jeff had arrived at Mitchel's boat rental. It was Todd's father's business but it was pretty much Todd's business as well since it was inevitable that one day in the future it would be all his. As he approached the rental booth, Jeff heard a voice that said, "Hey Jeff, how are you doing today?"

"Hey, Mr. Mitchel. I'm good. I'm just here to see Todd. Is he around?"

"He is down by the dock helping out some tourists. Do you want to wait here? He'll be back soon."

"No sir, I'm cool. I think I'll just go down and see him. He is expecting me."

Jeff walked down the dock and he could see his friend Todd giving some instruction to the tourists renting some boats. By Coast Guard law they were supposed to give anyone renting a boat a small class and test. They were pretty lax in how the test had to be really. So they made it more of a formality than anything. It was basically. "Do you speak English? Do you live on the planet earth? How do you make the boat go? How do you make it slow?" That was good enough for

Todd and his father since at the end of the day, it was only about making money. The only question that mattered to them was making sure the people understood the GPS so they did not get lost. They did not need to lose any boats or risk a lawsuit because some idiot got lost at sea for five hours and got scared.

Todd had shoved the guests boat away from the dock and he nervously watched them motor away. They always made him nervous. By they, he meant anyone he was renting a boat to. They always had certain looks on their faces. It was either one of a glazed look that they did not understand anything he had told them. Or it was that look that said, "Sure buddy, we will take good care of your boat." Then the second they were out of sight he knew they would be driving that thing like it's a rental and they were madmen at sea.

Walking up from the dock Todd noticed Jeff standing there. They gave each other a fist bump as Todd asked, "You ready to go?" Jeff looked at his friend and said, "Born ready." Todd told him, "Yeah, it's funny that you called and wanted to go out on the water because I was thinking about calling you and asking you anyway. I don't know.

Just had a feeling I wanted to be out on the water today" Jeff smiled as he said, "Great minds."

The two walked up to the rental shack and Todd grabbed a set of keys. His father looked up from his newspaper and asked, "You boys going somewhere?"

"Just taking the boat that I fixed this morning out for some sea trials dad. You know, we want to be CG compliant right?"

"How long do you plan on being out? Are you going to have time to repaint the shed later?"

Todd looked to his dad and said, "Yeah, we will only be a couple of hours. I figure as long as we are out there, we will try and catch some dinner." He grabbed some poles and other fishing gear.

The two walked away and back down to the docks. Jeff said, "The old man still treats you like a kid doesn't he?"

"Meh, I guess. He just wants to make sure I am ready to take over the business. I don't gripe about it. I mean, I have my whole life ahead of me, and it's already set-in-stone."

They got into a bigger boat. This was not one of the small one-person boats. It was a twenty-foot powerboat. It was one of a few boats they rented out for guys who wanted fishing trips or something to impress the ladies with as they took it for speed filled ride.

They were out at sea for about twenty minutes and without warning a heavy fog rolled in. The engine had died. Todd cussed out loud as he said, "Man, come on. I just fixed this one. Jeff, go back and look at the engine would ya?" Todd trusted Jeff with the boats as he knew Jeff had grown up around boats just as he had. He was a mechanic for one of the large boat retailers on the island. Jeff grabbed a bag of tools that had been laying on one of the seats and went aft to work on the engine. He had been tinkering with the engine for a few minutes and yelled out, "Okay, start her up!" Todd turned the key over and nothing happened. He tried again with still no results. The fog around them was starting to get heavy. Todd walked aft and grabbed a wrench. "Here let me show you something my dad taught me. Go to the console will ya?"

Jeff went to the console. With all of his might, Todd hit the engine repeatedly with the wrench as he yelled out, "Mother fucker! Mother fucker!" He turned to Jeff and said,

"Okay. Let's see if that worked." Jeff turned the key over and the engine started up. Todd put his arms out to his side in a self-praised posture as he said, "They don't do that at the shop, do they? Let's go home." Jeff throttled the engine and it took off. A few seconds later the engine made a strange shuttering sound. It sounded like it skipped a beat. The sound of the engine pitched up an octave as the boat slowed to not moving at all. Jeff pushed the throttle a little more. The sound of the engine increased, but the boat did not move forward. He brought the throttle down and tried reverse. The engine was running, it was just not moving the boat in any direction. Jeff killed the engine. He asked Todd to take the console and walked aft as he took off his shirt. He looked at Todd and said, "Hey, don't go anywhere", as he jumped off the boat into the water. Todd was standing at the console holding the wheel and the engine in place. It was so quiet out on the open water as the fog continued to roll in at a heavier pace. The visibility was around them was twenty feet. He heard Jeff yell, "Oh man, you are not going to like this." Todd already knew what was coming next. He said, "Tell me we still have a prop." As Jeff hoisted himself up on the boat he said, "We do NOT have a prop. So what do you want to do? You want to get on the radio and see if there is anyone nearby that can give us a tow?"

Todd shook his head back and forth as he said, "No man, my dad would never let me hear the end of it. We have to dive for that prop." Jeff laughed and said, "Dude you know it's at least thirty feet here right?"

Taking a deep breath Todd said, "Yeah. I can do this. I've free-dived that depth for lobster before. I am not taking this boat back to my dad without a prop. How can he trust me to run the shop one day if I cannot handle my own." Todd dove into the water and swam straight down as far as he could. The salt in the water stung his eyes as he tried to look for the bottom. With the heavy fog and lack of sunlight, the water visibility was dim and murky. He was almost to the bottom when he realized he could not see anything. He went back to the surface, took a breath, and went back down. With the same results, he came back to the surface out of breath. He lifted himself on the boat. Jeff asked him if he got the propeller.

Catching his breath he said that he had not. Jeff asked. "So are you ready to get on the horn and call for a tow? The weather is starting to pick up." Looking around the boat Todd saw a coiled-up hose at the bow that he had left there after rinsing the boat earlier.

He said, "No.", as he picked up the hose. Jeff protested, "Oh no man. You are not serious." Todd looked back to Jeff and said, "Listen it's real simple. You hold onto the hose and keep this end above water. I put this end in my mouth and go down." Jeff laughed in disbelief. "You have come up with some dumb-ass ideas in your life man, but this one takes the cake. You don't honestly think that is going to work do you?" Todd told him. "Come on man. Think positive." He jumped back in the water and put the hose to his mouth. He wrapped his lips and fist tightly around the hose as he dipped his face down into the water for a test run. He lifted his face out of the water after a few seconds. As he coughed up some water he said, "See. Works fine." He put the hose back in his mouth and dove down. The hose trick was not working as well as he thought. But as long as he used it only to take short breaths and hold it, it worked okay. He was scanning the bottom looking for the prop. They had drifted a little, so for all he knew they were already far away from it. He had to look though. Todd felt a tug on the hose. He felt it again. It was a tug in a three-beat motion. He went back to the surface. The sky was black. Jeff said, "Hey man, you need to come back up here. It is getting nasty out." Todd said, "I'll be fine." There was an earth-shattering clap of thunder. Todd was back on the boat in seconds. The two worked together to hoist up a canopy over the boat. It did not cover the whole boat, just the console area and the seat next to it. It was only the two of them so it would work. That was till the wind picked up its power as did the rain. The rain was coming into their covered area sideways. The wind was strong and pushed their boat along the open water. The swells were at least three feet as they progressed forward to wherever mother ocean was taking them.

The two could see the shadow of an island in the distance before them. They prayed that the wind would take them in that direction. The prayers worked as the wind shifted and pushed the boat rocking in the powerful waves toward the island. It was as if there was an imaginary force pushing the boat to the safety of the island and off of the treacherous sea. The boat came to shore as Jeff and Todd jumped off and into the shallow water. Together with the strength of two young men, they pulled the boat as far up on the beach as they could. They used line to secure it to a nearby tree and ran into the woods for cover from the torrential downpour. It was heavy as the raindrops felt like needles hitting their skin. The trees offered some cover. But they needed more. The dark ominous clouds were bringing with them a non-stop show of lighting that seemed to get closer to them with each strike. There was a sizzle in the air with the smell of ozone as a bright flash lit up the area around them. A tree only a couple of feet away split and sparked into a blaze as lightning struck. It was followed instantly by an ear-shattering clap of thunder. Huddled together under a tree for the warmth they looked at each other. Each was able to read the other's mind. They had to find some sort of shelter. They ran up a small trail nearby.

HELPLESS

Lillie was in her kitchen making some special tea when she heard the loud pounding on her front door. She smiled as she said, "Right on time." She opened the door and saw two men staring at her. They were shivering and looked startled as one said, "Ma'am. We are sorry to bother you. May we come in please?" The look in their eyes had a desperate look like two lost puppies.

She opened the door wide and said, "Of course. Come in. Come in. You boys should not be out in this." She poked her head out the door and looked up at the sky as she smiled and shut the door. She ushered them into the kitchen and handed them each bath a towel that was already conveniently sitting on the counter. "Wrap these around you. Sit down, boys. My name is Lillie. What are you doing out in that?"

The taller man with blonde hair said, "I'm Todd, this is Jeff. We were out on my boat. We lost our prop and as we were trying to retrieve it this storm came out of nowhere. Thankfully the wind brought us to this island."

With a sound of concern in her voice, Lillie said, "I have not seen a storm like this in years. This is strange. Here, you young men need to drink this. It will warm you up. Look at you. You are still shivering."

Jeff thanked her as he took a sip and asked, "You don't by chance have a phone we could use do you?"

"Oh, sweetie. I wish I did. But this is a small little private island. There are no phone lines that run out here."

"Do you have a radio we could use?" Todd asked.

"No, I am sorry honey. It is just me on this little island." She continued in a lofty voice as she said, "All by myself. I like it that way."

Todd and Jeff continued to drink the warm tea that was soothing to the soul. Not only did it warm their bodies, but had put them in a relaxed state. The room around them was starting to get slightly hazy. Almost like the fog on the water. Everything was starting to move in slow motion around them. The room started to spin slightly. Jeff looked to Todd and Todd said to him in a very slow and deep voice, "Hey man, are you feeling this? What is going on?" Jeff said back in an equally slow and deep voice, "I don't know man.

I think she put something in the tea." They both tried to get up and fell flat on their faces as their legs felt like molasses and were of no use to them. They looked up at the woman who had taken them in as she stood towering above them with a prideful smile filled with disdain. She had one hand on her hip. It could have been a smile. It was hard to tell as she appeared to lean to and fro and there were multiple versions of her when she moved. They felt themselves get picked up off the ground and back into the chairs. She was saying something to them but they could not make out the words. They were helpless as they could only watch as rope made its way around their arms and chest, binding them to the chairs. It was as if the rope moved on its own. It slithered around them and tightened like a snake about to devour its prey. The rope was sung and there was nothing they could do to escape the binding. The woman leaned into them one at a time as she grabbed their jaws and forced their mouths open. She inserted a pill into their mouths. Still holding them by the jaw she would tilt their heads back and slowly say, "Swallow." They did. They had no choice. The world around them faded to black.

LOST PETS ALWAYS RETURN

Jayden drove his truck off the ferry dock on Manta Ray. He was back on the Peeking Islands. This was not a vacation though. He was not here to party or enjoy the fun and frolicking that the historic seaport offered. He was here on a mission. He had to find out what this woman by the name of Lillie had done to him. She was in his every thought, both awake and when asleep. He could focus on nothing but her. Even if he were here on this trip to party it would not have been much of a party. The island was being thrashed by a sudden squall that formed without warning east of the island chain. It was a fierce squall that had come out of nowhere without warning. It was a clear day as the ferry had left Daytona. It is because of the suddenness that he was there at all. When the weather had started to pick up the ferry was already three-quarters to the Peeking Islands. Continuing the trip to the islands was the only choice the captain had. Otherwise, he would have turned around back to Daytona and canceled the trip. Jayden drove his car off of the boat ramp and past a shack at the end of the parking lot. The guard in the shack said, "Welcome to Peeking! Do you need a hotel?" Jayden said, "No. I'm good thanks! Heading out towards Martillo! I'll have a place to stay already! Are the bridges still open?"

The guard lifted the gate as he said with a laugh, "They are for now. But you better hurry. They might be closing them soon. All right! Stay dry! This one is going to be a doozy!" Jayden pulled his truck onto the Peeking highway and started his trek to the Isla de Cabeza Martillo. His white-knuckle grip was tight as he leaned forward to try to see through the thick rain. The windshield wipers were on the highest setting and had a hard time keeping the view clear. Jayden grabbed a rag off of his passenger seat as he used it to wipe off a thick foggy condensation building up on the inside of the windshield. As he crossed the bridge going from Manta Ray to Isla Sirena he could feel the wind push his truck. He focused straight ahead. Within a couple of minutes, he was on a bridge to Bear Island and then another to Isla de Cabeza Martillo. After getting off of that bridge he took a right and was heading south on Martillo. The rain was so thick he could barely see the road. He focused his attention on the white lines on the side of the road. It was the only way he could tell he was still on it.

He arrived at Mitchel's boat rental located on the southeast corner of Martillo. He parked his truck and ran to the rental booth. There was nobody there. He knocked loudly on the booth as he yelled out hello to anyone that would answer. There was nobody there. He ran down to the docks with the wind belting his face with rain that was hard as nails. He continued to yell out for anyone to respond. There was nobody there. Of course, why would there be in this weather? He wanted to get to Lillie's. He needed to be there. Nothing could stop him. He ran back to his truck and grabbed a wrench from the toolbox in the bed of the truck. While rubbing his water-soaked face he ran back to the booth and used the wrench to break open a padlock. He opened the booth and grabbed a key. Surrounded by lighting in the sky overhead he ran to the docks and looked at the floatable key chain in his hand. It had the number eighteen on it. He walked briskly on the dock with his hand acting as an awning over his eyes till he found the match. He felt some relief when he found that boat eighteen was one of the bigger boats and not one of the single rider boats. He had no idea how this would work if he took one of those out in this mess. Jayden started the boat and went to untie the line. The line was a thick rope that held the boat to the dock. Much like the thread that held his mind to Lillie. He gave the boat a good push as he jumped off the dock onto the boat and quickly returned to the console. As he pulled into the open water he took a left which took him under the south end of Martillo and out toward the open choppy water. He had no idea of how he was going to get to this island as he did not know how he got there the first time. He was going to rely on a lot of luck. So far, in getting just this far today, luck had been on his side.

The boat felt hard to control. As it hit each wave he fought to keep it on a straight course. There were times that the boat felt airborne. As it would come back to the water surface he would lean in the opposite direction that he felt the boat pitch to. It was not as if that would help. It was a natural reaction. The glow of the setting sun behind him made the moisture in the air turn everything into a blur. The rain beating into his eyes made it hard to see. Even by using his hand as a guide. His heartbeat was out of his chest as he still had no idea where he was going. He squinted and focused intently on the view in front of him looking for anything that might resemble an approaching island. He was in panic mode as he needed luck to run its course. Jayden took a breath as he closed his eyes and said with concentration, "Hear me, Lillie. Lead me to you. Feel me, Lillie. I am calling out to you. Bring me home. Bring me home." He said this as he continued to drive the boat in the fierce storm with his eyes tightly closed. He figured if his eyes were closed that meant he was not looking for it. If the only way to find this island was not to be looking for it, this seemed like a plausible plan.

He continued to yell out his chant loudly and in frustration. That was till he felt the boat come to a quick stop. The boat was not moving as he had grounded it on the beach. Rather than throttle down and turn the key he just pulled on the kill cord that was attached to his waist. Quickly he ran to the bow of the boat and grabbed the line that was attached to the bow. He jumped off the boat onto the sandy beach he had run aground and ran to a tree. Without haste, he tied the line around a tree. He noticed another boat tied similarly. It had the same markings on it that his boat did. That was from Todd's dad's rental company. He did not even know what to make of that. He did not have time to think about it. He had to make it to Lillie's house. If he was even on her island. This had to be her island.

DOMINUS MEUS

The cellar was lit dimly only by candles. It was slightly more than a dim light though as there were many candles. Perhaps even a thousand! Or perhaps that is least that what it looked like to Todd and Jeff in their current state of mind. There may have only been one hundred candles. Or maybe there were only sixty. With the vision that these two friends locked down in a cellar had, it looked like a thousand. Many were on shelves surrounding the two young men. Others had a random placement on the floor huddled together. One table appeared to be covered with candles of all different shapes and sizes. There was one formation of candles that did not seem so random. It was a circle that went all the way around them. Five lines inside the circle seemed to cross one another at specific points. Jeff and Todd could not tell it was a circle from their vantage point though. They sat side by side in two folding chairs. The effects of whatever they had been given were still weighing heavy in the bloodstream. There may have been a moment here or there when they would try to get up from the chairs. They could not. They could not even move their arms. They felt as if they were bound by rope. There was no rope there, however. It was only in their minds.

They felt a presence behind them and heard her speak. She came around to the front of them so they could see her. She said, "My two pets. Oh, don't worry. You will not be my pets for long. I have plenty of pets and like all pet's they must be fed. So maybe instead of calling you two my pets, perhaps I should just call you, dinner. They could hear breathing and feet scuttling on the floor behind them. She took out a long dagger and approached Todd. He could only look up to her in petrified fear. He could not move. He did not move. He closed his eyes and felt two hands on his shoulders. He felt a sheering pain in his neck and had the feeling that he was a bag of juice being attacked by a nine-year-old with a straw. He could feel his life draining away as his heartbeat slowed. In the chair directly next to Todd, Jeff was in the same situation as a creature unseen to him fed off the protein in his veins. They were both at the point when this all ends till, she yelled, "Stop! Now children. You must slow down and enjoy your meal. Not all at once. Save some for later. Save something for daddy. He is almost home. He will slice your dinner up into bite-size snacks for you so that you may get it all down." She stopped speaking as she looked up the stairway. She smiled and said, "Oh, well speak of the devil."

Heavy footsteps could be heard coming down the staircase. They came slowly as if there was no rush. There was all the time in the world. The footsteps stopped. Standing before Lillie was a figure. It was in a hooded robe. The face could not be seen but its eyes were illuminated like fiery coals. Todd and Jeff could smell a foul scent coming off it. It was a smell of rotting. It was a horrible stench that they could taste in the back of their throats. It stood before Lillie and spoke in Latin. She responded, "My Lord, what a pleasant surprise. I was just speaking of you. My children and I are very pleased to be graced by your presence."

The mysterious figure shouted one word at her as she responded in a defensive tone. "My Lord! He is on the way. He is my special case right now. I have given him much attention. I assure you he will be ready."

The figure continued to speak to her in Latin. The tone of its voice was slow and decisive. As it spoke it raised one arm to her face and a hand with long pointed fingers protruded from the sleeve as one finger pointed at her face. The figure seemed to be giving Lillie specific instructions. "The chosen one? Jayden? As I said, my Lord, he will be ready. I was not aware that you had such a special interest in him."

The tone that the figure spoke in was upset but did not yell. It spoke in a dry and calm manner.

"My Lord, he is on the way as we speak. I have called for him. He will be here. I have him under my complete control. Tonight is the final test for that. He will be sacrificing these two in your name tonight. He will do it because he knows it will make me happy. Then we will feast on the sacrifice in your name, my Lord."

The figure, breathing heavy with a slight hiss looked over to Todd and Jeff sitting in their chairs. It slowly walked to them. The energy of heat could be felt off it as the figure approached the two. Jeff was looking at this cryptic figure face to face as it bent over to him. The figure had to be at least eight feet tall. It had a large build. From the bottom of the robe it wore, there seemed to be boots, or were they hooves? All though he was nearly face to face with this figure he could not make out a face. He could only see dark shadows where there should be a face. The two fire-like coals pierced into his own eyes. He felt as if his mind were being read like a book. The figure held out its arm and a long-pointed finger protruded from the sleeve. It said something in Latin that almost seemed to be a whisper. As it spoke it put its finger on Jeff's neck. The pain he felt was searing as if someone had put a sharp and hot fire stoker to his neck. It was only for one second, but it lasted an eternity. As it removed its finger from Jeff's neck, he could still feel the pain. His skin felt irritated as if there were a dry and itchy rash on it. The figure then turned its attention to Todd and the same thing happened. This time Jeff could see what most likely was on his neck. At least he could assume it was the same thing. It was a number. It was a human number. It was six hundred and sixty-six.

At the same instant, both the creature and Lillie looked up toward the stairwell like two cats looking and following nothing in unison. She said with a smile, "He is here, my Lord. Allow me to do my job. I assure you. This one is mine. The figure walked back to Lillie and spoke, "Noli pati arrogantiam tuem." It then walked to a corner of the candlelit room and appeared to disappear into the wall.

HE'S BACK

Knowing it would be unlocked, Jayden burst through the front door of Lillie's house. He yelled out her name. She calmly walked into the living room and greeted him with a smile. "Jayden, my sweet boy. It is so pleasant to see you." She seemed to glow as she greeted him in the front living room. It was a glow that seemed to surround her presence. She was wearing a long robe. Despite it being black it was very revealing as it was a see-through robe. She was holding on to a glass jar. In her presence, he felt at peace. He was still breathing out of control as he said, "Lillie. I'm sorry to barge in. I cannot think of anything but you. I have an uncontrollable desire to see you. I don't know what is going on!"

She looked at him with a trustful stare. She said, "There, there my sweet boy." as she rubbed his cheek with her palm. He looked at her and he was mesmerized. He could not avoid her eyes. He felt a tingle of pleasure go up to his spine as she caressed his cheek and praised him. He was starting to calm down but was still out of breath as he tried to explain how he felt as if he had lost control of his life. She dipped a finger into the jar she was holding. She then put the finger to his lips as she hushed him. She rubbed her finger on his lips as she slowly inserted it into his mouth. He licked her finger slowly as he allowed it to come into his mouth. He started to suck on it. The flavor it had was like thick and sweet maple syrup. He closed his eyes as she returned her finger to the jar and back into his mouth. She set the jar down and with her free hand slowly rubbed the top of his head. As he continued to suck on her finger, she said things to him in a happy and soothing whisper that had made him feel at one and slightly aroused. She would whisper into one ear, and then the other. He felt electricity surge and pulse through his veins with every word she spoke. As he licked his lips he could feel a warmness overtake his body. While wrapping one hand around the back of his head, she used the other hand to pull his head into her chest and lightly massage the back of his head and neck. Her fingers worked their way through his hair like a snake slithering through the grass. He was starting to feel bliss.

She took a step away as she told him to follow her. He did as if he had no choice. It was like he was on a tether yet there was nothing physical connecting them. They walked into the kitchen and down the stairs into the cellar. Jayden was in a silent shock at what he saw. It was Jeff and Todd that were sitting in folding chairs next to each other. He said, "What the hell? What are you guys doing here?" What were they doing here he thought? He looked around the room and was just now noticing all of the candles. There was an ax. The one that had fallen off of the wall on his last visit to the island. Only now it was on a table. There was also a large dagger on the table. Shadows moved around on and off of the walls as the candles provided a light show of sorts all on their own. The floor around the chairs Jeff and Todd in looked damp. Along a back wall was a large wooden cross. It had leather restraining ropes attached to both sides. He looked back to Todd and Jeff as he said, "What the hell are you two doing here?" There was no response. He snapped his fingers in front of their faces. He waved his hand in front of their faces. Their eyes were open, but they were not responding. He could tell they were alive as their chests moved up and down to breathe. It was as if they were alive and not aware. He turned to Lillie who was directly behind him and put her finger to his mouth as she hushed him. She whispered in his ears. It was a sweet and happy whisper. She told him that he made her happy. She could tell by the smile on his face that he was feeling her bliss. She told him that he was becoming the best version of him. She added, "The only thoughts in your head are my thoughts. Because my thoughts are your thoughts. Do you remember when you were fully in bliss? Do you remember that feeling continuing deeper as your mind began to feel at peace? Suppose your mind could go anywhere it imagined. Now imagine you are going further into bliss. Every time you hear the sound of my voice, you begin to realize that the only thing that matters, is hearing the sound of my voice." Looking at him she could tell she was getting him into a deep trance. She could tell that, in his head, she was doing very naughty things to him. She said, "There you go. The more you drip. The deeper you drop. The deeper you drop the more you drip. Now drop... Deeper." She grabbed the back of his head tightly as she put her lips to his and thrust her tongue deep down his throat. She could feel his muscles tighten up as his body started to contort and convulse. She held on to him tightly, not allowing him to fall on the ground. She released her grip as she walked to the table. She came back to him with the ax in her hand. She said, "You make me happy. When I am happy you are happy and you make me so happy. Your pleasure comes from making me happy. You are such a sweet boy. Do you want to make me happy?"

He nodded his head up and down as he said, "Yes Temptress."

While handing him the ax she looked him deep into his eyes with her smile and said, "Imagine how happy I would be with you if you were to chop them up. You want to kill them. You will kill them. Obey"

He grabbed the ax and slowly walked toward Jeff and Todd who sat in a state of being aware but not awake. Jayden stood before the two with the ax in his hands held high above his head. He noticed a tear roll down the side of Jeff's cheek. He dropped the ax as he looked back to Lillie in a state of confusion. "PET!" She yelled out as she pointed her finger at him and then to the ground. Jayden went to his knees. Lillie went back to the table and came back with a dagger. He looked at Todd and Jeff who were only a foot in front of him. They said and did nothing. She bent down toward Jayden and used the dagger to cut open his shirt completely. She cut a long line from the collar to the bottom. She ripped the shirt off of him and tossed it to the ground. She then put the dagger up against his shoulder. He could feel the prick of the blade poking into his skin. She smiled as she asked, "You like this, don't you? You like it when I threaten you like this. You like it because you know I will not hurt you. You can trust me. You do trust me. Because you make me happy. Do you trust me?" He could feel a small stream of his blood trickle down his chest as he said, "Yes Temptress."

"Such a good boy!" She said as she filled him with bliss. With the dagger in his skin, she lightly and slowly dragged it down his chest, over his belly, and to his waist. She poked it in a little deeper as he jumped slightly and smiled. Grabbing the waistline of his shorts and holding on she cut through his shorts and his boxers as she removed both. The blade cut through his clothing like it was going through butter. Jayden was kneeling on the hard cement floor. His blood was dripping down his body as in one motion Lillie leaned into him and licked the blood from his waist to his shoulder. She looked down at him as she licked her lips and said, "You taste so good. You make me happy. You are a sweet boy. Now you will kill them for me. Obey. That would make me so happy. You will kill them because I am your Temptress, and you are my pet." She handed him the dagger.

Jayden stood up and with the dagger in his hand, looked down to Todd sitting before him. He was a millisecond from bringing the blade down onto Todd. He heard a voice. It was a voice that had always been there but just not heard recently. It said, "Turn the blade on her. You know what must be done."

Lillie noticed Jayden hesitate. Putting her hand on his shoulder she shoved him back to the ground on his knees. She waved the ax back and forth up and down with violence in her heart as she brutally chopped up Todd and Jeff. She did not stop till the job was done and they were in pieces. The blood from both had spattered all over the cellar. It had spilled all over Jayden's naked body. Jayden could only watch from his knees. He knew this could not go on. He knew he must do something. He could not. He could not go against her. She was Temptress. She made him happy.

FRACTIONATION

His eyes were dark and swollen as he looked at himself in the mirror. He was naked and covered from head to toe in blood. It was the blood from Todd and Jeff who he had just watched Lillie savagely murder with an ax. She was standing next to him. She was also naked. She was not covered in blood. She looked clean and wet. He looked down in his hand and noticed he was holding a blood-soaked sponge. He could only assume that he had just given her a sponge bath. He had given his Temptress a sponge bath in a candle-lit room and he did not even remember that. He did not remember. The last thing he remembered was standing above Todd as he was about to swing away and take off his head with a vengeance. But now, here he stood in the bathroom naked and covered in blood. Lillie took the blood-soaked sponge from his hand as she said, "You are such a good boy."

She looked down at him as she could see his penis twitch and start to become erect. "Now be a good boy and clean yourself up." She said as she took the bloody sponge from his hand and replaced it with a fresh one. He dipped the sponge in the sink to get it wet. He would then rub it on his body wherever she told him to. He did this because it made her happy.

As he finished she handed him a towel and told him to dry himself off. He did and she walked him to the bedroom he had stayed in before. Candles sat lit on the floor surrounding the bed as well as being on the dresser. Lillie told him to lay down on the bed on his back. He was naked and laying on the bed as Lillie walked to the side of the bed. She was dressed in a tight leather skirt and leather corset. She stood at the side of the bed and sensually ran her fingers up and down his chest. She started to whisper triggers and commands into his ear.

His mind and his body responded appropriately since they had been programmed to do such. She was taking him into another trance. He eagerly let his mind slip away as he anticipated the reward of bliss. As she dropped him deeper into a trance, she had taken a candle from the floor by the bed and started to drip the wax on him. She would slowly run it over his whole body as he would shiver in a burst of bliss. He was enjoying the pain and she took it to the next level as she revealed the dagger. He smiled as she told him that he trusted her. He trusted her because that is what she had told him. Those were his thoughts as his thoughts were the thoughts she put in his brain. He did not have to think. She would think for him. She used the dagger to make narrow and shallow incisions in his body. By his reaction, she knew she was in his head. A favorite hobby of Lillie's was toying around with the minds of her pets. Especially this one. He was so reactive to her every command. It was so easy. Almost, too easy. To her, it was a game to bring him directly to the edge. Using her commands and triggers to take his mind to the point that he would explode in a fury of passion. It was fun to get him to that point and then take it away. She would watch his body thrive and she could tell he was moments away from feeling pure bliss. Then she would count him out of his trance. Stealing the moment of bliss away from him. Once she had awoken him, she would take him deeper down. She could play this game for hours. She enjoyed taking him, or any pet for that matter on the roller coaster called fractionation. She could see pre-cum oozing out of him. She said, "Good boy. Remember that the more you drop, the more you drip. You want to drip because it makes you drop... deeper. So now drop...deeper for me." Tick, tick, ding.

I AM YOU

It was the early hours when Jayden awoke. It was probably around 3 AM. As Jayden brought his brain from sleep he rubbed his belly and felt a hardened substance. It was wax from earlier. He must have dozed off mid trance as he did not even remember her leaving. He stood up to rub the wax off and heard a voice. It said his name. It was coming from the front yard below. He went to the dresser and opened it up. He was relieved to find extra clothing in there. Left behind from a friend of Lillie's a long time ago no doubt. Either way, it beat walking around naked since his clothes were sliced up and covered in blood. It was jeans and a hoodie. He put them on and walked out on the front balcony.

Below him, he saw a misty figure. It vaguely looked like a small girl. She looked to be about nine or ten. She was in a white dress. It was the kind of dress that a young girl would wear to church on Easter Sunday. She whispered out his name again as she said, "Come out here." Jayden grabbed the dagger that he had just seen laying on the dresser. He put it in the pocket of the hoodie. He then tip-toed down the stairs and slowly opened the front door as he crept out of the house.

He was on the lower balcony standing in front of the door. He looked into the darkness and saw the figure again. She said, "Come on, follow me." He left the property and had lost sight of the little girl. He stopped and whispered. "Hey, little girl. Are you there?" She popped her head out from behind a tree. She put her finger to her mouth as she said, "Yes. Ssh. Follow me." They played this cat and mouse game till they got to the beach. Jayden was alone again. He looked all around him and he did not see the little girl. He was nearly startled when he heard her say his name. He turned around quickly and saw the girl. She was no longer a misty figure she looked real. She said, "Listen, I don't have long. You need to take care of this mess. You know what you must do."

Jayden asked, "Who the hell are you?"

She said, "I am you. Well, I am the righteous side of you. I am the side of you that makes the good decisions. I help keep you in line with God."

"So you are my good angel on my shoulder is what you're saying."

She tried to explain, "No. I am, in fact, you. I am only one part of you though. I am the good part."

Jayden asked her, "So if you are me, how come you don't look like me? How come you look like a little girl on her way to church?"

She said, "I don't know. You're the one that manifested me. I am nothing more than light and energy. You only see me as a human because it makes it easier to talk to me. Maybe this is how you view the righteous version of yourself."

"So what are you doing here now?"

She said, "I'm here to help you make the right decision. Your entire life you have strived to be a righteous person. Yet you always seem to fall into the same pits and run the same loop."

"What do you mean by loop?" he asked.

She explained to him. "This lesson is either pass or fail. There is no bell curve. You go through your life and if you fail any lessons, you are bound to loop back till you get them all right."

"Your saying reincarnation is a thing? I thought that was a Buddhist belief."

The little girl said, "No. Reincarnation would be coming back as someone or something else for a different lesson. You are coming back as yourself in the same life with all the same lessons to learn over again. Think of it as being held back a grade."

Jayden continued to try and learn more as he asked her, "If I do something wrong and I get thrown back into this…"

"Loop."

"Right, Loop. If I get thrown back into the loop how will I know which life lessons I am trying to improve on? I mean, up till now I did not even know I was being held back a grade so to speak. Are there signs?"

"You've seen them many times." She told him. He asked her when.

"Have you ever had a moment when you feel as if you've done this before or you're having a conversation with someone that you have had before?"

He was happy when he finally had known one answer to what she was talking about when he said, "Yeah, it's called Déjà vu. Everyone has that." He paused then his face lit up as he asked, "I get it. So every time I feel as if I've done something I've already done, that is the loop's way of letting me know that, I've done this before. I did not make the right choice that time so now I have to see if I have learned. If I make all the correct choices in life I get to move on?" She laughed and said, "Now you've got it. Kind of. Remember that you do not move on right away after doing everything right. Do everything right then you go one more time to prove that the righteous is implanted in you."

"Wait, so basically I have to have two consecutive lives that are one hundred percent? If they are not, I am back at square one."

"You got it." She said with a smile.

"Well, that sucks."

"I don't make the rules, I only explain them in a way you will understand. Think of it this way. All you have to do is pitch two consecutive no-hitters. You can do that, I've watched you do it."

He had a big heavy sigh and asked, "Okay. So why do you come to me only now? How come you are only showing up now to get me back on the right path?"

"You have never needed me before. So therefore you have never called on me before"

Jayden told the manifestation of his good self, "But I did not call on you now."

"Sure you did, otherwise we would not be talking."

Jayden laughed as he said, "Well if you are only a manifestation created by my mind we are not really even talking. If anyone were to walk by right now it would look as if I am talking to myself?"

She said, "Essentially. I guess if that is how you want to look at it."

"So all of these people I see in the streets that look they are talking to themselves, they are not crazy, they are talking to their angel?"

"Maybe. Listen. We don't have a lot of time. You need to get back to the house soon. She will be up. I need you to understand what is going on here. This is something that you need to fix now. There has always been a battle of righteous versus evil in your head. But that is the problem. The two balance each other out in a matter of speaking. Right now you are stuck in a spiritual black hole. Realize that evil is birthed from corruption. Evil is self-destructive to itself. But the corruption will always be reborn if one does not learn from mistakes. History will always repeat itself on earth because humans refuse to learn from their mistakes. But to balance it out, you have goodness. Which comes from innocence. Innocence can only come from a world without evil. Because evil corrupts every time.

Jayden asked, "So it sounds like darkness will always win and the loop continues?"

She said, "No. Think of it this way. If you walk into a dark room and flip on a light switch what happens?"

"There will be light in the room."

She told him, "Right, and all of the darkness leaves the room. But if you walk into a dark room, there is still some amount of light coming in from somewhere, whether it be a crack on under a door or whatever."

Jayden said, "So you are saying that the evil will always be devoured by the good but the evil can never fully consume the good."

"Right."

Jayden asked, "But isn't it all about balance? For every right, there is a wrong. For example; if I find something, it is because someone else lost it right?"

She told him, "It is all how you want to look at it. Just because I say I love you does not mean someone else in the world has to say I hate you. The problem with that line of thinking is that you sleep well at night knowing that the people you screwed over that day probably deserved it. It is the line of karma that people believe in for their personal justification. But what if you look at it in a positive light? Good breeds good. If you do something nice for three people maybe that expands to nine good deeds at the end of the day."

"I am totally confused. What does this all come down to?" She told him, "I brought you out here because you need to do the right thing. You know what that is. The answer is in your hoodie pocket." She walked away, surrounded by other manifestations as she vanished into the trees.

Jayden was so lost and confused. That was too much information at once and it all seemed to contradict itself. Which he thought was a problem with the world today. There was so much hate fueled by hypocrisy. The world is always at war because each side believes they are right. Or even worse, one country is at war within itself because each side believes they are right. In a way, aren't both sides right if they believe in what they are selling? What if perspective is truth? A person's perspective is how they see it. Therefore, perception must be their truth. But what if there is an opposition that enters the room with a different perspective? Would that not be his or her truth as well? Can there be two truths? Jayden was getting into his head way too deep. He wanted to drop down and go to sleep. He needed a simple answer.

He stood on the beach looking at the sea. Maybe the answer was out there. White flakes had started to lightly fall from the sky. They were everywhere and covered everything they touched. They were very small in size. Jayden thought, is it snowing in Florida? He had never seen snow before. This would be so exciting! Maybe this was his answer. He had never seen snow before. That was a change. So maybe God was showing him that change, no matter how unlikely it may seem, it is possible. It is not possible to snow this much in Florida! Yet it is. This stuff was coming down and it was covering everything it touched. So maybe it is possible to change his mind about his Temptress that had controlled him so much. She was leading him down a dark path. She had consumed him. She was darkness. He was the light. So maybe it was time to hit the switch and let the light devour the darkness. He had his answer. He must kill Lillie. He took a couple of seconds to think of a plan. He put his hands in the front pocket of the hoodie. He felt the dagger. His eyes lit up as he said, "That's it." He gathered some palm fronds and tossed them out on the beach in a way that looked most random. He placed the dagger under the palm fronds and ran down the beach excited with his plan and a new lease on life. He put his arms out and face up as

he collected the falling white flakes from the sky.
He was happy to catch them on his tongue.

LIGHT RISES

He had made it back to the house. He walked through the front gate and to the backyard via the wrap-around balcony. He had a plan. He would somehow lure Lillie out to the beach and kill her there. He had to get her away from this house though. This was her home so she was probably strongest here. He wanted to go to her room and get her now. He could not do that. She would not react well. A pet never wakes its master. The pet only begs its master it does not demand of it. Anyway, it was the middle of the night. She would no doubt be in the backyard soon for her late-night naked frolicking with the moon and nature. The fact that he was thinking strategically was a good sign to him. It meant he was regaining control of his thoughts. He made it to the backyard. The snowfall he had witnessed at the beach and on the run back to the house was nothing compared to what he saw here. It was as if God said, "Snow on this one spot more than any other." Then he noticed the brick oven. It was lit up as a fire was burning bright. He looked up to the top of the chimney and noticed what he had earlier thought of as snow was billowing from the top of the chimney. That was not snow. It was ash.

He rushed over to the oven itself and looked inside, covering his face as it was blasted with heat. He saw what looked very much like two skeletal remains. He was hit by a massive number of memories. It was as if there was a movie playing out of him. He was watching himself from a third-person perspective. He could see Lillie putting him under her trance. He watched himself twitch and convulse as she whispered things in his ear. He could see himself bound up and suspended as she decorated him with rope. He watched himself enjoy it with a stupid schoolboy grin on his face. He punched himself in frustration. "Oh, how could you have been so stupid?" Then a final memory popped in his head. He was in a cellar as Jeff and Todd were being chopped up violently by Lillie. Only it was not her that did the chopping. It was him. He was very angry now. He wanted to run to the cellar, grab that ax and kill her now. But he could not. This was her home. This was where she had the most power over him. He had to be patient and stick to the plan.

For what seemed like a couple of hours, Jayden had been sitting on the back porch looking out over the yard. It may have not been a couple of hours, but it was long enough for the fire in the brick oven to have burned down to a glow.

He had spent the time stewing in silence waiting for the bitch to come into the yard. He would convince her that he had something to profess to her. He would tell her it was something of great importance. It could not wait. He knew her mind. She had put her mind inside of his after all. He knew that if she thought he had something to profess to him she would assume he wanted to give himself body, mind, and soul to her. That is all she wanted from him anyway. He was nothing to her. He was just another soul to collect in the barn and cellar. He knew this because her thoughts were his thoughts. He would play to her ego. This would require the best poker face ever. It would require one hell of an acting job.

He was focused on his thoughts and only his thoughts. Any other thoughts in his mind would be blank. He must strongly hold on to his righteous thoughts to keep the evil of Lillie out of his mind. He was not hers. He was his own. He had the power within to make the evil that had been implanted to turn on itself. He conditioned himself to believe in and to stay true to himself. Resistance to her was not futile. It was possible.

He must not obey. He must not accept. Her words, her awful trigger words meant nothing to him. He implanted these affirmations into his head just as she had implanted her words into his mind. He was bound to become a better version of what she had made him. He was not perfectly righteous. He knew that. He would have to use evil to beat the evil. Evil does not always play by the rules. He was going to have to break some rules. He was about to commit murder. Murder is evil. But he would use this evil to create a better good in the world. By committing this act of evil he would save future souls from falling prey to her evil. He most certainly was not of the light, but he was no longer of the dark. He would be grey. He was the balance between light and dark that would make things right. This was the choice he had made. He was one with himself.

While he waited for her to come outside he played what was now his now third-person memories over in his head. He studied these memories like an actor who studies a script. He wanted to behave and act as if everything were normal. He had to know the mindless Jayden as well as he knew himself. He had to convince her to walk on the beach, away from the house. He heard her footsteps in the kitchen. He took a deep breath. In his head, he could almost picture himself on a movie set. He saw a movie director looking at him through an imaginary screen that he made with his hands. The director said, "Okay, picture this. Your name is Jayden. You are a mindless pervert that gets off on a Temptress saying simple words and phrases to you. Ready on sound, ready on tape. Here we go, folks." Another man that was holding a clapperboard dryly said, "Finale scene. Jayden lures Lillie to the beach. Take one." There was the sound of a loud single clap. The director pointed at Jayden as he said, "Lights, Camera, and…action!" Lillie walked through the door and looked at Jayden as she smiled and said, "My sweet boy." He faked a body twitch and said, "Yes Temptress."

She walked onto the balcony and looked down at him sitting in a chair.

"My sweet boy. You have done so well. You are my best subject ever. You have become a better version of yourself." Lillie said to Jayden as he looked up to her with eager eyes of admiration.

"Thank you, Temptress."

She put her hand to his face and caressed under his chin. He looked up to her with puppy dog eyes and said, "Temptress, I have a favor to ask if I may." She looked to him with a bit of dismay in her eyes. "Silly pet. You do not make any requests of me. You are mine. Remember? You have no requests as your thoughts are the thoughts that I implant into myself." She paused and continued, "But you have been a good pet. Such a sweet boy. I will at least entertain your request. Tell me, pet. What is it?"

Jayden cleared his throat as he swallowed down some self-confidence. I would very much like to join you tonight for your dance with the moon."

She asked with a playful laugh, "My dance with the moon?"

He said, "Yes. Many times I have watched you out in the yard. You dance with the moon and seem to surround yourself with nature. It reminds me of the time you taught me to be one with nature in the yard."

She took a quick pause as she asked, "You remember that?" Realizing he had just made a slip he thought quickly to get out of that.

"Yes, my thoughts are the ones that you put in my head. I remember all of your lessons. I remember all that you have done to make me a version of myself. It is how I remain your loyal subvariant. Because I am yours."

"Go on, my pet."

"Thank you, my Temptress. I want to become one with nature again. I enjoyed that lesson. I want to take it all in once again."

She looked to him inquisitively and said, "You are in luck, my sweet boy. I was just about to do just that. I do not see any harm in allowing you to join me. Come with me."

"Wait."

"what?" She asked

"I don't want to do it here. I want to do it out on the beach."

"Why the beach? What is wrong with here? Do you feel this is not good enough?"

She reached down toward his lap and rubbed her hand over his crotch. Her cleavage was very revealing to any sort of reward that could be coming his way. He could feel himself swell under his pants. It was not the swell of a subvariant under the command of his master though. It was the body's natural reaction to being touched and rubbed in that spot. His body would have reacted this way under normal conditions. He was still in control.

Keeping to his script but also trying to still sound like a mindless subvariant he said, "Your yard is perfect my Temptress. I love it here. I enjoy being anywhere you are. I live to make you happy. I do feel at one with the water though. I feel a special lightness with sand under my feet. I was hoping that being there could help me get to the next level. I want to get to a higher level for you. I want to be able to serve you better. I want to make you happy. When you are happy, I feel bliss. I want to achieve ultimate bliss. Plus there is something I must confess, or profess to you."

Lillie starred into his eyes for what seemed like forever. His heart pounded with a heavy beat. What would her response be? Would she beat him? Would she punish him? He grew nervous as his plan seemed to meet its failure.

She smiled. "Okay, my pet. I will take you to the beach. But first, you must do something for me. I will be right back."

He sat in the chair wondering what was next. Was she on to him? What was her bargaining chip going to be? He clasped his hands together tightly and nervously. He then released the tight grip as he told himself to remain calm and stick to the plan. He must not falter. He must not let this go on. He looked up into the yard as he saw the little girl in the white dress. She was standing in the middle of the yard. With her hands, she was making a "keep going" gesture. He nodded his head up and down. She then put her fingers to her mouth and he could somehow hear her make the sound of, "ssshhh." Then she vanished into thin air.

Lillie returned to the porch and stood before Jayden with a mug. It was a mug filled with her tea no doubt. That sweet magical tea would sweep him into a deep trance. He had enough control of his thoughts to continue this mission. He had enough control to overcome Lillie and her words. He could not resist the power of that tea though. He knew that if he drank from that mug, it was over. She handed Jayden the mug and said, "This will help you in your lesson at the beach. This will help you elevate yourself in your enlightenment. You will feel bliss at the beach if you drink this. Imagine pure bliss. Obey." He grabbed the mug. How was he going to get out of this? He had not planned for this type of counterattack. He should have. He knew her mind as her mind was his mind. His thoughts were her thoughts. How could he not see this coming? There was no plan B for this. As he slowly put the mug to his mouth there was a slight and sudden cold breeze. For a split second, he saw the little girl in the white dress. She made a snap with her fingers.

Lillie looked down at her pet as he put the mug to his mouth. She felt a sudden chill as a quick and sudden breeze swept across the porch. She heard what sounded like a twig snapping in the yard. She turned around and saw nothing. There was no one there.

Just as Jayden had put the mug to his mouth and the chill had hit the air, Lillie had turned completely around. She seemed startled. She seemed surprised. All of her attention was on the yard. It was only for one second. This was long enough for Jayden to do what came next. As she turned her attention to the backyard, he dumped the tea in a flowerpot next to the chair he was sitting in. He then put the mug back to his mouth. As Lillie turned back to him, he looked up to her with anticipation. He looked to her eager for direction.

She put her hands over his hands that held the mug full of the tea that would fill him with warm tingles and thoughts. She tilted the mug into his mouth and instructed him to drink. He acted as if the mug were full and faked drinking tea and swallowing. He was thinking of himself as such a good actor. He must have been. She smiled as he took down the imaginary tea from the empty mug. She started to speak to him in a provocative tone.

"My sweet boy. Remember what it is like to feel completely relaxed. You remember and because you remember, it is easy for you to drop, deeper, for me. The more you hear my words the easier it is for you to drop, deeper. The deeper you drop the more you drip."

She continued to go through her spiel laced with trigger words designed to put him under her control. These were the words she had implanted in his mind to make him a better version of himself. Jayden feigned body twitches with a faux look of bliss on his face. He knew what the words were supposed to do to him. He acted out those reactions like a pro. As she began to count him out of a trance, she told him he was a good pet that must always obey. She asked him, "My sweet boy. Are you sure you want to walk to the beach? We can simply achieve everything you want here in my backyard."

Jayden looked at her with a glazed look of happiness on his face as he dryly said, "Yes, yes, please." He repeated this phrase in a way that it was said to a rhymical pattern. She then reached to a table that was next to the chair as she said, "Okay pet. I will take you for a walk. But like any pet, you must be on a leash." From the table, she had taken a leash. It was a thin chain attached to a leather collar. She put the leather securely around his neck then pulled on the chain. She said, "Get up, pet. Obey." Jayden stood up as if under her spell and awaited her next instruction with anticipation. Lillie tugged on the chain as she said, "Come, my pet, it is time for your walk."

Jayden left the yard and on to a trail that would take them to the beach. He did this under the lead of Lillie as she tugged on the leash that bound him to her. His plan was working, as far as he knew.

DROP. DEEPER.

Lillie walked on the beach as she tightly held the leash around Jayden's neck. The night was clear and every star in the sky could be seen. Moonlight splashed off the calm waves as they lightly caressed the sand on the beach with a gentle touch of love as they would slip back into the sea only to come back seconds later for another short tease. Imagine it as a never-ending loop that would repeat itself.

She asked, "You have me out here on this beach. Tell me now my sweet boy? Why did you bring me out to the sea?"
With a sense of nervousness quivering in his voice, he said, "I have something I must profess to you."
She stopped and asked, "This is something that could not be professed at the house?"
"I wanted to be out here, in nature. I wanted to take in the strength of mother nature to give me the power to profess what I must. Just as you have taught me to do my Temptress."
"Be a sweet boy and tell me this now."
He looked at her with intense admiration. He looked her deep in the eyes with passion and said, "I want to profess my never-ending devotion to you Temptress. My devotion to making you happy. Because when you are happy, I am happy.

And my only pleasure comes from pleasing you. I want to be your pet."

She laughed. "You are such a sweet boy. You already are my devoted pet. I already own you. What is there to profess that has not already been done?"

"I am your pet yes. But I want to be your forever pet. Never to leave the binds you have put around me. Your binds give me security. I will never return to the mainland. I want to devote the rest of my life to serving you in any way you see fit."

A grin hit her face and her lips curled up. She looked at him and said, "So be it…PET!" She put her hands on his shoulders and thrust him down to the ground on his knees. Keeping a hand on the top of his head she said, "Profess pet. Profess your devotion to your Temptress. Your Goddess of bliss."

"I profess to be forever loyal to you Goddess Temptress. I swear my devotion to you and will do whatever your bidding asks."

She said, "Not like that. Profess only as a pet should." She shoved his head to the ground. Worship me. Praise me. Honor me. Lick my feet."

She smiled as she looked down at her subservient. He groveled like a dog at her feet just as he should. She felt great pleasure in watching him kiss and worship the feet that carried her. She had molded his little mind exactly where she wanted it. She shoved the front of her foot into his mouth as he almost gagged. She said in a powerful voice, "Do not gag on the feet that you worship. Suck on my toes. You cannot get enough of them. You want more. You need more, pet! Obey!"

She looked down on him as his master. She watched as he sucked on her toes as if it were the best candy he had ever eaten. She pulled her foot away from him and he looked at her in a panic. "Oh don't worry little one. We are not done yet. She took a step back as she took her clothing off. First, she unbuttoned her top and let it slide off of her back as it hit the sand behind her. She then removed her tight jeans. As she slid them off, her thick thighs were revealed to Jayden. She could see his eyes open wide with anticipation. She looked down to him with scorn as he begged her to keep going. She said, "Let me hear your devotion to me."

With deep breaths, he swore to her that she was his Goddess. She was all that mattered in the universe. His praise was building her up and filling her head. She slid off her panties she rubbed them hard in his face. She said, "You want what these cover. You need what these cover.

You need my juices in your mouth. You want my juices as you want my tea. You cannot survive without them. Are you a good boy?"

On his knees, before her, he said, "Yes Goddess Temptress. Bless me with your juices." She grabbed the back of his head and forced his face between her thighs. She looked down at him and laughed as her submissive pet was butter in her fingertips. She commanded that he lick deeper and he did. For a pet, he was pretty good at this. She said, "I think from now on I am going to call you slut. You seem to enjoy this in a way that only a slut would. Are you my slut?" He said "Yes Goddess Temptress." She smacked the back of his head as she said, "Don't talk now. You may only answer by nodding your head up and down slut." She forced his head up and down as she asked. "Do you understand?" He moved his head up and down at a fevered pitch. She put her hand on his forehead and pushed him away. Still on his knees before her, he gazed up to her as he wiped his mouth. She gave him a powerful backhanded slap across the face. She told him. "Do not wipe my juices away! My juices are a delicacy to you. You need them. She rubbed herself, getting her hand wet, and rubbed it in his face as she commanded him to lick her fingers.

With two fingers under his chin, she pulled him off the ground. She instructed him to take off his shirt and he did without hesitation. She grabbed him by the back of his head as she pulled him in toward her chest. She told him, "Worship me, my slut. Worship me, as only my slut would know-how." His face was buried in her chest. He would lick and suck on both of her breasts as if it were the last chance he would ever have to do so. She pulled him in tight. He felt as if he could not breathe. If these were his final moments, asphyxiation was not a bad way to go. He started to suck hard on her nipples. She would let out her moans and tell him to bite. When he bit he could feel her fingernails go down his back. They were sharp. He felt as if eight separate razors were digging into his back. It was a pleasurable pain that was followed by the warmness of his blood dripping down his back. She would rub a hand across his back and lick the blood off of her fingers and palms.

Without warning, she pushed him away and stood back. She looked at him. She was excited that he could only look to her in anticipation of what she would have him do next. She told him to remove his pants. He did as he put them down on the sand next to his feet. She told him to lay down on his back. As he lay in the sand, he tilted his head back and tried to look behind him. He was looking for a pile of palm fronds on the beach. He knew they should be there because he had put them there himself only hours ago. When they walked onto the beach he had manipulated them to this specific spot for good reason. This was all done under the guise that she was the one that had chosen this spot. He was a clever boy. He rolled his eyes back as far as he could and noticed he was about six inches short of the fronds. He wiggled himself back so that they were under his head. She looked down at him and said, "I suppose I can allow that. You have been such a sweet boy I will allow you a little bit of comfort. You may use those fronds as a pillow if you choose. You are my sweet boy. She could see his body convulse as she said that. "You have made me very happy. I think I am going to reward you with something no pet has ever been given before." He had her exactly where he wanted her. She was correct in her statement though. She was about to break a cardinal rule of being a Temptress. No Temptress would ever even consider having sex with a subservient. Especially one that was human. Subservient human seemed like such an oxymoron. Perhaps just this once would be okay. He was a pet as just any other pet. One day he would be replaced. For this one moment though, she would break the rules and allow him to have her. Evil has been known to sometimes break the rules.

She straddled herself over his hips. She looked at him and said, "You are already dripping. That is good. Such a sweet boy. The more you drip. The more you drop… Deeper!" She snapped her fingers hard.

He was quivering. She said, "You are not going to get off so easy slut. You are going to do all the work from where you lay. I will sit on top of you till you make me happy. Do you want to make me happy?" He said, "Yes, yes, please."
She grabbed his penis and inserted it into herself as she slid down onto him.
"Now I want you to thrust for me." He complied. She would tell him he was a good boy. She did this because every time she said the phrase he would thrust into her twice as hard as the time before. She kept praising him as each praise made him go faster and harder. She felt exhilarated with the power she held over him. She felt greedy for power and the greed felt good.

He could tell he was close to climax. He could feel it coming up in his body. He must hold on. He must go longer. He must not orgasm till she did. He thrust into her harder and faster than ever before. She seemed to enjoy it this way. He needed to bring her to climax, and he did. It came almost without warning. She tilted her head back as she seemed to howl. From her mouth came screams of pleasure. Some were high pitched and some sounded like a growl. He wanted this to go on longer. Could a life like this be so bad? To give it up seemed maddening. But he was also drawn to the praise of a manifestation off to the side in the bushes that only he could see. They both knew what he must do. He knew what must be done because this could not go on.

As she reached her peak of climax she started to thrust hard herself as she closed her eyes and said in a low voice, "I honor you with this seed my dark Lord, I bequeath you with this gift." With her eyes shut, Jayden had his chance. He reached his hand over his shoulder to the palm fronds. He grabbed the dagger he had hidden there earlier. The power of his orgasm made it nearly impossible to get a firm grip on the knife. He looked into the face of evil and found strength provided by his inner righteous self. As the sharp blade of the dagger created a wide gap across her throat he could feel his hot juices continue to build in his shaft as they dropped, deeper from his tip to the inside of her.

    She opened her eyes only in time to see a flash of the moon reflecting off the blade coming at her. She had no time to react or protect herself. She felt the blade cut deep into her neck as searing hot blood splattered out to the pet below her. She smiled as it was almost a pleasurable pain. Her eyes rolled to the back of her head as she collapsed onto her subservient, still inside of her, while she gagged on her blood.

    Jayden pushed her heavy body off him and stood up and wiped his face. He put his clothes back on and looked around. In the trees, he could see the manifestation of his good self. She was still dressed in her Sunday's best. He looked at her and yelled out, "So are we all good?" She answered back to him in a whisper that he could somehow hear and said, "Finish the job." He looked down at the corpse of Lillie. He knew what the manifestation was talking about. There was still much to be done.

DARKNESS FALLS

He ran through the woods and back to the house. He knew all that must be done. This had to all be erased. He ran into the house and down to the cellar. He pulled the chain on the light as he ran down the stairs. It reeked of death down there. He wondered how he could have never noticed that before. Dried blood was all over the cement floor. He could hear voices. It was a mixture of many voices overlapping each other. Some were far away and muffled. Others sounded as if they were next to him whispering. Some were there to support him. He could hear them say, "Finish the job. Release us. Burn it all down." Others wanted to bring him harm. He figured they were the ones that were close by. He could feel them. It was not in just a mere feeling of their presence. He could physically feel as if fingers were poking at him. Poking at his ribs in a very uncomfortable manner. He tried to brush the invisible hands and fingers away from him as he screamed to get off of him. He frantically looked around the room. He would open a closet door and be starring at a variety of sexual devices. He would see ropes, whips, chains, and a collection of knives. He saw things that he could not even begin to figure out what they would be used for. No doubt they had been used on him down there in Lillie's dungeon.

He could not remember. He yelled out, "Come on! Help me out.
Gas! Anything that starts a fire." A cabinet in the far corner opened on its own. A voice said, "Finish it. Burn it do the ground." He ran to the cabinet and saw a gasoline tank. He whispered, "Please be full." He started to spill it on the floor. He put the tank down on the ground as he felt his pockets and yelled, "Fuck!" A book of matches fell of a table filled with candles. "Thank you!" he yelled out. He nervously fiddled with the matchbook. He lit a match and it instantly went out as he felt a blast of air go across his hand. "Oh fuck you. That's how you want to play?" He stuffed the matchbook in his pants pocket and grabbed a handful of candles off of the table. He picked up the gas can and ran to the top of the stairs. He felt hands trying to grab at his ankles. They could not manifest enough to get a firm grip.

He stood at the top of the stairs as he lit a match and put it to a candle. He tossed down into the cellar and watched the floor ignite. He could hear screams coming from the cellar below. He watched as shadows seem to sink into any darkness they could find. White dots of light whisked by him quickly as he could swear he heard them give him thanks and tell him to finish the job. Do what had to be done. He dumped gasoline in every room on the first floor. He made sure to save some. There was still the barn. He lit another candle as he stood at the front door and tossed it into the house. He did light another and threw that in as well. As they rolled across the floor, a fire had started.

He took his gas can and ran down the hill toward the barn. He could hear the drums beat an angry and furious beat. He opened the door and went in to finish the job. He felt a large overwhelming presence at the door. It made the air thick. He could not walk in. He felt himself get physically shoved back. They knew what he had done. The word was out. Bad news travels fast in herds. He could hear angry voices tell him he must die. He was not getting in, that much was for sure. He edged his way around outside of the barn as he poured out the remaining gasoline on the outer walls. He only was able to make it a quarter way around before running out of gasoline. He lit a match held it to a wet part of the wall. It went up immediately and some flame caught his hand. He dropped the can and remaining candles as he ran away from the barn. Pausing only once to turn around and watch as it started to burn. He ran out across the field and into the woods. He followed a trail and was on the beach. Running across the beach he could see the two boats. He ran to the boat he had come in and quickly untied the line from the tree. He fumbled with the knots he had tied earlier and cursed at himself for making such intricate knots…and so many of them. Then he paused. He looked down at his pants and laughed as he looked up at the sky. It was not a funny laugh. It was the laugh of a hopeless situation. He already knew the answer to what he was thinking. These were not the clothes he wore out here. He had to check anyway. He reached in both pockets. Just as he suspected, they were empty. What he was looking for, what he needed was in the shorts he had worn out her that were now trapped under a burning inferno that he had started. He cursed himself for being so careless. He had planned this out so perfectly. Right down to the last detail. Except for one important one. That would be the key to the boat. Why did he not just leave the key with the boat? He went down to one knee and tried to think. He looked up and saw his answer. The other boat that Jeff and Todd had come on. He looked to the sky and said, "Oh please Jesus, let there be keys there. If there are keys to that boat I swear I will go to church every Sunday. He got on the boat and frantically searched every inch. There were no keys. He was stuck on an island that according to locals did not exist. He was stuck on this island with a few dead bodies and a lot of angry restless souls.

He walked down the beach. He looked down with a defeated purpose. He ran through his plan in his head trying to figure out how he could have forgotten about such an important detail. Then another detail hit him that he had forgotten about. He stopped dead in his tracks as he said out loud, "No, it is not possible." Of course, with everything he has experienced since meeting this woman, anything was possible. He started to fear that he would go back to where he left Lillie and she would miraculously be gone. Just like in the movies when the protagonist leaves the body of the killer behind only to later find their body missing. He went into an immediate run in the direction of where he had left her body. He was so focused on the thought of his antagonist getting up from death and now stalking him around the island for the final kill that he almost did not notice her as he nearly tripped over the dead body. He looked over her and said, "Nope. Still there, just as I left you."

Jayden continued to look at her dead naked body. It was laid on the beach naked with its throat slashed open. He studied her hard. She was beautiful still. Despite being evil and dead. Sexy would be a better word. He could see how he had fallen for her so hard. Every detail of her naked body had so much appeal to it.

He sat down on the sand next to her. He sat with his legs crossed, his arms resting on his legs with his hands clasped together. He stared into the air in front of him. He looked at her. He reached over and touched her belly and gently rubbed it with his hand. He tried to think about how he had allowed himself into this situation. She was beautiful, that's how. But how did it all happen? Was it that magic tea she was feeding him? What had been in that? What else had she made him take? Was it the trigger words and phrases he had allowed her to put into his head? Or was it something as simple as her being intoxicatingly gorgeous?

He reached over and grabbed her hand. He pulled her body over, partially onto him as he lay back into the sand. There he was, laying on a beach with Lillie as she rested her head on his chest and had a hand on his chest. He held her in his arms and ran his fingers through her hair as he looked up at the cloud cover that was glowing orange from the fires below. He tilted his head as he kissed her on the cheek. He closed his eyes and he dropped, into a deep sleep.

A DAY ON THE BEACH

The beach was crawling with investigators, police, medical personal, and coast guard. Many boats along with two helicopters had parked on the beach. This would probably turn into one of the most bizarre cases any of them had worked. The only survivor sat on a large rock formation wrapped in an olive drab military blanket. He was surrounded by investigators as they tried to conduct an on-site investigation. As they would ask questions his mind would drift off as he would look over to Lillie. She was still on the beach as well. There were a few investigators that took pictures of her from every angle.

Further down the beach an officer stood by two boats that had been pulled up to shore and tied off to trees. The boats had the markings of Mitchel Boat Rental. The officer looked directly at a man standing in front of him. He asked, "Mr. Mitchel, these are your boats?"
"Yes officer, These are mine. I am Dan Mitchel, the owner of Mitchel Boat Rental and those are my boats. Can I see my boy now?"
The officer said, "Mr. Mitchel, your boy's body is currently part of a crime scene. Can you tell me again what he was doing here?"
Dan Mitchel was visibly upset as he said, "Listen I've answered all of your questions

multiple times already. My boy, Todd, and his friend Jeff…Have Jeff's parents been notified yet?"

"They have Mr. Mitchel. You were saying your son Todd and his friend Jeff were what?"

Dan said, "They were taking a boat out for sea trials and they were going to do some fishing. That was the last I heard from them. It was the middle of the night I had not heard from him. So I came down to the shop to at least see if the boat was there and he was back. The boat was not there and I found another boat missing. I called the coast guard and gave them the tracking information on the boats. I have GPS tracking beacons on all of my boats. They called me and told me they had found the boats. I came out to retrieve them and I find this mess and all of you out here. Where is my boy? I want to see my boy! What the hell is going on here?"

A detective came over and pulled the officer aside as he whispered something to him. He nodded his head up and down as he said, "Yes ma'am." The officer came back to Dan and said, "Mr. Mitchel. Thank you for your time and patience. This is Detective Paris, she will take you up to the house."

The morning sun was bright on Jayden's eyes as investigators seemed to repeat the same questions and phrases differently. It was almost like when Lillie would put him under trance. He could vaguely remember it sounding like her voice overlapping itself as she would implant multiple phrases in his head. This was pretty much the same. Except for in this moment, there was no bliss. He was distracted as he squinted into the sun and looked down at the beach. There was a woman in a suit that had just gotten off a boat. She was raising quite the commotion. The woman had taken something out of her pocket and shown it to those trying to stop him from going any further. They then pointed in the direction of the investigation.

She approached the investigators and said, "Ah hello. Excuse me. Hello? Where is Jayden Pink?" The woman in the suit looked at the man wrapped in the olive drab military blanket and asked, "Are you Jayden Pink?" Without saying a word Jayden nodded his head up and down. An officer stepped in front of the man and said, "Excuse me Ma'am, who are you? This is a closed investigation site."
The woman in the suit presented a card to the officer as he said, "I am Gabriella Perez-Ruiz,

attorney at law and this man you are questioning is my client. She leaned into Jayden as handed him a card and said, "Hi Jayden, don't say another word to these people. I've got this. We are going to get you off this beach." Jayden looked to Gabriella as he shook his head back and forth and said, "I can't afford an attorney." Gabriella told him, "Don't worry Jayden, we are going to take your case pro bono. Do you accept me as your legal representation?" Jayden looked at the business card and nodded his head up and down. The attorney turned to the officers and said, "Okay, this man is my client and you cannot be speaking to him now. You will get him cleaned up and you may continue this investigation in a more suitable location with me by his side." She looked back to Jayden and said, "Remember, not one more word to them till you and I have had a chance to talk. I will see you later." She walked away and was seen talking to someone who appeared to be in charge of the scene for only about a minute. The man who seemed to be in charge approached the interrogation area and announced, "Okay, listen up. There will be no more questioning for now. Mrs. Perez-Ruiz is going to escort Mr. Pink back to the station. Officer Reed and Detective Ramirez, would you travel with them please?" The detective and officer got on the boat with Jayden and his attorney. They sped off in the direction of Isla de Cabeza Martillo.

MADNESS

Gabriella Perez-Ruiz sat at her table in the courtroom next to her client, Jayden Pink. She sat with her hands clasped so they would not shake. She was nervous. She was a great defense attorney with an almost flawless record. This case was going to be a challenging one for her. She knew this. If it had been up to her, she would not have taken this. It was her firm that assigned this to her. They were doing it pro-bono and her boss saw this case as one with potential for headlines. He believed that she could win this one. If she did, that would mean great things for the firm. She thought about the charges against her client. Three brutal murders, double arson, boat theft, and rape. Rape, that must have been another reason the firm chose her to represent this case. It would not look good in a jury's eyes if it were a man standing up for another man accused of rape. Perhaps if the jury saw that it was a woman defending his words that there must be room for forgiveness. She did not have a lot going in her favor though. The one thing she did have is that her client's story was unbelievably insane. It was something that could only be perceived in a movie. If this were to happen in real life, the only explanation is that the person is insane. That was her angle. That is how she was pleading this case. That is how she would win.

Her thoughts were interrupted as a bailiff announced the entrance of the judge. "All rise! For the honorable Justice Ronald Henderson. This is for case number 0731981. The State of Florida vs. Jayden Pink." Every person in the courtroom stood as the judge entered. He came from a room in the far corner and walked directly to his desk. He sat and instructed everyone to be seated. Looking at the bailiff he said, "Thank you." He introduced the case as he read from papers that he produced from a manilla folder then gave counsel on both sides instructions on how he expected his courtroom to be run. After that, he looked to those gathered in attendance and reminded them that this is a court of law, not a circus. Everyone must always remain quiet. Any distractions would result in contempt of court. He then asked the bailiff to bring in the jury. Twelve people entered the room. They were a balanced mixture of gender and races. Judge Henderson then instructed the jury on the case they were about to hear. He said, "You will make your final decision based on the facts of the case. You will also go by the law that I give you and not the law that you think you may know. As a reminder, the state is perusing the death penalty. It is imperative that you listen to all the facts and take the time to reach your decision. For a death sentence to be reached there must be a unanimous agreement. As a reminder, what goes on in my court, stays in my court. That means you do not talk about this case with your friends, family, or media. You do not talk about it as you are walking around this courthouse. You are not allowed to discuss this case with each other till both sides have had a chance to present their closing statements. You may not post about this case on social media. Failure to follow any of my instructions will result in your expulsion from the jury and you may also receive contempt of court. Does everyone understand?" He paused. "I need to see everyone's head move up and down. Does everyone understand?" The entire jury, most of whom had never done this before, and were unsure how to reply nodded their heads up and down in silence. "Good. Before we begin, during jury selection you all have been given the non-specifics of this case. You know the charges and you know that the state will be recommending the death penalty. You all have already been asked this by Judge Cune during the selection process and I will ask again. Is there anyone that believes they will not be able to sit on this jury for religious or medical reasons? Should this be you, please raise your hand." The jury sat in motionless silence. The judge shuffled his papers onto his desk and looked to the courtroom as he said, "Would the state please make your opening statement."

A man in a suit walked from his table in the courtroom. He was tall with dark hair. It was peppered with specs of grey and he was cleanly shaven. His suit was not flashy, but it was not cheap. He stood before the judge as he said, "Thank you, your honor." Then he turned to the jury.

"Ladies and gentlemen. Thank you for your time. You are here today to listen to the facts of a brutal murder gone horribly wrong. Not just one murder, but three. Three separate murders of the most heinous degree. I will be straight-up honest with you. The facts that will be presented to you, in this case, will be graphic. The murders committed by the accused were completed most horrifically. I will not be sugarcoating this for you. I cannot, for all I must present to you are the facts. I am here to present to you the facts of not only three separate murders, but also two charges of arson, one of grand theft of a water vessel, and rape. These occurrences all took place. They are irrefutable. Let us go over these facts. The defendant killed his two friends. But wait, he did not just kill them. It was a brutal murder with no remorse. The accused used an ax to kill his friends, his friends. After that, he chopped the bodies of his friends into pieces and threw them into a BBQ pit in an attempt to burn them beyond recognition. Thankfully it takes more heat than a BBQ pit can produce to cremate a human body, otherwise, we would not know what had happened to these two, fine, young boys that were upstanding members of the community. The third murder was even more disturbing than the first two. He took a dagger and savagely cut the throat of the property owner. He committed this disturbing act on this innocent woman's property, her private island. He then raped her. Or did he rape her before the murder? I apologize for being so graphic. I know these images cannot be easy for you to imagine. I am sorry, but these are the facts. He then with no rhyme or reason took it upon himself to burn her barn and house to the ground. Let's not forget, to even get to the island, he stole a boat. He stole a boat from the company that is owned by his friend's dad. This friend is one of the same young men that he wickedly murdered with an ax. I have not even yet gotten to the worse part. The part that will show this was all done with no remorse. I will show, by way of facts, that the defendant was discovered on the beach, sleeping on his back. He had the naked body of the deceased, the lifeless body of a defenseless woman with her throat slashed wide open draped over himself in a cuddling fashion. I will show you that traces of his semen were found inside her body. This will indicate the rape. As if a disgusting hate-induced murder was not enough, he had to defile this lady in her final moments on earth. These are the facts. Facts do not lie. Now, the defense over here, she is going to try, try her best to paint you a picture of a young boy gone wrong. She is going to try and convince you that he is insane and had no idea what he was doing. She will try her best to teach you something called hypnotism. Yes, ladies and gentlemen. Hypnotism. The same thing that you have seen magicians use on stage to make people dance like chickens. She is also going to try and get you to humanize this vile man. She will tell you that he could be any one of us. Make no mistake, he is not a part of this community. He is not one of you. He is not human. He is a demonic man with nothing but pure evil on his mind. That is why the state will be asking you, as unpleasant as it may seem, to put this man, this man who came from somewhere else and murdered some of our own, to death. These are the facts, this is why you are today."

The prosecutor clasped his hands together and did an almost about-face movement from the jury as he walked back to his desk. It was now time for the defense to make her opening statement. Gabriella approached the bench and said, "Thank you, your honor." She then approached the jury.

"Good morning folks. I thank you for being here today. My name is Gabriella and this young man sitting over here is Jayden. Yes, he has a name. It is not, the defendant. It is not the accused, nor is he a brutal demon. He has a name. His name is Jayden. That is one tactic that the state is going to use on you in this case. They already have. They are going to dehumanize Jayden to you. If you do not think of him as human, it will be easier for you to put this young man to death. They are also going to use the word, facts, a lot. They will drill that word into your brain. They are also going to use many", she paused as she appeared to think for a couple of seconds, "colorful adjectives in front of the word, facts. They will use words like; brutal, vicious, and heinous. This is not mad-libs ladies and gentlemen. Listen to the facts, yes, I ask of you to please ignore the adjectives. It is a mind trick the prosecution will use on you to trigger or implant thoughts in your head. It is a clever way for them to tell you, their story. Remember a time that you have been seduced into buying snacks at the theater. Because you remember this, you will be able to see that the state is using subtle tricks of the mind to trick you into buying their story.

Ticks of the mind. That is what this case is truly about. Jayden has been accused of triple murder, arson, boat theft, and rape. This case is not about whether he did all of those things. I will tell you right now, he did. All of those except the rape. We will circle back to that later. Right now, know that, yes. He did commit a triple murder, he did steal a boat, and he did burn down two buildings. Now that we have that out of the way, we can focus on the why.

Jayden is not a demonic murderer with a thirst for blood. He is an easily influenced young boy whose mind was corrupted by a woman who does represent evil. Try to remember when you were young. Remember to a time when you have not yet settled into your thoughts and beliefs on life. What would it be like to be that person now? A person that is naïve and trusting to the world around them. Just pretend that you are not old enough yet to have determined who you are. Once you can imagine that person you will realize that you were also at one time, easily influenced by those around you with more experience in life. Because you can picture that person you will begin to realize that any young mind can be coerced into another's bidding. The more you think about this, the more realize it to be true. You will realize that this could happen to anyone. Any person could have their thoughts stripped from them without any knowledge of their own. It could happen to you. It has happened to you. Remember any time that you have bought a product because you have seen it advertised in repetition. The words that the advertiser used to trigger thoughts in your brain are what drove you to that purchase.

It goes much deeper than that in the case of poor Jayden here though. We are not talking about making a purchase because of slick advertising. We are talking about a young boy whose mind was taken over by evil and was forced to do acts his innocent, young mind would not normally allow him to do. We will show you, through facts," She paused as she turned away from the jury and looked towards the prosecution, "that young and easily influenced Jayden had his mind warped by one much stronger and experienced than his own. We will show you, that his mind was seduced by not only trance-inducing drugs but by something much more powerful. It is called hypnotherapy. Through facts and science, we will show you that hypnotherapy was used to take over Jayden's mind and remove him from his cognizance.

As for the rape. There was rape. Contrary to what the state says, it was Jayden that was raped. Not only by the body but of his mind. Through forensic evidence, we will show you that by use of hypnotherapy and drugs that Jayden was raped. This case is not as simple as it has been just made to sound. It is not a matter of did he do it? It is a matter of why he did it."

Dr. Kasim took the witness stand and was sworn in and verified by the judge as an expert in her field.

The prosecutor approached the witness stand and asked said, "Dr. Kasim, you are a doctor for the NCAA and it is your job to test student-athletes for anabolic steroids. Is that correct?"

"Yes."

"You were responsible for testing Jayden and his teammates. Is that also correct?"

"Yes."

"As required by the NCAA, Jayden was tested after April 5 of this year. Is that correct?"

"Yes."

"Were the results of Jayden's test, positive for use of anabolic steroids?"

"No."

"Did you find traces of any other drugs in his body, such as LSD or other mind-altering drugs?"

"No."

The prosecution thanked the doctor and Gabriella approached the witness stand.

"Dr. Kasim, you said that there were no traces of mind-altering drugs found in Jayden."

"That is correct."

"Does that mean they unquestionably were not there?"

"Unquestionably. No."

"Why is that Doctor?"

"We are only looking for anabolic steroid use. We are not looking for anything else."

"Why do you only look for steroid use, Doctor? Are you not supposed to be checking on the student athlete's health?"

"We only look for performance-enhancing drugs. Checking for anything else in a student athletes' system could affect a potential professional career if anything were found and they lost their position on a team. It could result in lawsuits."

"So, when you state that no mind-altering drugs were found inside of Jayden, you do not mean that they were not there. You mean you just did not look."

The doctor paused and then said, "That is correct."

"Does that mean that they were not there?"

"Not necessarily."

"Why is that Dr. Kasim?"

"We only test for anabolic steroids. Looking for anything else would open up a whole other can of worms."

"Thank you, Dr. Kasim."

The prosecution approached the stand where Pepper was sitting.

"You and Jayden were dating, yes?"

"I would not say we were dating exactly."

"What would you say it was?"

"I would say it was more like bosom buddies."

There was a low stifle of laugher in the courtroom.

"Bosom buddies?"

"Yes."

"Could you describe what that means exactly?"

"We had sex."

"Sex. So, he could be described as a sexual deviant."

Pepper laughed, "Jayden? Sexual deviant? No. He was actually quite vanilla."

"What do you mean by vanilla.?"

"He was shy in the bedroom. He had to be coaxed."

"And it was you that did the coaxing?"

"Yes."

"Did you use drugs or alcohol to do this coaxing?"

"No."

"Well then, tell us, how did you two become bosom buddies if he was, vanilla."

With a smile, Pepper waved her hand across her face as she said, "Look at me."

There was more stifled laughter in the courtroom as the judge reminded those in attendance to remain quiet.

It was now time for Gabriella to ask her questions of the witness.
"Pepper, you described your relationship with, Jayden as bosom buddies."
"Yes."
"That implies that it was nothing more than a sexual relationship."
"Perhaps."
"There are records of conversations via letters and postcards that appear to go much deeper than a relationship much more than just sex."
"Okay."
"Would you care to expand on that?"
"I am not sure what you mean."
"Reading over the letters and postcards it appears that the two of you had more than just a sexual relationship. It appears that there were feelings on both sides that go beyond that. Tell me, other than the sex, what else attracted you to Jayden?"
"He was a caring soul with a good heart. He seemed to put the interests of everyone around him before his own. He had a good sense of humor. He also seemed like a natural-born leader

that at the same time was willing to follow and be open to others' thoughts."

"Would you say he was controlling?"

Pepper laughed, "Jayden? Oh no. He was always open to my suggestions. He did everything I asked of him. He was very easy going in that way."

Gabriella continued her line of questioning that would show that Jayden was controlled by Pepper and that there was a relationship that went much deeper than sex.

Both sides had called several witnesses to the stand. One of the star witness was a psychologist. Her testimony took an entire day and it showed him to have dissociative identity. Given the fact that he was hearing voices telling him what to do along with the use of what she referred to as trigger words. He was shown to two or more personality traits. While he was in a state of consciousness and awareness he was also in a state of having fugues. Because of everything his subconscious mind had seen, he was unknowingly suffering from PTSD. The case went back and forth between showing Jayden as a cold-hearted murderer and a man who was a victim of mind-control by a vicious and seductive woman.

After all the witnesses had been questioned, there was one more. It was the one that surprised everyone in the courtroom. It was Jayden.

The prosecution stood before Jayden on the witness stand and asked, "Did you kill your two friends, Jeff and Todd?"
"No, sir."
"You did not? Then why were your prints found on the ax that you used to chop them up?"
"I do not know."

"I suppose you would also have us believe that you did not kill Lillie?"

"It was in self-defense."

"But you were found, cuddling, with her naked body on the beach. Your hands were covered in her blood."

Jayden did not reply.

"Well?"

"Well, what?" Asked Jayden.

"You did not respond to what I said."

"I did not hear a question."

The prosecutor paused, "If you did not kill Jeff and Todd, who did?"

"She did."

"Who is she?"

"Lillie."

"Was that before or after you killed her?"

"Its complicated."

The prosecutor paused again. "Explain why it was your prints that were found on coffee mugs that had traces of ecstasy."

"It was not ecstasy. It was an ancient family recipe put into tea. Oh, I mean…"

Realizing that he had just made it sound as if it was his recipe, he paused and said, "It was a recipe that she had used that altered my mind."

"When you say she, who do you mean?"

"Lillie, she controlled my mind with her tea."

Jayden took a deep breath of frustration. He turned to the judge and asked, "May I just tell you what happened? In my own words? I have a prepared statement that tells what really happened."

Gabriella stood up and said, "Objection, your honor! I have not seen this statement and do not know anything about it." The prosecutor said, "He is still my witness, I have no problem with him reading this statement."
Gabriella pleaded with the judge, "Your honor, I strongly urge the court to allow me time to confer with my client over this. I did not know of this statement and have no idea what is in it." This was not entirely true. She did know of the statement and knew exactly what was in it. It was all part of her plan. She knew that the prosecutor would push Jayden's warped mind and bring him to a point that he would voluntarily bring forth his own words. She knew that the story, in his own words, sounded crazier than anything the defense could bring out of him. By denying her knowledge of this statement, she was committing perjury in a roundabout way, she knew this. To her though, it was worth the risk as it was Jayden's own words that would save him from the death penalty. With a deep breath, the judge

asked, "Would counsel please approach the bench?"

Both the prosecutor and Gabriella approached the bench. The judge turned off his microphone and spoke to both counselors in a hushed conversation that lasted approximately five minutes. Both counsels returned to their desks as the judge announced to the court, "We are going to take a fifteen-minute recess. When we do, Mr. Pink will read from his prepared statement"

Jayden sat at a desk on the defense side of the courtroom. He was dressed in a suit that seemed to be tailored to fit perfectly. No doubt it was picked out by his attorney. He had a nervous look on his face. He leaned into the microphone, cleared his throat, and spoke.

"My name is Jayden. I have heard my story retold from two different angles. I wish to speak to the court today to tell you from my side. My attorney has advised against this, but again, it is important to me that this all be heard from my point of view directly.

This all starts with a visit to the Peeking Islands. Let me say, that I love this community as I have been visiting here all of my life. I consider this my home away from home. I was coming here this time to visit a girl I had met. Her name is, Pepper. On my first day in town, before meeting with Pepper I stopped by Billy's. While I was in there, some of the locals told me about a sixth island in this five-island chain. They called it, David Key. They told me it was a place where either devil worshippers, vampires, or some sort of cult lived. There did not seem to be a consensus among the group. They all seemed to have their own twist on the story. Either way, I took it all as a bunch of locals trying to mess with a tourist. That tourist being me.

Later that evening I met up with Pepper and her friends at a boat ramp by Mitchel's boat rental. We were taking part in a bonfire. I told them about my encounter at Billy's earlier in the day and inquired about this mythical island. They all had their versions of the story as well. I still wrote this off as just a story that people tell. Where I am from, we also have urban legends that are passed down throughout the years. This mythical island they spoke of, supposedly had seven bridges, and if you backtracked where you came from, there would only be six. They also mentioned a barn that would appear out of nowhere along with tribal-like drum music. It had all the makings of a creepypasta. Just like at Billy's, I wrote it off as locals messing with the naive tourist.

After a few drinks and many stories later, it was someone's idea to do a boat race. We used boats from Mitchel's boat rental since Todd Mitchel's dad owned that. During the race, I got left behind by the group lost at sea. It was dark and my GPS was not working. While lost at sea I felt as if I were being stalked by evil forces. I could even see them, hear them, and smell them. One was like a giant Hydra creature with multiple heads. The weather had taken a turn for the worse. It was raining, foggy, and the sky was filled with lightning. I somehow, by the grace of God, hit the shore. I was on land that I did not recognize. I tied my boat up and decided to explore. My line of thinking was that I would come across people that could help me out and direct me back to where I needed to be.

It was while I was walking around the island that I did cross seven bridges. I also heard drum music. I was a little creeped out but thought of it as an odd coincidence. I was not sure if it was real or if my mind was playing tricks on me. My real-world thoughts were that if I heard music, that meant people. People, meant that I could find help. I chose to continue my trek.

I did come across a barn. It appeared that was where the music was coming from. I walked inside the barn and there was not a soul in there. At this point, I was starting to become scared. I was walking around an open field and this is when I met, Lillie.

She took me to her house and gave me a chance to dry my clothes and warm me up by feeding me. It is at this point now, that my memories of everything start to get a little foggy. I did not know it at the time, but Lillie was feeding me tea that had been laced with something that worked as either a hallucinogenic drug or perhaps something that worked like ecstasy. I do not know for sure, and I realize that traces did not show up in my system. That is because whatever she gave me, was something she made herself. It was all-natural herbs as she put it. I spent the next couple of days with her on her island. I did not want to, but at the same time, I felt compelled to. I knew that I should not stick around, but I felt that I must. I felt as if I had two choices between good and evil. Apparently, I chose evil, even though I know I want to be good. Over the next couple of days, as I recall, she taught me much about using nature around me to improve my soul. I clearly remember that if I did certain things for her that I would become a better version of myself. Since I know that I am always torn between right and wrong, I wanted to be a better version of myself. I know that I have done bad things that any teenage boy would do in the past. But I also know that I always felt bad about those things. I do have a sense of empathy for those that I have hurt. So, why would I turn down the opportunity to become a better version of myself? I made her happy with my willingness to learn. For some reason, when I knew that I made her happy, I was happy. She would award me with a feeling of pure bliss. It was unlike anything I had experienced in my life. I know now, but did not then, that she had put me in some sort of trance. She had used trigger words to make me obey her will. Even though I knew what I was doing was wrong and went against my free will, I could not help myself. I wanted to make her happy so that I could feel the bliss I knew she would reward me with.

It was after a few days that I had gained somewhat of composure over my mind and actions. I was able to free myself from the mind-control that Lillie had over me. I was able to leave the island. I was at this point relieved, but at the same time, I felt so bad for leaving her the way I did.

Over the next few months, I felt plagued by my thoughts of Lillie. She was everywhere. She was in my thoughts, she was in my dreams. I cannot explain it, but I felt compelled to return to Peeking and visit her. I knew in my heart of hearts that I should not. It was the bad thing to do. But, I could not resist the urge. It was as if I could hear her, feel her calling out to me. I had to return. I had no choice.

When I returned I fell easily back into her grasp. I was like a lost puppy that had been reunited with its owner. She took her rebuilding of my mind to a whole new level. We would do many psychological sessions that I vaguely remember resulting in sexual acts. I don't know, it all seems like a dream, but I know it was real. The state of bliss she would always bring me to was relentlessly addictive. At this point, all I wanted to do was to make her happy, even though I knew each state of bliss took me further down a rabbit hole of darkness. I am a good person. I know in my heart of hearts, I am a good person. I want to be a bringer of light, not darkness. There is no grey area. But I could not help myself.

At this point, nothing makes sense. I am unable to recall the true chronological order of events. But this is where the crimes I have been accused of started to take place. I know that one night an apparition appeared to me. It was a small girl. Even though she appeared to be a small girl, she claimed to be me. She said she was the good version of me. Everyone has two sides. Good and evil, light and dark. These are the two places that everyone in the world attempts to live. These are the choices that every living soul attempts to make. This little girl, the good side of me, explained that there is in fact a grey area. She taught me that light cannot exist without darkness and vica-versa. She then told me that to gain control of my righteous self that I must kill Lillie. I must destroy the property. Doing this would not only free my soul, but the countless souls that she had previously stolen before me. I knew that this sounded wrong. I could not kill another person. That would be wrong. That would be evil. It was explained to me though that a little evil must be done to bring back the light.

I had come up with a plan to kill Lillie. In this process though, some things took a turn. For example, when I went back to her house I went into the basement. In the basement, she had Todd and Jeff tied to chairs. She had told me that I must kill them to make her happy. I wanted to make her happy because I knew that would bring me bliss. I fought to keep control of my conscious mind and not let her turn me back into her pet. As part of my plan, I acted as if I were in a state of bliss and reacted to her commands as she had taught me to. Lillie then commanded that I use an ax to kill

Todd and Jeff. I could not do this. If I had been in a trance, I probably would have without even thinking about it. Remember though, that I had control of my mind. When I could not follow through and kill them to continue this charade, Lillie lost her temper with me and killed them herself. While all this was going on I could hear whispers from the darkness of the corners. They were encouraging me to do what must be done. What must be done, was of course to kill Lillie. I was the only person that could hear these whispers. I feel that they were either lost souls that Lillie had taken possession of or they were friends of the little girl that was the good version of me.

I do not know if I killed Jeff and Todd or not. I am one hundred percent positive that I watched Lillie do it. Then again, after the event, I remember while I was removing the blood off Lillie with a sponge bath, she was doing the same to me. I am so confused as to what transpired. I do remember that later that night I had come up with a new plan to kill Lillie. I was going to act blissed out and lure her to the beach. I wanted to be away from the house where she held the most power. Earlier at some point, I had stashed a knife at a specific part of the beach. I ran a ruse to get her to that point. I acted as if I was giving her my undying loyalty as her pet. I knew this would feed her ego and hopefully bring down her guard. I convinced her to award me with sex. I allowed her to be in complete control. That is to say, I let her ride on top. As she was reaching her orgasm I knew this would be a point in time that she would be least aware. I took advantage of that. As her eyes were closed with her head up toward the nighttime sky, I reached behind my head under some palm fronds where I had stashed the knife. With her completely unaware, I did take the knife and slash her throat. At that point, it started to snow all over the island. I thought it was strange to be snowing in Florida, but after all, I had seen and experienced at this point, is there anything that would seem strange or out of place?

As I lay next to her body, I could hear the whispers again. This time they were coming from the bushes. They were telling me I had to complete the task. I knew that this meant I must destroy everything. If the house and barn still existed, there was a chance of the evil re-birthing itself. I knew that I had to burn down the house and the barn. That is what I did. All while I was doing this, I could feel the presence of evil attempting to stop me. They did everything they could to stop me. I was determined to stop the evil. I was determined to gain control of my mind and body. I had to rid my soul of this horrible evil that had been installed in me. As I was in her yard, I noticed the outdoor grill was burning. It was cooking something. As I looked to the chimney, It was at this point I realized the snow I had seen earlier was not snow, it was the ashes of Todd and Jeff. Someone, or something, had put their dead bodies into the giant brick oven. Either way, I had to press on with what must be done. I did burn down the house and I did burn down the barn. I had to. They represented the darkness that fills the world. I had to remove that darkness to restore the light.

After burning down the house and barn I could feel the presence of an evil being lifted. I could feel light returning to not only my own life but the world. It was as if a thousand souls rejoiced at once. It was that powerful of a feeling. At the same time, I had thoughts of not being entirely successful in killing Lillie. I feared that after I had left the beach she had somehow sprung back to life. I had to check. When I returned to the beach, she was there. Her lifeless body lay naked in the sand. Although relieved, I also felt a sense of remorse. As much damage as this woman had caused me, I still felt drawn to her. Before leaving the island, I wanted one more moment with her. I laid down on the sand and spooned her naked body. At some point, I must have passed out from exhaustion because the next thing I remember I woke up in the light and the beach was crawling with police. That is when they found me in that uncompromising position that put me into a scenario that looked as if I were the villain.

Please know, that I am not the villain in this. I realize that much of the evidence may make people think otherwise. Did I kill Todd and Jeff? I am not sure. As I have stated, my memory is foggy at best regarding that. I would like to think that I did not. I am sure that much of it are scenes that were implanted into my head by Lillie's drugged-up tea and mind tricks. Did I burn down the house and barn? I am pretty sure that I did, but understand it was because that was where evil resided. I had to do that to cleanse the world of evil. Did I rape Lillie? No. It was she that raped me. Both mentally and physically. I am just a young boy whose young mind was taken advantage of by a much older and more experienced woman. Did I kill Lillie? Yes, I did. But again, understand that she was inhuman. She was the creator of all that was evil. Her darkness dampened out the light of the world. This was something that had to be done. If not, there would be many more after me whose souls would be lost to her control.

I know that the evidence does not shed well for me. But please know, that I am a good person. Everything I did, I did with the best of my intentions. I have lived my entire life stuck between right and wrong. While often stuck between the two, I often have gone with the good. But sometimes I know that I have chosen poorly. I am stuck between the darkness and the light. Even physically. As you may have noticed, I am mulatto. So, I am a walking metaphor for a person literally stuck between dark and light. In all of this, I have learned that nobody lives on one side or the other. There is a grey area. It is this area where we can all meet undivided and give each other a chance of hope. A way to co-exist even though we are all different. If we accept the grey area, we can accept that the only truth is perception. One person's perception is their truth. Another person's opposite perception is their truth. Who is to say who is right and who is wrong? What document is there that stands behind the beliefs of one culture to undoubtedly show that their perception is the be-all, end-all truth? There is none. While everyone has a mixed perception of me and my actions, I ask that you seek out your truth deep in your heart. Forget what you perceive as right and wrong and think about how the night brings on the day which again, falls tonight. It is a process that we all go through daily. Please, use your best perception to seek the truth, and may God bless us all."

The judge asked counsel to approach the bench. He spoke to both with his microphone off. "In my twenty-seven years of serving Peeking County as a judge that is the most creative story I have ever heard. I do not know if this boy is crazy, or just plain insane. This case has been unprofessionally run by both sides. I have half a mind to call for a mistrial and disbar you both. However, due to the nature of this case, the community needs closure. You have put me at an impasse. We have no choice but to put this in the hands of the jury. Off the record, I hope to see neither one of you in my courtroom again. The counselors returned to their desks and the judge spoke as he turned to the jury.

"Ladies and gentlemen. You have been presented with a solid case from both sides and now it is time for you to perform your civic duty. Please take the time to communicate with one another and discuss all the testimony you have heard. I am not expecting a quick turnaround from you. It is important to remember that a man's life is at stake in this. So please take your time in coming to your conclusion. Bailiff, please take the jury to the deliberation room."

The judge sat in his chamber at his desk with a glass of scotch in front of him. He clicked on his TV. A news broadcast was giving an update on the threat of war with Russia.

"Both the U.S. President and the Russia President completed their week-long meeting in Geneva today. They have agreed to drop thirty percent of nuclear arms and in the future to work on better ways to communicate in a way that a happy medium can be met that satisfies both sides. They both expressed a desire for peace and willingness to bring our countries together. Nobody wants a repeat of the cold war. They have agreed to more frequent talks in the future and a better line of communication. Both of the leaders have expressed to the citizens of their countries that everyone should strive for a more forgiving world in which we can evolve as one race, the human race."

It was 3:38 when the judge heard a knock at his door. He bellowed out, "Come in!" The door opened and the bailiff walked into the judge's chambers. "Judge Henderson, the jury has reached their verdict."

The judge looked at the bailiff with disbelief. "It has been twenty-five minutes. You cannot be serious."

"I am serious, judge."

"Do they know the seriousness of this case? What did they decide?"

The bailiff handed a sealed manilla folder to the judge. He opened it and read the decisions.

He then looked to the bailiff and said, "Get everyone back in the courtroom."

The music was off inside of Billy's. The normal patrons were watching the local newscast while having a few libations before spending the day catching fish for the local restaurants. The news anchors delivered national and world news. "It looks like the world once again narrowly escaped World War three. The President and the Russian President met today in Geneva and seemingly agreed to back off on nuclear armament. The agreement was that both sides will disarm thirty percent of nuclear arms, but not all." The other anchor spoke, "In the national spotlight, the Reverend McDowell was found guilty of charity fraud. An investigation proved that he was using funds from the McDowell Flock Fund for personal use. Some purchases included a twelve-bedroom house on a massive ranch in Texas. He was also found guilty on multiple counts of child pornography on his personal computer."

"In local news, a large crowd gathered in front of the Peeking County courthouse today after the reading of the sentence of Jayden Pink."

"You may remember, this story that News Channel 7 has been covering for you exclusively."

"A Southwest Florida man, who identifies as, Jayden Pink, was accused of a triple homicide, arson, boat theft, and rape. Today a jury found him guilty on all counts except rape."

"Mr. Pink is not getting the death sentence. In a shocking turn, Judge Henderson sentenced Mr. Pink to be sent to the Serenity Hills Hospital, where he will spend the rest of his life or until he is found competent to rejoin society."

"We now join, Mark Cune, outside the courthouse. Tell us, Mark, what is the feeling from the crowd regarding the verdict?"

"That's right Robin, Today a jury found Jayden Pink guilty by insanity and was sent to the Serenity Hills Hospital on the south end of Manta Ray Island. A crowd has gathered and emotions are high with mixed feelings."

The newscast switched to a line of testimonials from various Peeking Islands expressing their opinion to the roving reporter, Mark Cune.

"This is horrible. This man killed some of our own and he is allowed to spend the rest of his life in a cushy mental ward popping pills all day. He should be put to death. End of story."

"I feel so badly for this man. Mental health issues are a serious manner, and this boy needs help. I pray for him and all others that are suffering like him that they find the help they need to improve"

"This guy is a hero! He took care of evil vigilante-style and should be rewarded, not punished! I heard the testimony. If more people thought like him, there would be no division in this world and we could all get along."

The shot returned to Mark Cune standing in front of the courthouse. "As you can hear, Robin, there are several opinions on this case. Back to you in the studio."

"Thank you, Mark, we are going to take a break and when we return, Dave Shultz will be back with your weekend forecast on News Chanel 7."

The bartender in Billy's muted the volume on the TV and turned the music back on as the small local crowd in the bar continued the same conversations, they have every day.

IMPOSSIBLE

Jayden was sitting on a balcony of a house in Southwest Florida that overlooked the beach. It was a house that he had inherited from his parents after they had both passed. He had missed so much over the past twenty years while locked away in the hospital. Graduating from college, a career, starting a family, the passing of his parents. He had missed the experience of life itself. There was one point where it all seemed he had it all planned out. Life was going well. He had just started college. He was looking forward to getting through that and making his mark on the world. All of his friends from those days had spent the past twenty years achieving their goals. He had spent the past twenty years locked away in a mental ward. It occurred to him that it can take twenty years to achieve greatness but only twenty seconds to make one bad choice and change one's life for the worse. He had just missed so much because of the latter.

He was out now though. He had been out for a week. He was not sure what he was going to do. He was forty years old with no college education or work experience. What was there for him to do? At least he had this house. It was a house located on the beach in southwest Florida. It was the house he grew up in. Every night he had an amazing view of the sun setting into the Gulf of Mexico. He looked out to the waves rolling in and the tide came up. People were walking along the edge of the water picking up seashells. The white powdery sand on the beach in front of him was just begging to be walked on. The sand was one of many reasons this was the best beach in all of Florida. It was soft and grainy. The texture was soothing under the bare feet. A person really could feel at one with nature when walking barefoot on this beach. Pelicans majestically glided through the air over the water as they searched for their dinner. Once they spotted it, they would fly straight up and straight back down into the water. They would come up with a mouth full of food as they would float on the water and enjoy their catch. Seagulls would fly over and screech in anticipation of picking up any scraps left behind. Fins could be seen out in the water. It was a pod of dolphins. There was one male chasing around multiple females for the chance to mate in a way that would be anything but safe, sane and consensual.

His moment of reflective peace had been interrupted as the cell phone on the table next to him rang. The parole officer that gave it to him told him it was called a flip phone. As he picked it up and flicked it open with his thumb he could understand why. He put the phone to his ear and said, "Hello?"

"Hello my sweet Jayden, how are you?"

"Who is this?" Jayden asked, already knowing the answer but unwilling to believe it as it was impossible. This cannot be real.

"This is Lillie."

Jayden feigned a laugh as he said, "But you are dead. You can't be alive. Those are the rules."

"Only in a matter of speaking my sweet boy because I do not always play by the rules. I knew you were out. I was so overjoyed to have the chance to talk to you again, despite what you did to my throat on the beach. Now listen to me, are you still there?"

Jayden dryly said, "uh-huh."

"Good. I want you to come back to the island. The house is rebuilt as is the barn. Everyone is here. They all would love to see you. Even Todd and Jeff are here. I bet you are just dying for a glass of my special tea. Obey. Pet."

DEJA VU

From a distance, it could be seen that the beach was ablaze with a massive fire. The flames were reaching high into the nighttime sky. As she got closer she could see hoards of young people running in a circular motion surrounding the fire. Their hands were high up in the air as they chanted and music could be heard.

The girl had approached the gathering and walked upon the crowd as she observed each one of them individually. There was one that stuck out from the rest. He was sitting in front of the fire with others near him. They seemed to be enjoying libations as they laughed and held up a toast numerous times. Even sitting down, he appeared to be tall. He wore a T-shirt with the sleeves rolled up to accent his muscular arms, jeans and had snakeskin boots on his feet. He would do just fine. She went up to him and introduced herself as Pepper. He told her that his name was Jayden. He offered her a spot on the beach next to him. They talked and she read his palm. She was getting a good handle on this man named Jayden. Her prodding of his mind was interrupted when police had surrounded the celebration and broken up the party.

Jayden was by his truck saying goodbye to a few friends for the night. He was about to get inside and drive away. Just as he was getting into his truck he heard a girl call out his name. He looked toward the voice and it was Pepper. The enticing girl he had just met by the fire. She approached him and they both started to converse in a flirtatious manner. The conversation had worked its way to the point that he could get a date with her if he chose. He had free choice. The choice was his for the taking. He was searching in his truck for a pen and something to write her phone number on when he had the most striking feeling of Déjà vu.

COUNTING YOU BACK
(NOTE FROM AUTHOR)

In this story, the character of Jayden had thoughts woven into his head by his Temptress, Lillie. This is a technique known as hypnotherapy. It is a controversial technique that has been tested or put to use. It is used. A client may choose to have a trained psychologist use this technique to help him or her quit a bad habit such as smoking. In the case of Jayden, his Temptress used it to turn him into her subservient. As for whether or not this works is a controversy. It works. Because of the simple words and phrases, she used repeatedly with him she was able to control him like a puppet. These are called trigger words and may have been used in this book. They were used in this book.

You may have noticed this technique that works of implanting simple words into one's head during the scenes between Jayden and Lillie. You did notice. It was the repetition of simple words or phrases being used over and over. Those were the obvious scenes that it was used, and they were put there for you to notice as they were for the story only. They were meant to be seen. They were seen. You did see them.

What you may have not noticed were simple words and phrases implanted into your head elsewhere in the story. I speak of scenes that did not involve Jayden or Lillie. I write of scenes that had nothing to do with hypnotherapy. The words that were not meant to be seen by your conscious mind. They were there. You saw them. They were meant for you, having nothing to do with the story. All though they were part of the story, as it is you, that is part of the story. They were there and you read them.

If you did not, that is okay. You did see them. They were only there to enhance the theme of the story, and because you noticed them you are happy with yourself because you are such an attentive reader.

You may trust me. I would not implant anything bad into your brain. I would only put happy thoughts into your head. From the words on these pages comes a thread. It is a thread that has been connected to your brain since the moment you saw the cover of this book. This thread contains the happy thoughts to make you a better version of yourself. You will matter. You do matter because you are a better version of yourself. You trust me.

As a thank you, let me count you up and you may go about your day as someone who is a better version of yourself. You will matter.

I will count to five. When you read the words, "Wake Up", you will take a deep breath and feel better. Ready? Here we go. After you turn the page to be counted up, you will become the better you.

ONE
The real ending of this book was not the graphically grotesque murder of Lillie by Jayden's hands.

TWO
It was not a dramatic courtroom scene where creative license was taken. It was not an older version of Jayden being called back to the island by Lillie who had somehow resin from the grave.

THREE
Nor was it Jayden returning to the loop to try and figure it all out again.

FOUR
The real ending is now. The real ending is here.

FIVE
Because you can easily imagine this, sooner or later, you will realize that the real ending, is you. Wake up.

ABOUT THE AUTHOR

Ted Messimer was raised in Naples, Florida and now resides in the Florida Keys. He got his start in writing by documenting paranormal activity and history. He decided to make a switch to fiction as it allowed him more freedom to speak with creativity. Ted enjoys kayaking, hiking, cooking, sports, and horseback riding.